ARTHUR SLADE
CHRISTOPHER STEININGER

ORCA BOOK PUBLISHERS

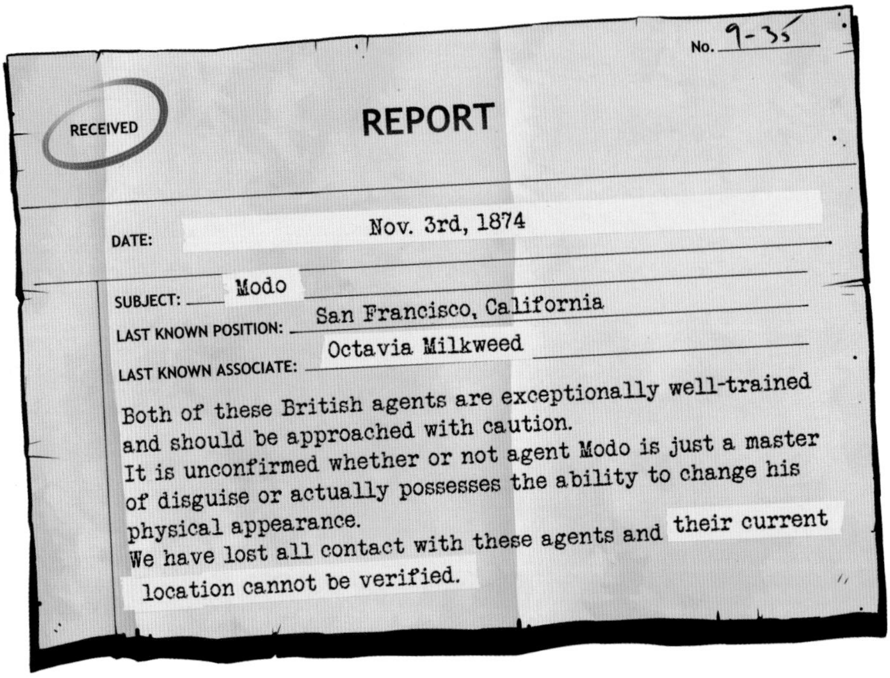

No. 9-35

RECEIVED

REPORT

DATE: Nov. 3rd, 1874

SUBJECT: Modo

LAST KNOWN POSITION: San Francisco, California

LAST KNOWN ASSOCIATE: Octavia Milkweed

Both of these British agents are exceptionally well-trained and should be approached with caution.
It is unconfirmed whether or not agent Modo is just a master of disguise or actually possesses the ability to change his physical appearance.
We have lost all contact with these agents and their current location cannot be verified.

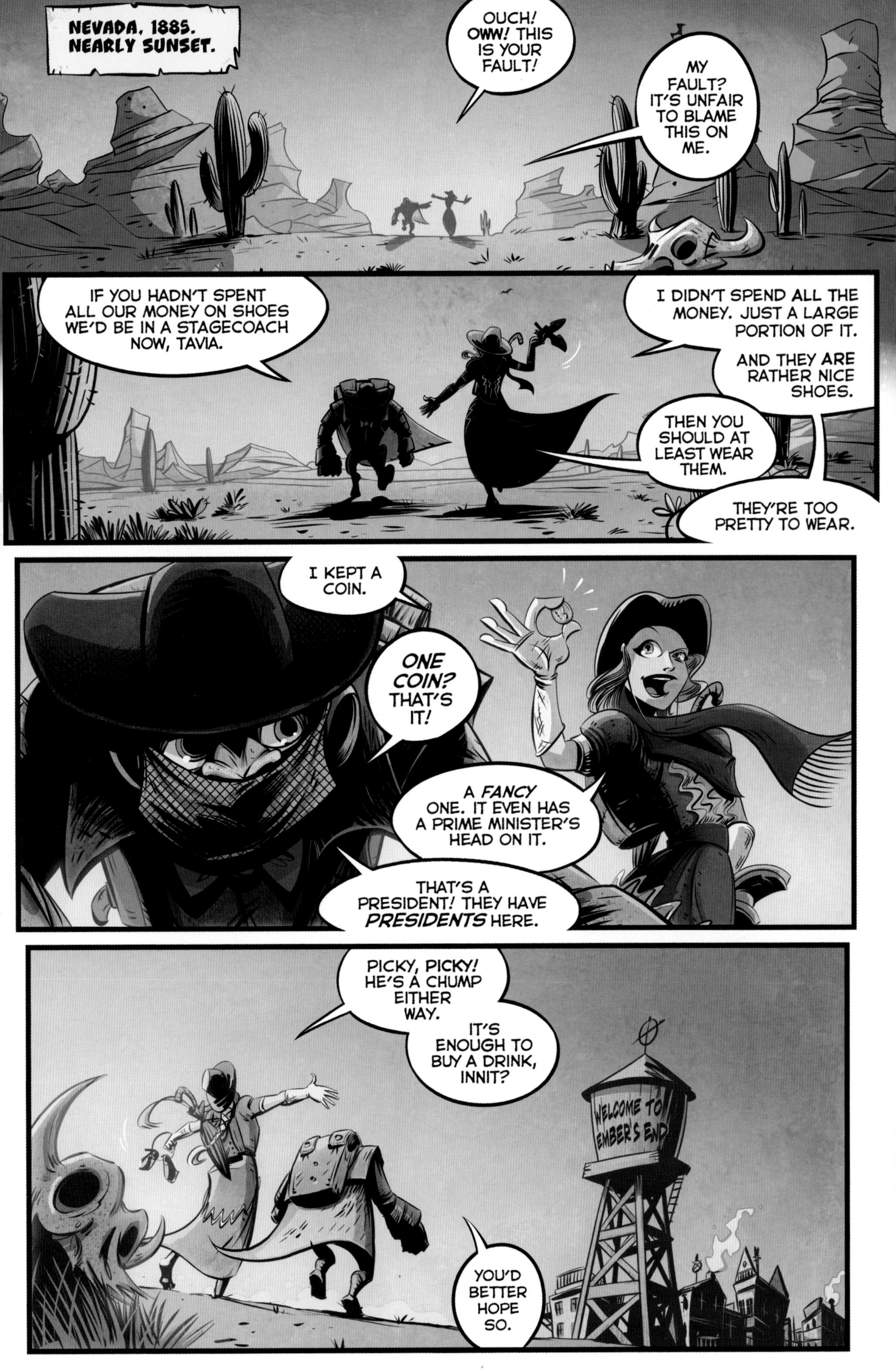
NEVADA, 1885. NEARLY SUNSET.
OUCH! OWW! THIS IS YOUR FAULT!
MY FAULT? IT'S UNFAIR TO BLAME THIS ON ME.
IF YOU HADN'T SPENT ALL OUR MONEY ON SHOES WE'D BE IN A STAGECOACH NOW, TAVIA.
I DIDN'T SPEND ALL THE MONEY. JUST A LARGE PORTION OF IT.
AND THEY ARE RATHER NICE SHOES.
THEN YOU SHOULD AT LEAST WEAR THEM.
THEY'RE TOO PRETTY TO WEAR.
I KEPT A COIN.
ONE COIN? THAT'S IT!
A FANCY ONE. IT EVEN HAS A PRIME MINISTER'S HEAD ON IT.
THAT'S A PRESIDENT! THEY HAVE PRESIDENTS HERE.
PICKY, PICKY! HE'S A CHUMP EITHER WAY.
IT'S ENOUGH TO BUY A DRINK, INNIT?
WELCOME TO EMBER'S END
YOU'D BETTER HOPE SO.

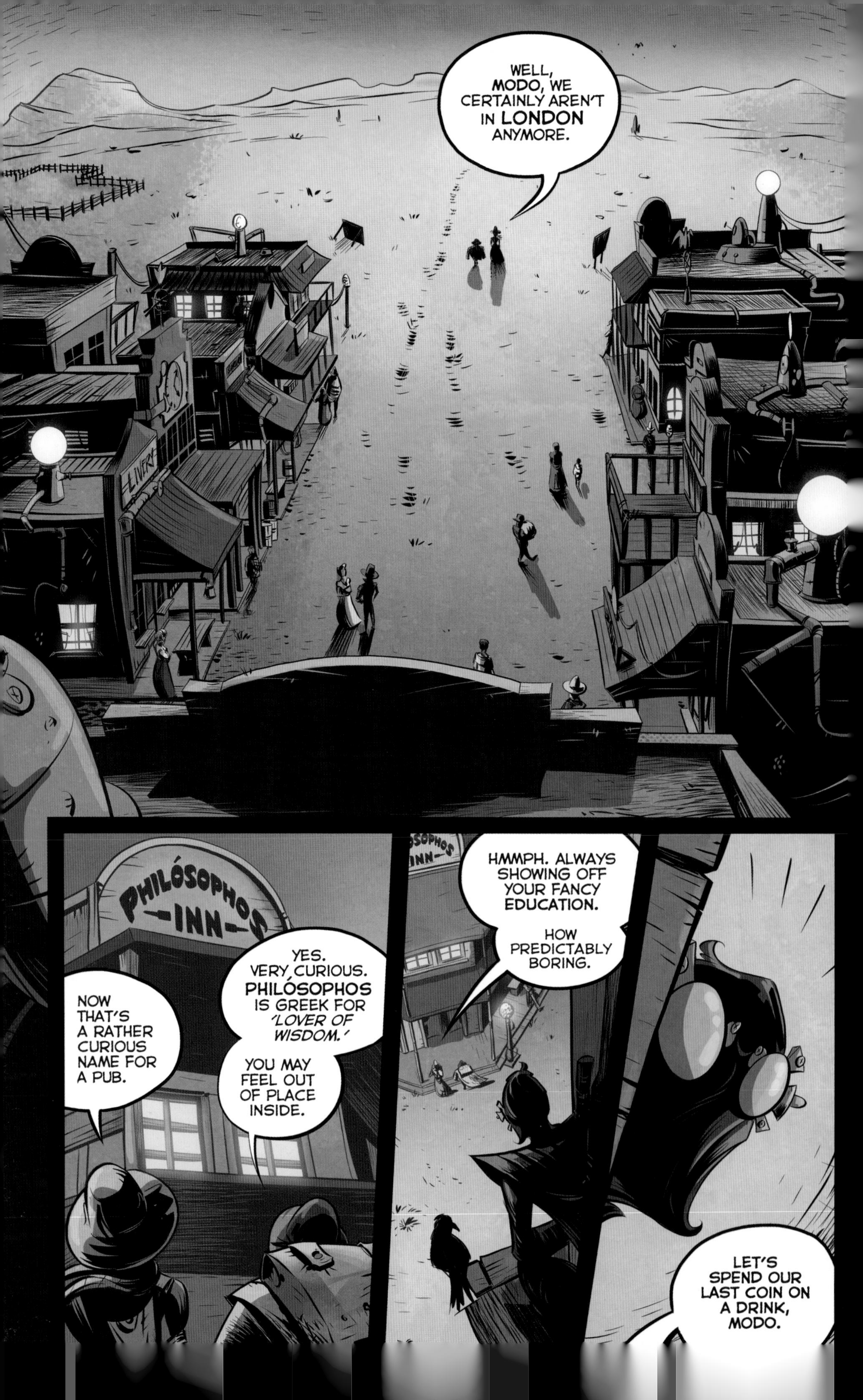
WELL, MODO, WE CERTAINLY AREN'T IN LONDON ANYMORE.
LIVERY
PHILÓSOPHOS —INN—
NOW THAT'S A RATHER CURIOUS NAME FOR A PUB.
YES. VERY CURIOUS. PHILÓSOPHOS IS GREEK FOR 'LOVER OF WISDOM.'
YOU MAY FEEL OUT OF PLACE INSIDE.
HMMPH. ALWAYS SHOWING OFF YOUR FANCY EDUCATION.
HOW PREDICTABLY BORING.
LET'S SPEND OUR LAST COIN ON A DRINK, MODO.

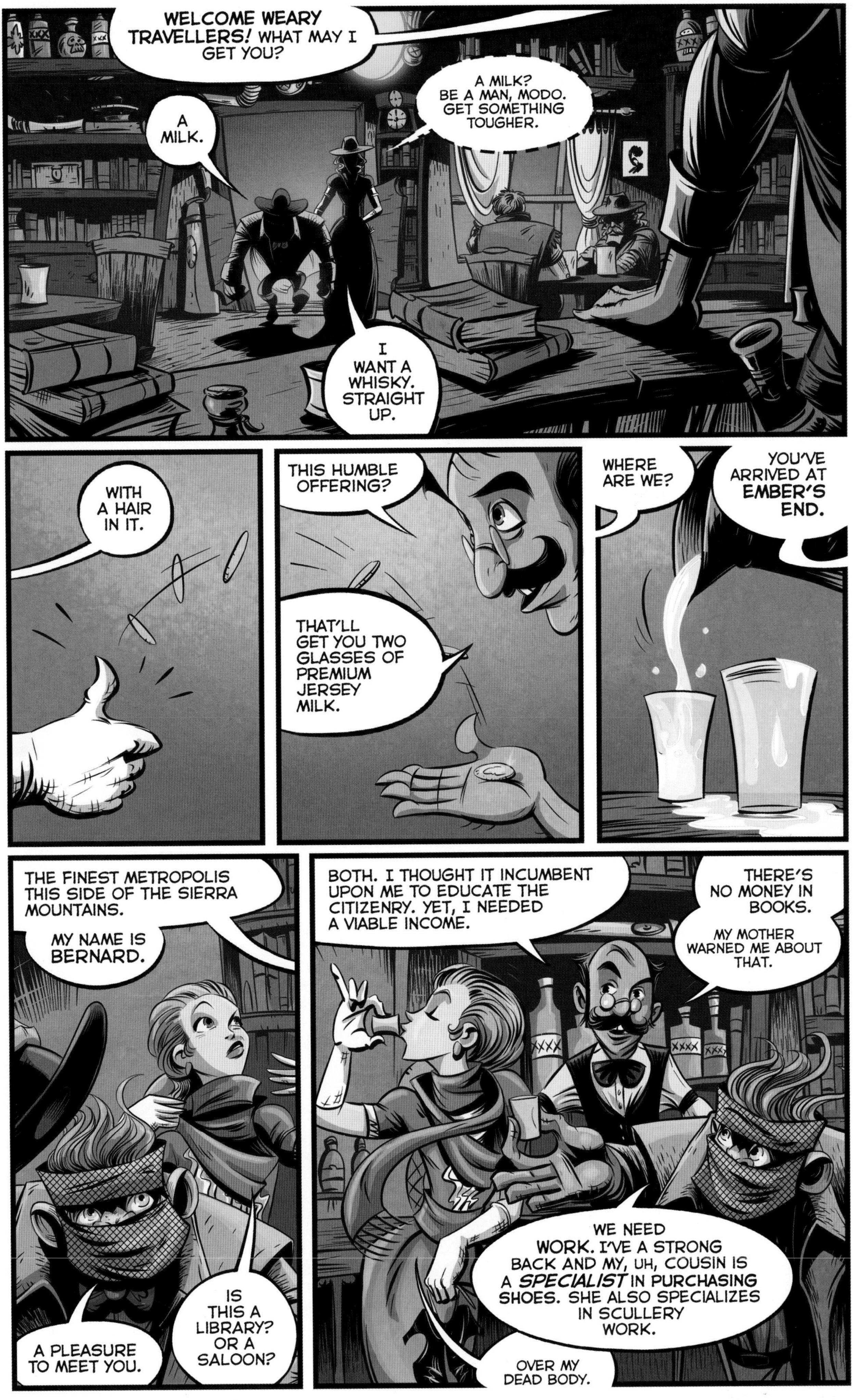
WELCOME WEARY TRAVELLERS! WHAT MAY I GET YOU?
A MILK.
A MILK? BE A MAN, MODO. GET SOMETHING TOUGHER.
I WANT A WHISKY. STRAIGHT UP.
WITH A HAIR IN IT.
THIS HUMBLE OFFERING?
THAT'LL GET YOU TWO GLASSES OF PREMIUM JERSEY MILK.
WHERE ARE WE?
YOU'VE ARRIVED AT EMBER'S END.
THE FINEST METROPOLIS THIS SIDE OF THE SIERRA MOUNTAINS.
MY NAME IS BERNARD.
A PLEASURE TO MEET YOU.
IS THIS A LIBRARY? OR A SALOON?
BOTH. I THOUGHT IT INCUMBENT UPON ME TO EDUCATE THE CITIZENRY. YET, I NEEDED A VIABLE INCOME.
THERE'S NO MONEY IN BOOKS.
MY MOTHER WARNED ME ABOUT THAT.
WE NEED WORK. I'VE A STRONG BACK AND MY, UH, COUSIN IS A *SPECIALIST* IN PURCHASING SHOES. SHE ALSO SPECIALIZES IN SCULLERY WORK.
OVER MY DEAD BODY.

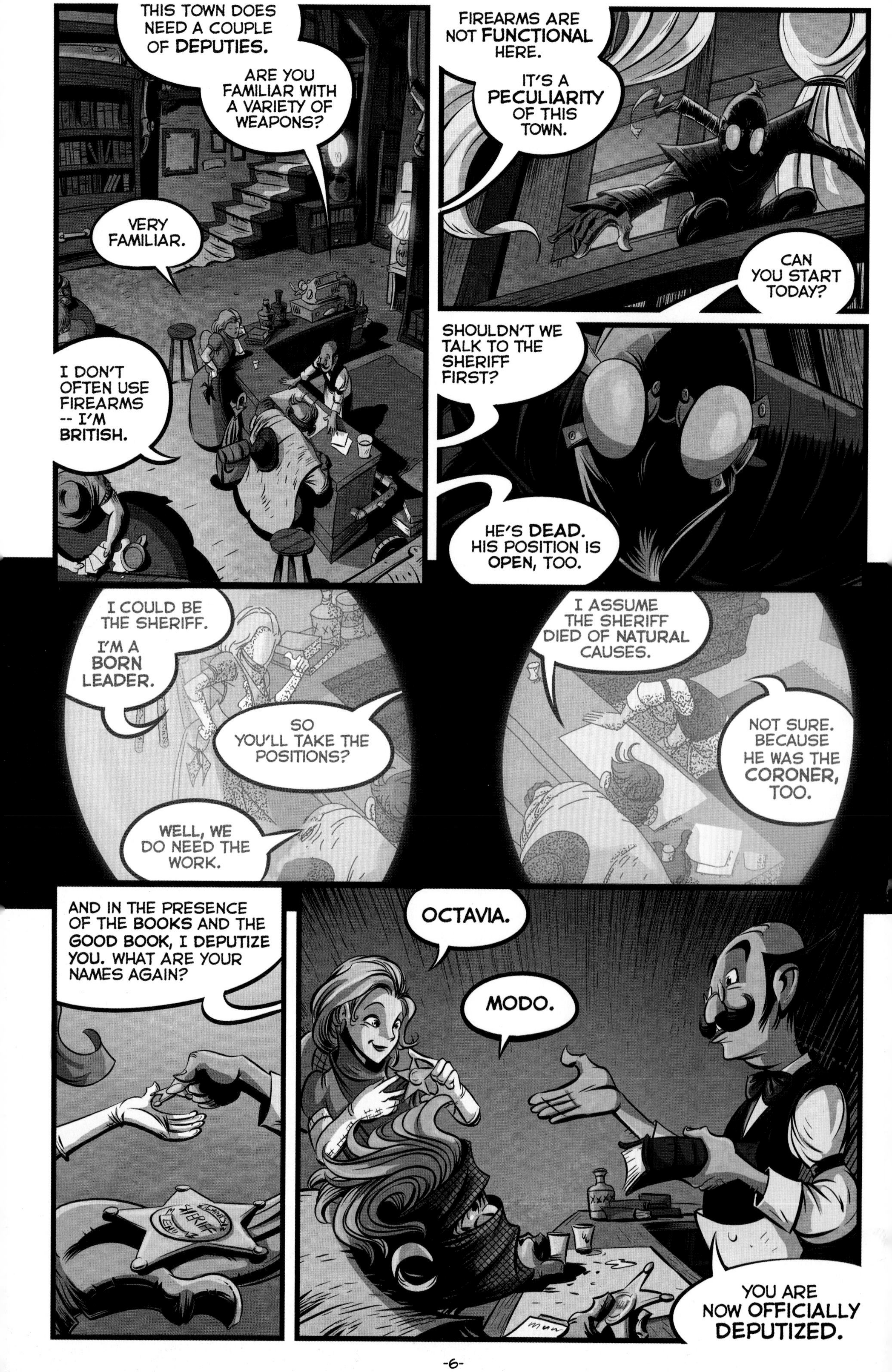
THIS TOWN DOES NEED A COUPLE OF DEPUTIES.
ARE YOU FAMILIAR WITH A VARIETY OF WEAPONS?
VERY FAMILIAR.
I DON'T OFTEN USE FIREARMS -- I'M BRITISH.
FIREARMS ARE NOT FUNCTIONAL HERE.
IT'S A PECULIARITY OF THIS TOWN.
CAN YOU START TODAY?
SHOULDN'T WE TALK TO THE SHERIFF FIRST?
HE'S DEAD. HIS POSITION IS OPEN, TOO.
I COULD BE THE SHERIFF.
I'M A BORN LEADER.
SO YOU'LL TAKE THE POSITIONS?
WELL, WE DO NEED THE WORK.
I ASSUME THE SHERIFF DIED OF NATURAL CAUSES.
NOT SURE. BECAUSE HE WAS THE CORONER, TOO.
AND IN THE PRESENCE OF THE BOOKS AND THE GOOD BOOK, I DEPUTIZE YOU. WHAT ARE YOUR NAMES AGAIN?
OCTAVIA.
MODO.
YOU ARE NOW OFFICIALLY DEPUTIZED.

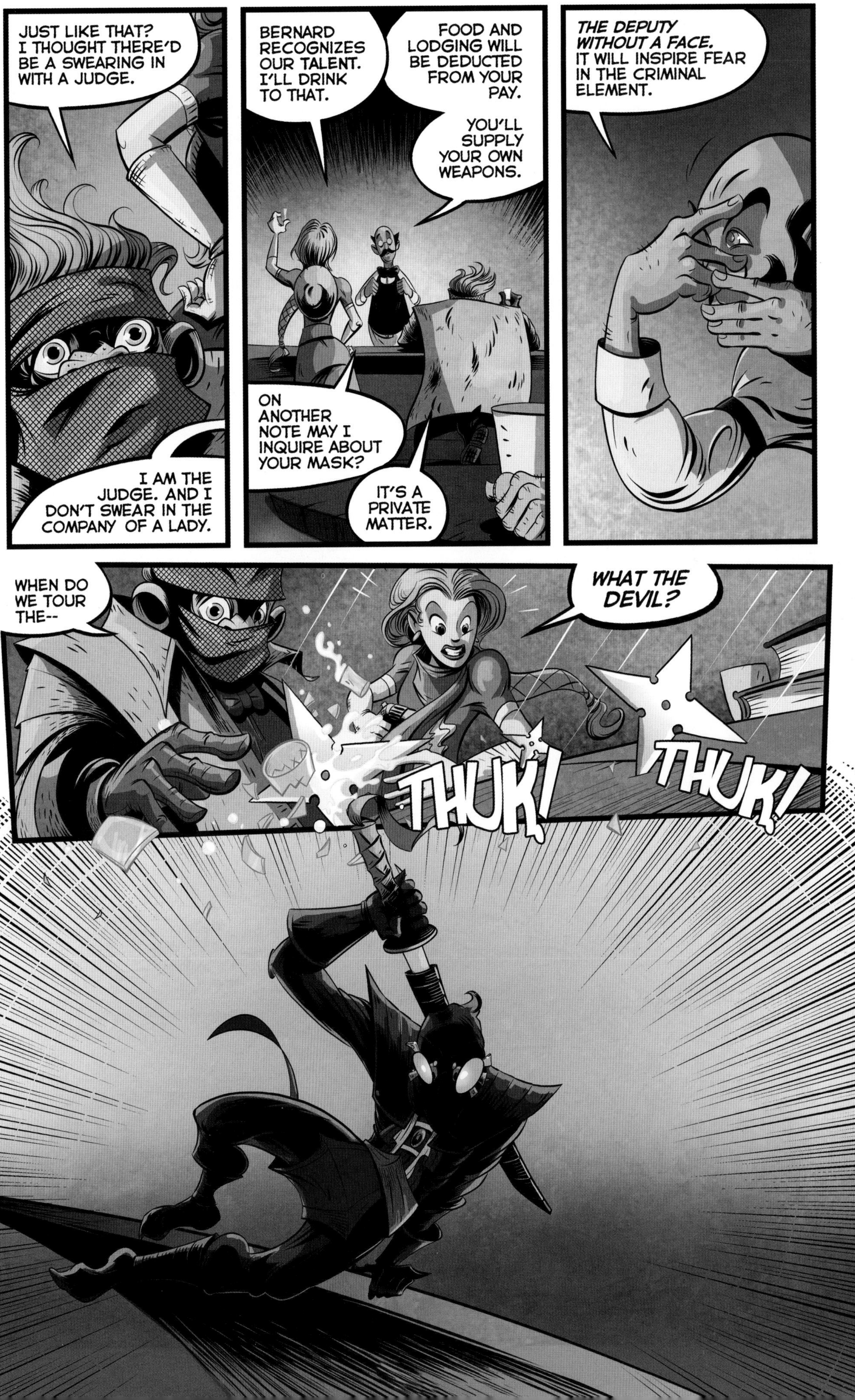
JUST LIKE THAT? I THOUGHT THERE'D BE A SWEARING IN WITH A JUDGE.
I AM THE JUDGE. AND I DON'T SWEAR IN THE COMPANY OF A LADY.
BERNARD RECOGNIZES OUR TALENT. I'LL DRINK TO THAT.
FOOD AND LODGING WILL BE DEDUCTED FROM YOUR PAY.
YOU'LL SUPPLY YOUR OWN WEAPONS.
ON ANOTHER NOTE MAY I INQUIRE ABOUT YOUR MASK?
IT'S A PRIVATE MATTER.
THE DEPUTY WITHOUT A FACE.
IT WILL INSPIRE FEAR IN THE CRIMINAL ELEMENT.
WHEN DO WE TOUR THE--
WHAT THE DEVIL?
THUK!
THUK!

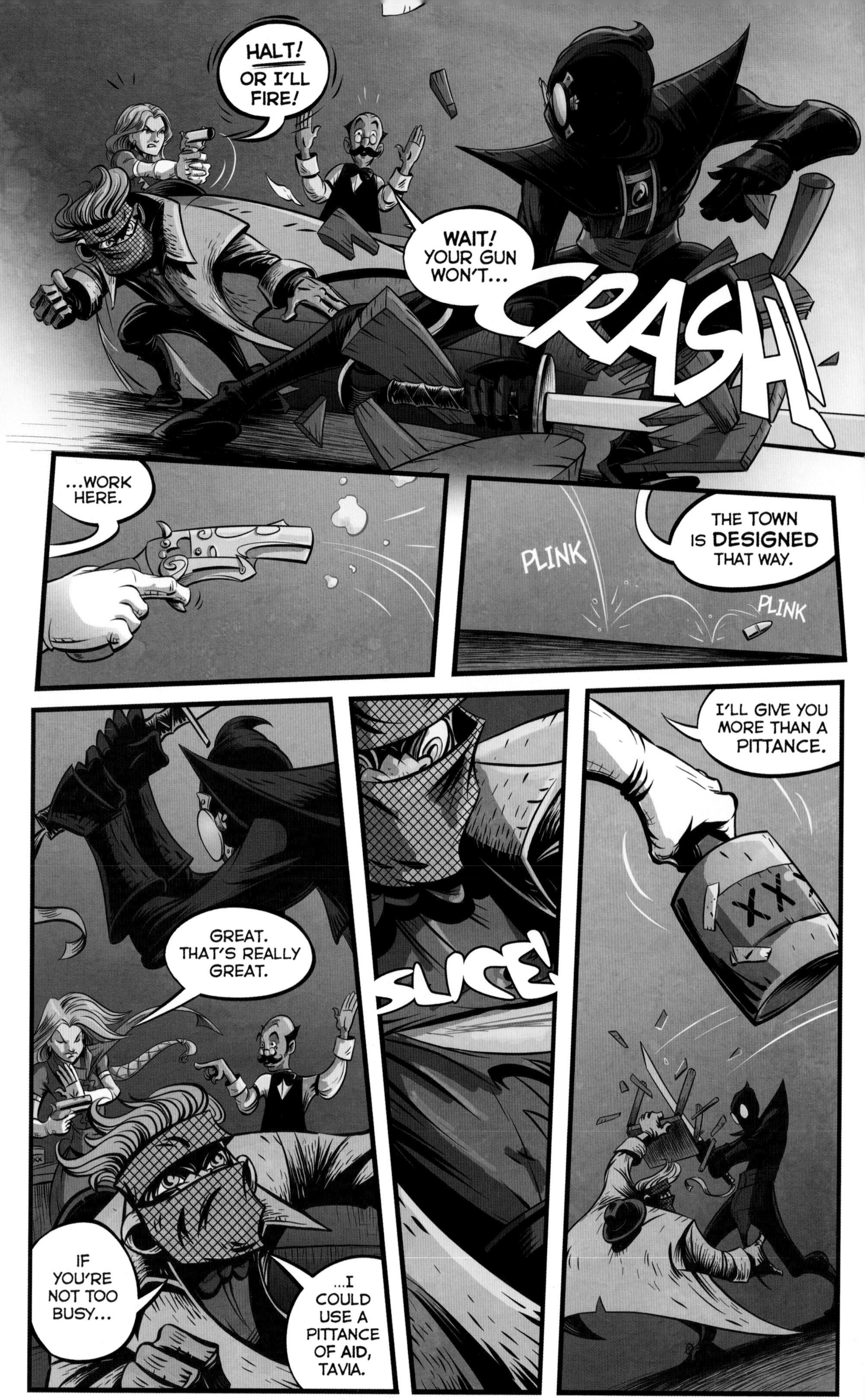
HALT! OR I'LL FIRE!
WAIT! YOUR GUN WON'T...
CRASH!
...WORK HERE.
PLINK
THE TOWN IS DESIGNED THAT WAY.
PLINK
GREAT. THAT'S REALLY GREAT.
IF YOU'RE NOT TOO BUSY...
...I COULD USE A PITTANCE OF AID, TAVIA.
SLICE
I'LL GIVE YOU MORE THAN A PITTANCE.

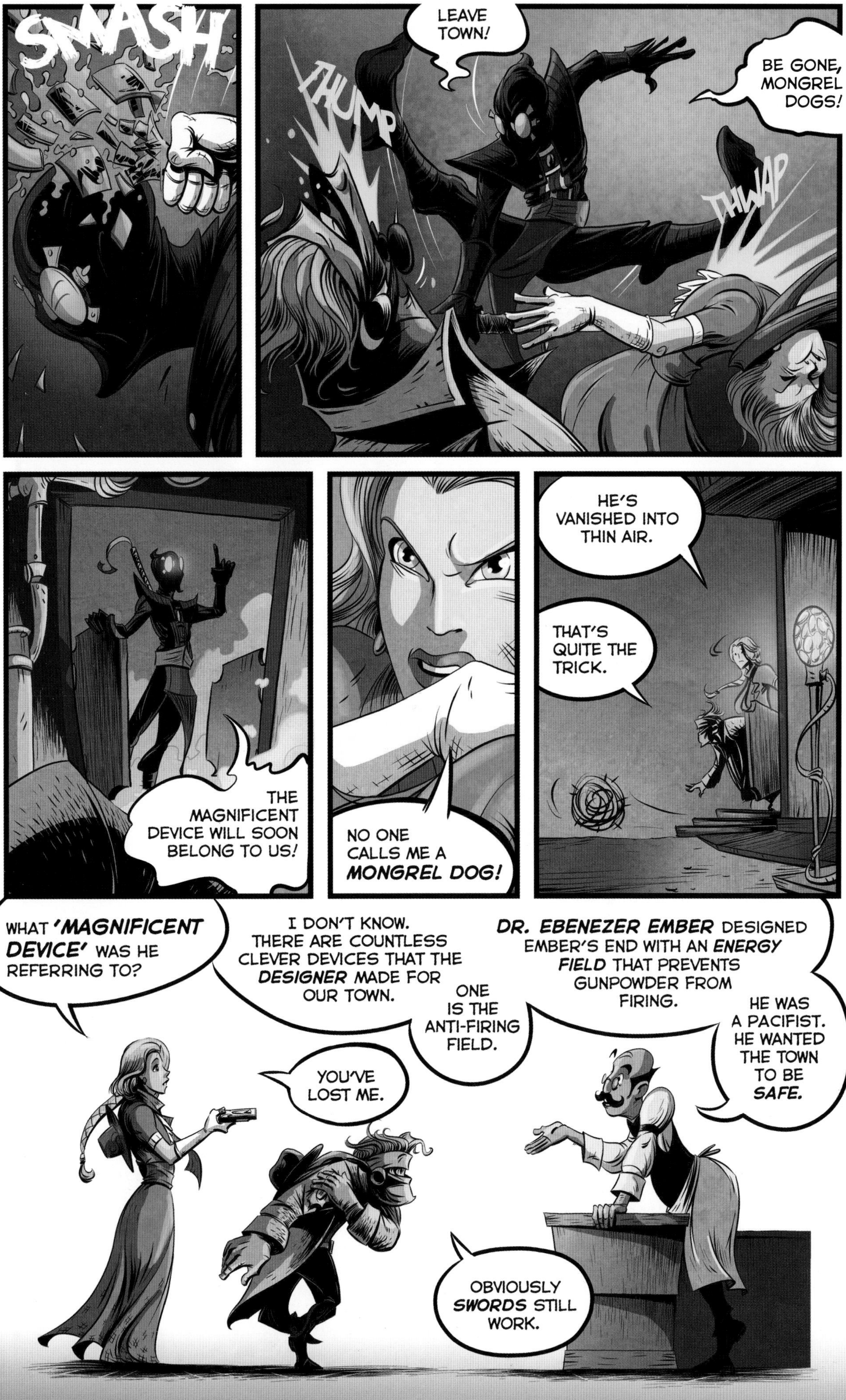
SMASH
LEAVE TOWN!
THUMP
BE GONE, MONGREL DOGS!
THWAP
THE MAGNIFICENT DEVICE WILL SOON BELONG TO US!
NO ONE CALLS ME A **MONGREL DOG!**
HE'S VANISHED INTO THIN AIR.
THAT'S QUITE THE TRICK.
WHAT ***'MAGNIFICENT DEVICE'*** WAS HE REFERRING TO?
I DON'T KNOW. THERE ARE COUNTLESS CLEVER DEVICES THAT THE ***DESIGNER*** MADE FOR OUR TOWN.
ONE IS THE ANTI-FIRING FIELD.
DR. EBENEZER EMBER DESIGNED EMBER'S END WITH AN ***ENERGY FIELD*** THAT PREVENTS GUNPOWDER FROM FIRING.
HE WAS A PACIFIST. HE WANTED THE TOWN TO BE ***SAFE.***
YOU'VE LOST ME.
OBVIOUSLY ***SWORDS*** STILL WORK.

DO YOU AT LEAST KNOW WHO OUR SWORD-WIELDING FIEND IS?
HIS CLOTHING SUGGESTS HE'S A *NINJA*. THERE ARE RUMOURS ABOUT A PACK OF RUFFIANS WHO ARRIVED A FEW DAYS AGO.
COME TO THINK OF IT--THAT'S ABOUT WHEN THE SHERIFF DIED.
THE EVENTS MAY BE CONNECTED.
I'LL INFORM THE TOWN OF YOUR APPOINTMENTS. OUR *FIRST* FEMALE DEPUTY!
I HOPE I LIVE TO ENJOY THE FAME.
WITH LUCK YOU WILL. I'LL SEND A SPECIAL NOTE TO *MISS EMBER.* SHE INHERITED THE TOWN FROM HER FATHER.
WHAT TYPE OF COMMUNICATION SYSTEM IS THAT?
PNEUMATIC TUBES. THEY GO TO EVERY BUILDING IN TOWN.
NEAR INSTANTANEOUS COMMUNICATION. ANOTHER OF DR. EMBER'S *BRILLIANT INVENTIONS.*
IMPRESSIVE. CAN IT FETCH YOU A *DRINK*, TOO?
NO. BUT I CAN. ANOTHER MILK COMING UP.
MAKE THAT TWO.

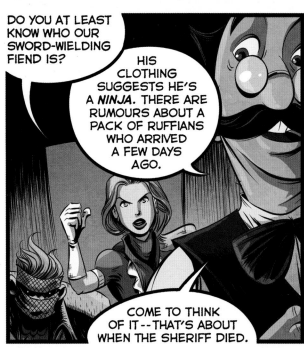

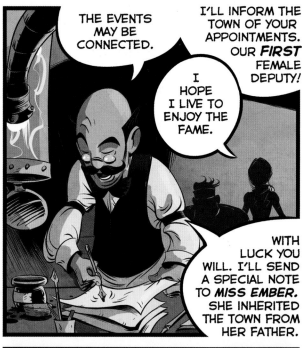

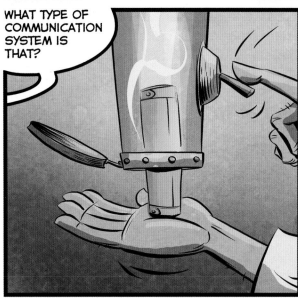

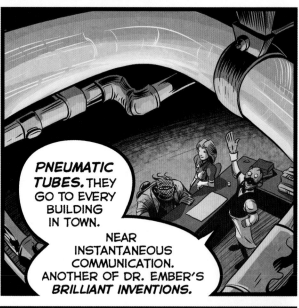

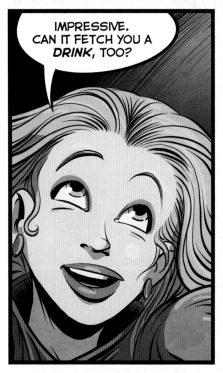

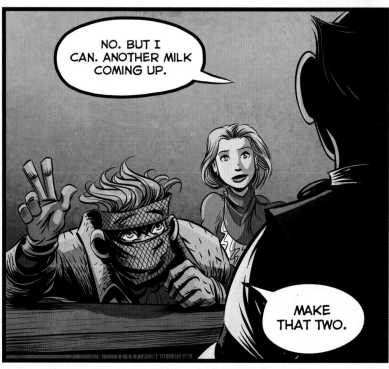

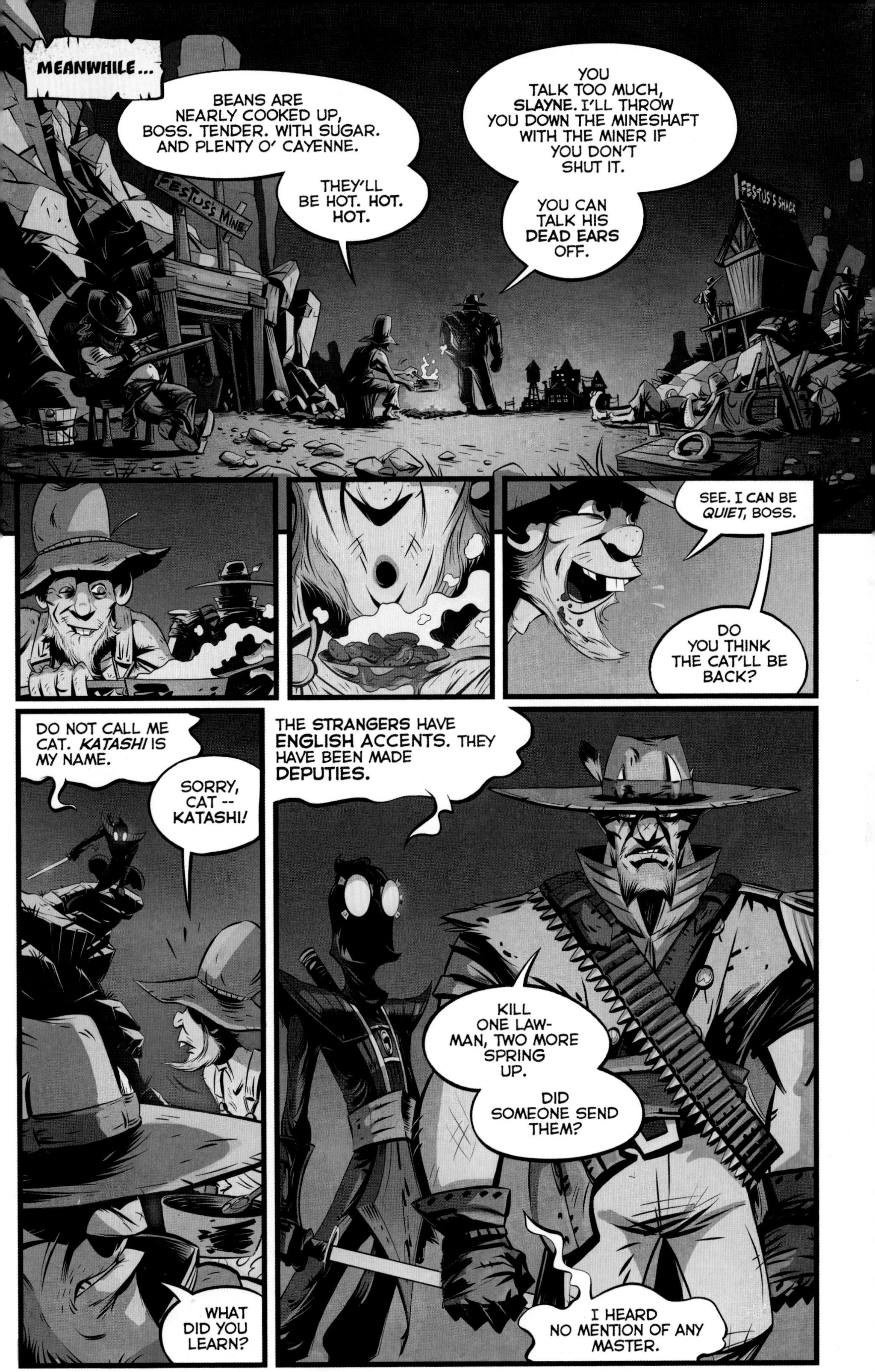
MEANWHILE...
BEANS ARE NEARLY COOKED UP, BOSS. TENDER. WITH SUGAR. AND PLENTY O' CAYENNE.
THEY'LL BE HOT. HOT. HOT.
YOU TALK TOO MUCH, SLAYNE. I'LL THROW YOU DOWN THE MINESHAFT WITH THE MINER IF YOU DON'T SHUT IT.
YOU CAN TALK HIS DEAD EARS OFF.
FESTUS'S MINE
FESTUS'S SHACK
SEE. I CAN BE QUIET, BOSS.
DO YOU THINK THE CAT'LL BE BACK?
DO NOT CALL ME CAT. KATASHI IS MY NAME.
SORRY, CAT -- KATASHI!
WHAT DID YOU LEARN?
THE STRANGERS HAVE ENGLISH ACCENTS. THEY HAVE BEEN MADE DEPUTIES.
KILL ONE LAW-MAN, TWO MORE SPRING UP.
DID SOMEONE SEND THEM?
I HEARD NO MENTION OF ANY MASTER.

THEN **CHANCE** BROUGHT THEM HERE.

YES.

THE LUCKY AND THE DEAD, THAT'S WHAT THEY ARE.

WE'LL HAVE TO ADD THEM TO THE LATTER CATEGORY.

WHY DON'T WE TAKE THE **DEVICE** NOW, BOSS?

THE **EMBER GIRL** CAN'T STOP US.

DON'T ASK QUESTIONS, SLAYNE.

YOUR JOB IS TO COOK. THE GIRL IS NOT THE DANGER. HER FATHER IS.

BUT HE'S **DEAD.** EVERYONE IN TOWN SAYS SO.

DEAD OR ALIVE, HE'S STILL A DANGER.

DR. EMBER HAD A MIND LIKE **CLOCKWORK.**

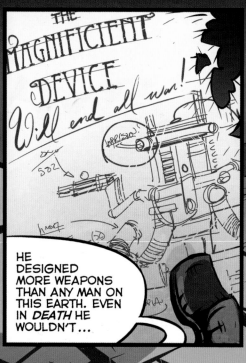

THE **MAGNIFICENT DEVICE**

Will end all war!

HE DESIGNED MORE WEAPONS THAN ANY MAN ON THIS EARTH. EVEN IN *DEATH* HE WOULDN'T...

"... LEAVE HIS DAUGHTER UNPROTECTED."

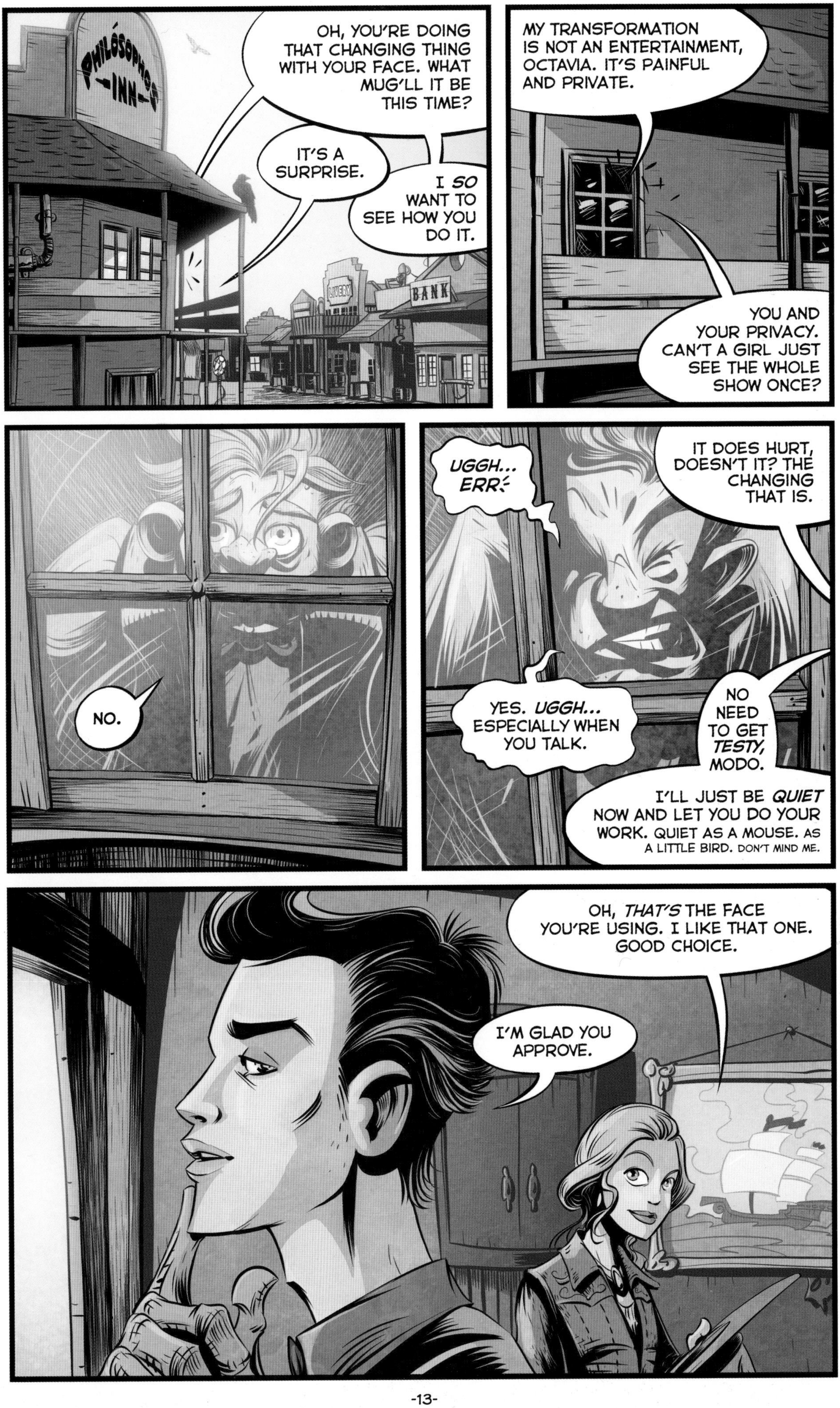
PHILOSOPHOS INN
OH, YOU'RE DOING THAT CHANGING THING WITH YOUR FACE. WHAT MUG'LL IT BE THIS TIME?
IT'S A SURPRISE.
I SO WANT TO SEE HOW YOU DO IT.
LIVERY
BANK
MY TRANSFORMATION IS NOT AN ENTERTAINMENT, OCTAVIA. IT'S PAINFUL AND PRIVATE.
YOU AND YOUR PRIVACY. CAN'T A GIRL JUST SEE THE WHOLE SHOW ONCE?
NO.
UGGH... ERR...
IT DOES HURT, DOESN'T IT? THE CHANGING THAT IS.
YES. UGGH... ESPECIALLY WHEN YOU TALK.
NO NEED TO GET TESTY, MODO.
I'LL JUST BE QUIET NOW AND LET YOU DO YOUR WORK. QUIET AS A MOUSE. AS A LITTLE BIRD. DON'T MIND ME.
OH, THAT'S THE FACE YOU'RE USING. I LIKE THAT ONE. GOOD CHOICE.
I'M GLAD YOU APPROVE.

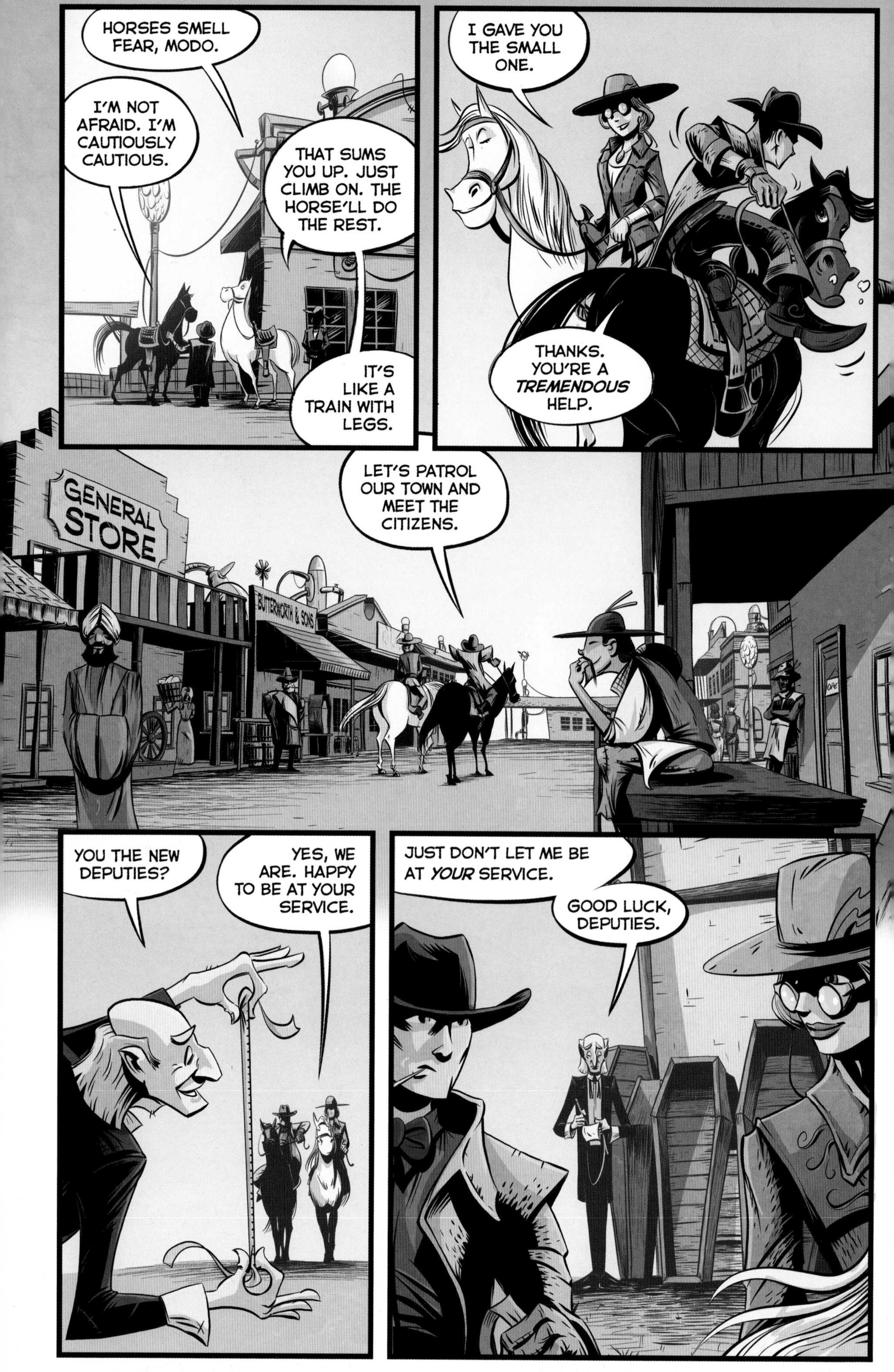

HORSES SMELL FEAR, MODO.
I'M NOT AFRAID. I'M CAUTIOUSLY CAUTIOUS.
THAT SUMS YOU UP. JUST CLIMB ON. THE HORSE'LL DO THE REST.
IT'S LIKE A TRAIN WITH LEGS.
I GAVE YOU THE SMALL ONE.
THANKS. YOU'RE A *TREMENDOUS* HELP.
LET'S PATROL OUR TOWN AND MEET THE CITIZENS.
GENERAL STORE
BUTTERWORTH & SONS
YOU THE NEW DEPUTIES?
YES, WE ARE. HAPPY TO BE AT YOUR SERVICE.
JUST DON'T LET ME BE AT *YOUR* SERVICE.
GOOD LUCK, DEPUTIES.

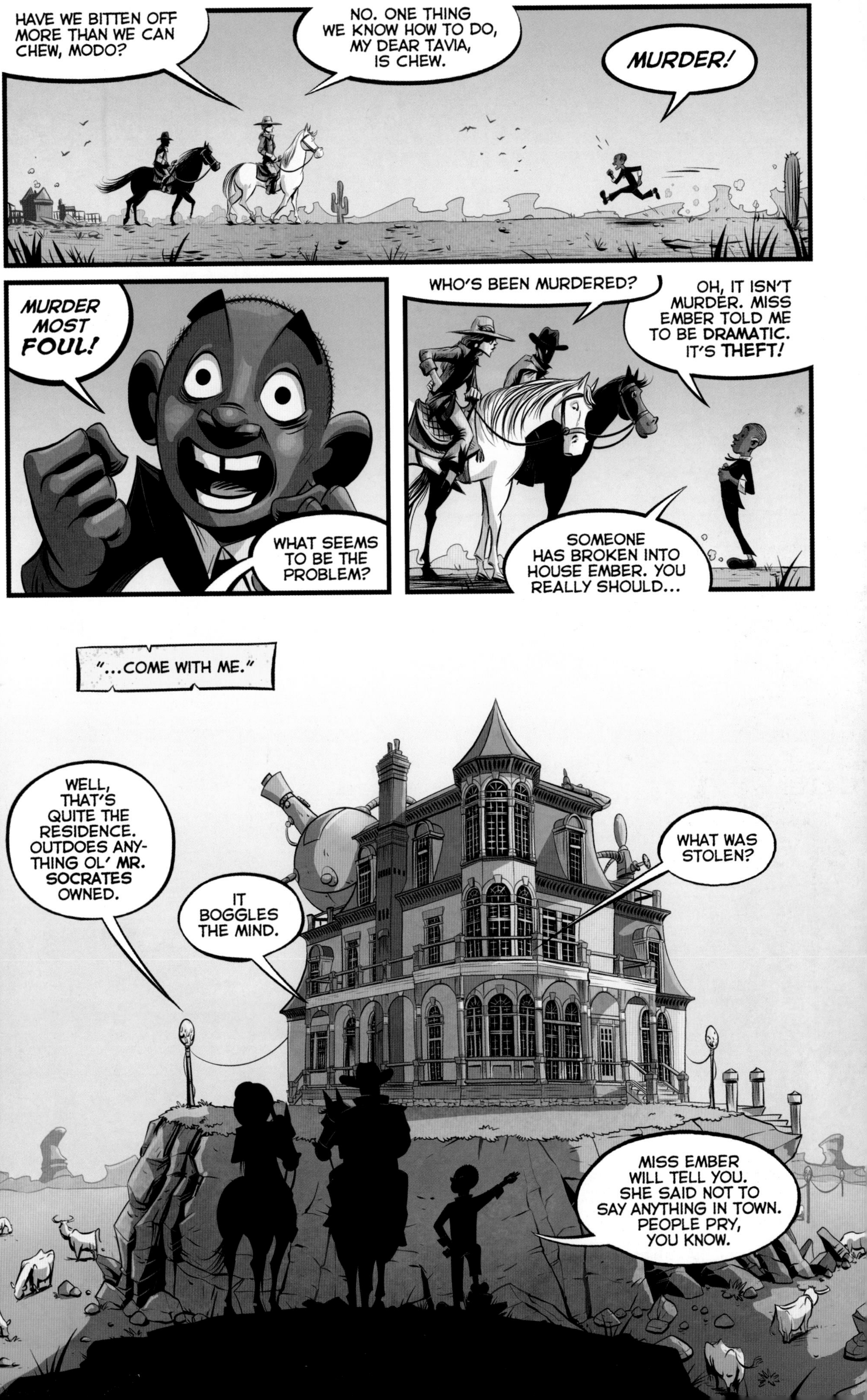
HAVE WE BITTEN OFF MORE THAN WE CAN CHEW, MODO?
NO. ONE THING WE KNOW HOW TO DO, MY DEAR TAVIA, IS CHEW.
MURDER!
MURDER MOST FOUL!
WHAT SEEMS TO BE THE PROBLEM?
WHO'S BEEN MURDERED?
OH, IT ISN'T MURDER. MISS EMBER TOLD ME TO BE DRAMATIC. IT'S THEFT!
SOMEONE HAS BROKEN INTO HOUSE EMBER. YOU REALLY SHOULD...
"...COME WITH ME."
WELL, THAT'S QUITE THE RESIDENCE. OUTDOES ANYTHING OL' MR. SOCRATES OWNED.
IT BOGGLES THE MIND.
WHAT WAS STOLEN?
MISS EMBER WILL TELL YOU. SHE SAID NOT TO SAY ANYTHING IN TOWN. PEOPLE PRY, YOU KNOW.

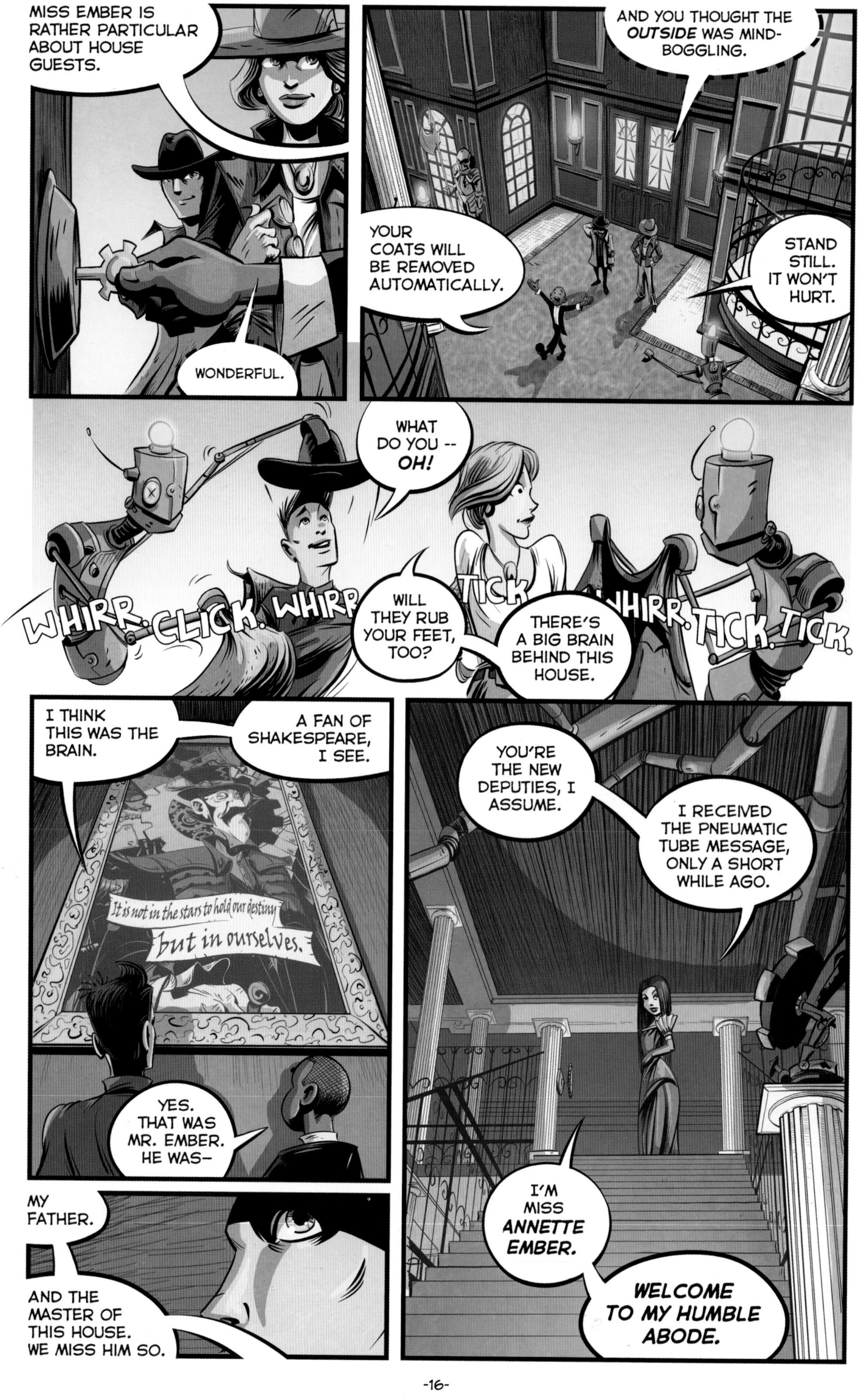
MISS EMBER IS RATHER PARTICULAR ABOUT HOUSE GUESTS.
WONDERFUL.
AND YOU THOUGHT THE *OUTSIDE* WAS MIND-BOGGLING.
YOUR COATS WILL BE REMOVED AUTOMATICALLY.
STAND STILL. IT WON'T HURT.
WHAT DO YOU -- *OH!*
WHIRR. CLICK. WHIRR
TICK
WILL THEY RUB YOUR FEET, TOO?
THERE'S A BIG BRAIN BEHIND THIS HOUSE.
WHIRR. TICK. TICK.
I THINK THIS WAS THE BRAIN.
A FAN OF SHAKESPEARE, I SEE.
It is not in the stars to hold our destiny
but in ourselves.
YES. THAT WAS MR. EMBER. HE WAS—
MY FATHER.
AND THE MASTER OF THIS HOUSE. WE MISS HIM SO.
YOU'RE THE NEW DEPUTIES, I ASSUME.
I RECEIVED THE PNEUMATIC TUBE MESSAGE, ONLY A SHORT WHILE AGO.
I'M MISS *ANNETTE EMBER.*
WELCOME TO MY HUMBLE ABODE.

THIS IS FAR FROM HUMBLE.

MY PARTNER MEANT TO SAY, *"THANK YOU."*

WE'RE AT YOUR SERVICE.

WHIRR. CLICK. WH...

BERNARD MENTIONED THAT YOU WORE A MASK.

I HAVE A MINOR AFFLICTION.

HEALED NOW?

GOOD.

WHIRR. TICK. TICK.

I'VE EXPERIENCED THE THEFT OF A FEW *ITEMS*.

LET'S START IN MY *OBSERVATION ROOM*.

YOU WATCH THE TOWN FROM HERE?

CREEPY.

MY FATHER SPENT MANY HOURS WATCHING *HIS CREATION*. EMBER'S END WAS HIS SECOND CHILD.

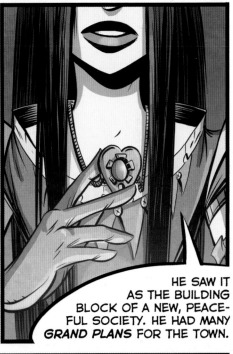

HE SAW IT AS THE BUILDING BLOCK OF A NEW, PEACEFUL SOCIETY. HE HAD MANY *GRAND PLANS* FOR THE TOWN.

THE THIEF ENTERED HERE AFTER CLIMBING *FIFTY FEET* OF *ROCK*.

IMPRESSIVE. WHAT DID HE STEAL?

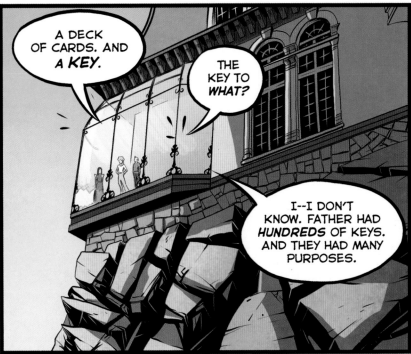

A DECK OF CARDS. AND *A KEY*.

THE KEY TO *WHAT?*

I--I DON'T KNOW. FATHER HAD *HUNDREDS* OF KEYS. AND THEY HAD MANY PURPOSES.

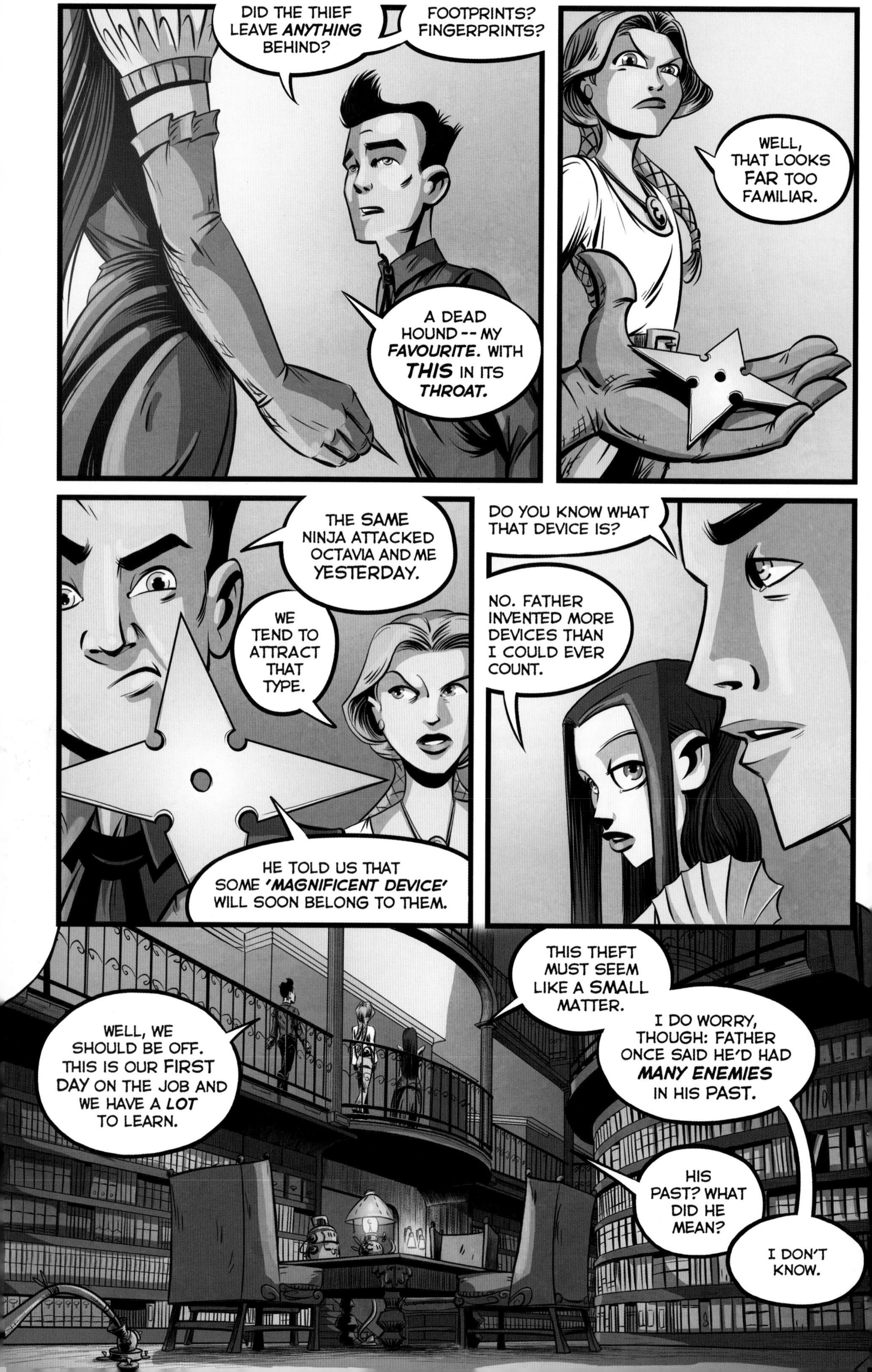
DID THE THIEF LEAVE *ANYTHING* BEHIND?
FOOTPRINTS? FINGERPRINTS?
A DEAD HOUND -- MY *FAVOURITE*. WITH **THIS** IN ITS *THROAT*.
WELL, THAT LOOKS FAR TOO FAMILIAR.
THE SAME NINJA ATTACKED OCTAVIA AND ME YESTERDAY.
WE TEND TO ATTRACT THAT TYPE.
HE TOLD US THAT SOME *'MAGNIFICENT DEVICE'* WILL SOON BELONG TO THEM.
DO YOU KNOW WHAT THAT DEVICE IS?
NO. FATHER INVENTED MORE DEVICES THAN I COULD EVER COUNT.
WELL, WE SHOULD BE OFF. THIS IS OUR FIRST DAY ON THE JOB AND WE HAVE A *LOT* TO LEARN.
THIS THEFT MUST SEEM LIKE A SMALL MATTER.
I DO WORRY, THOUGH: FATHER ONCE SAID HE'D HAD *MANY ENEMIES* IN HIS PAST.
HIS PAST? WHAT DID HE MEAN?
I DON'T KNOW.

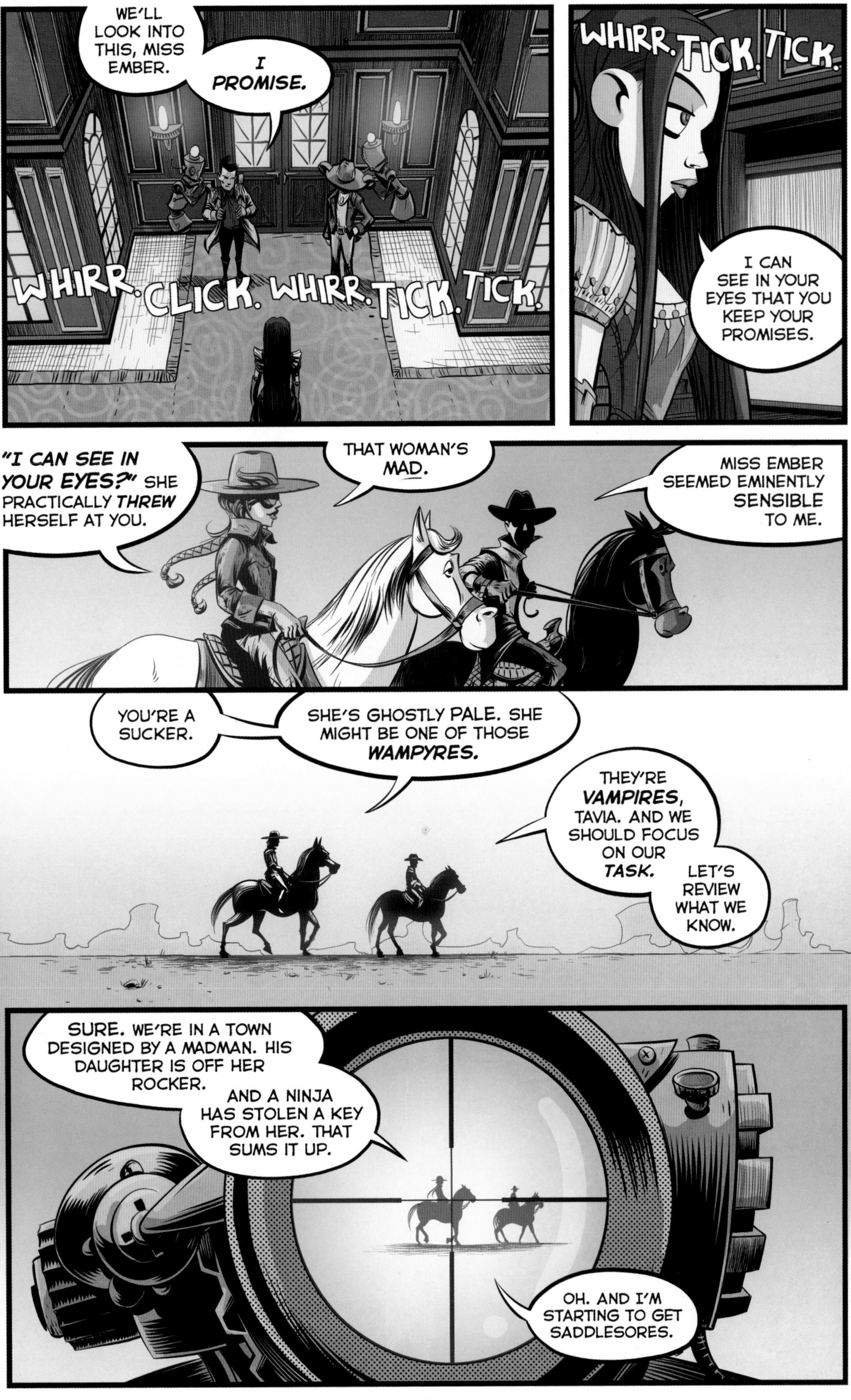
WE'LL LOOK INTO THIS, MISS EMBER.
I PROMISE.
WHIRR. CLICK. WHIRR. TICK. TICK.
WHIRR. TICK. TICK.
I CAN SEE IN YOUR EYES THAT YOU KEEP YOUR PROMISES.
"I CAN SEE IN YOUR EYES?" SHE PRACTICALLY THREW HERSELF AT YOU.
THAT WOMAN'S MAD.
MISS EMBER SEEMED EMINENTLY SENSIBLE TO ME.
YOU'RE A SUCKER.
SHE'S GHOSTLY PALE. SHE MIGHT BE ONE OF THOSE WAMPYRES.
THEY'RE VAMPIRES, TAVIA. AND WE SHOULD FOCUS ON OUR TASK.
LET'S REVIEW WHAT WE KNOW.
SURE. WE'RE IN A TOWN DESIGNED BY A MADMAN. HIS DAUGHTER IS OFF HER ROCKER.
AND A NINJA HAS STOLEN A KEY FROM HER. THAT SUMS IT UP.
OH. AND I'M STARTING TO GET SADDLESORES.

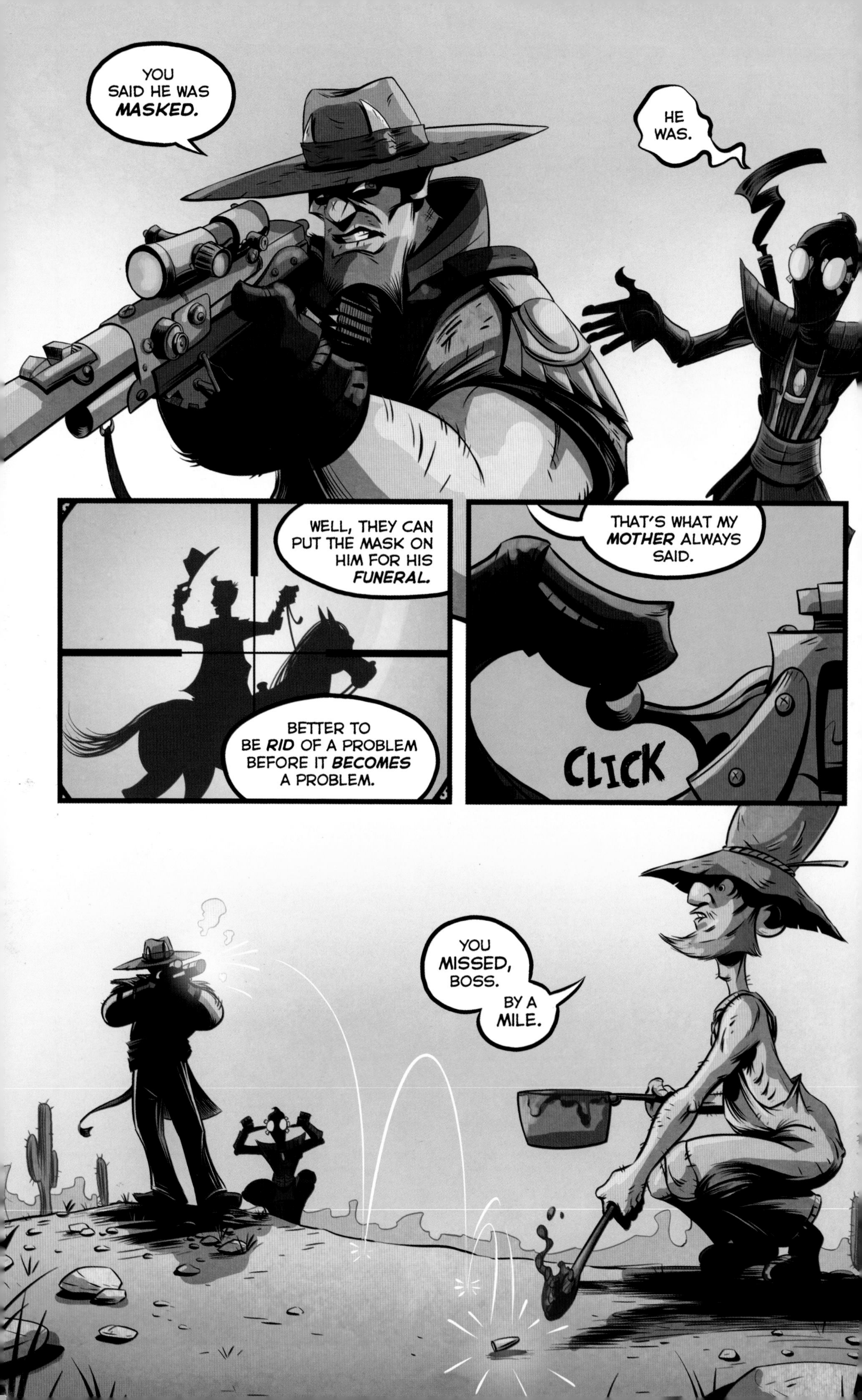
YOU SAID HE WAS *MASKED.*
HE WAS.
WELL, THEY CAN PUT THE MASK ON HIM FOR HIS *FUNERAL.*
BETTER TO BE *RID* OF A PROBLEM BEFORE IT *BECOMES* A PROBLEM.
THAT'S WHAT MY *MOTHER* ALWAYS SAID.
CLICK
YOU MISSED, BOSS.
BY A MILE.

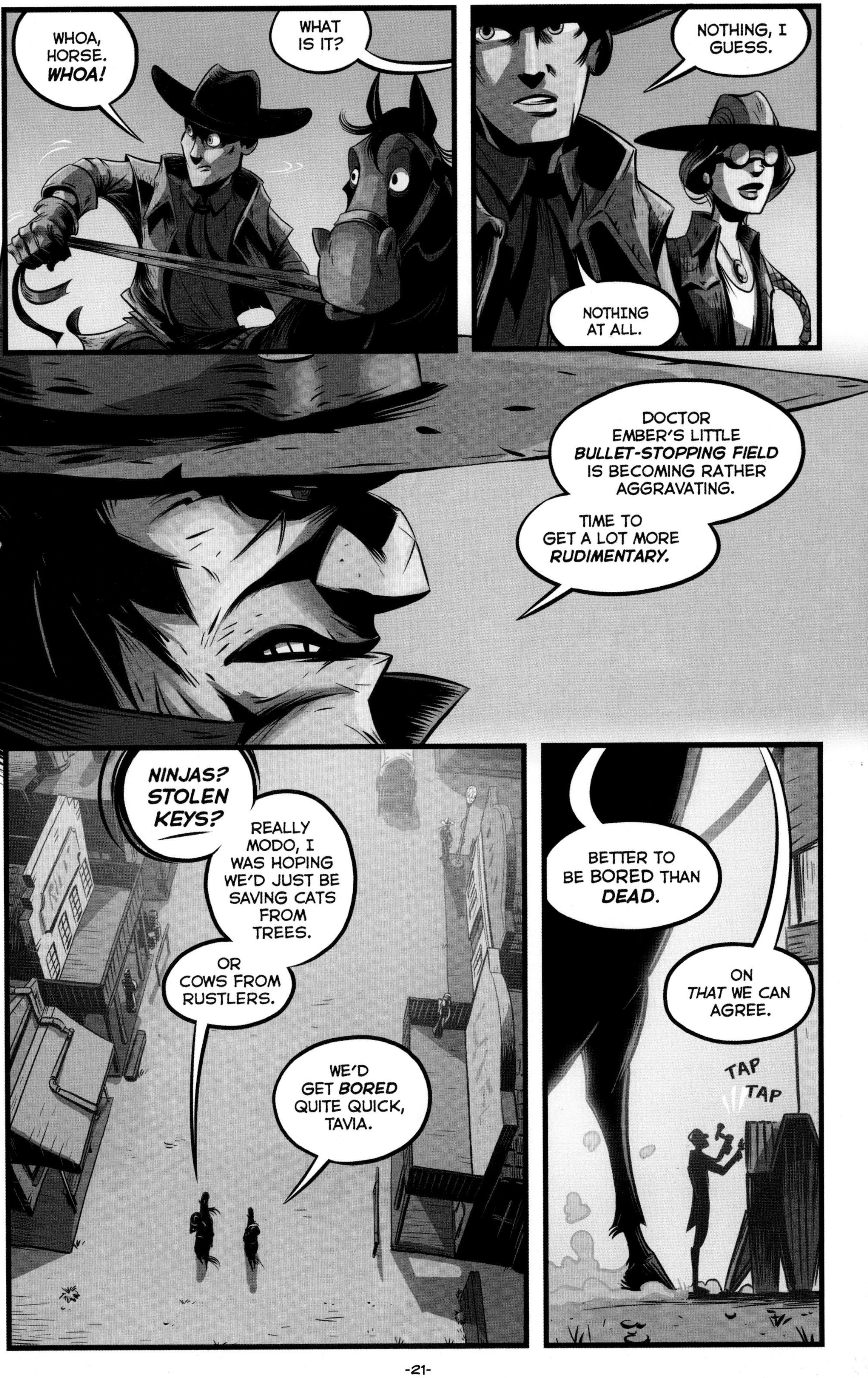
WHOA, HORSE. *WHOA!*
WHAT IS IT?
NOTHING, I GUESS.
NOTHING AT ALL.
DOCTOR EMBER'S LITTLE *BULLET-STOPPING FIELD* IS BECOMING RATHER AGGRAVATING.
TIME TO GET A LOT MORE *RUDIMENTARY.*
NINJAS? STOLEN KEYS?
REALLY MODO, I WAS HOPING WE'D JUST BE SAVING CATS FROM TREES.
OR COWS FROM RUSTLERS.
WE'D GET *BORED* QUITE QUICK, TAVIA.
BETTER TO BE BORED THAN *DEAD*.
ON *THAT* WE CAN AGREE.
TAP TAP

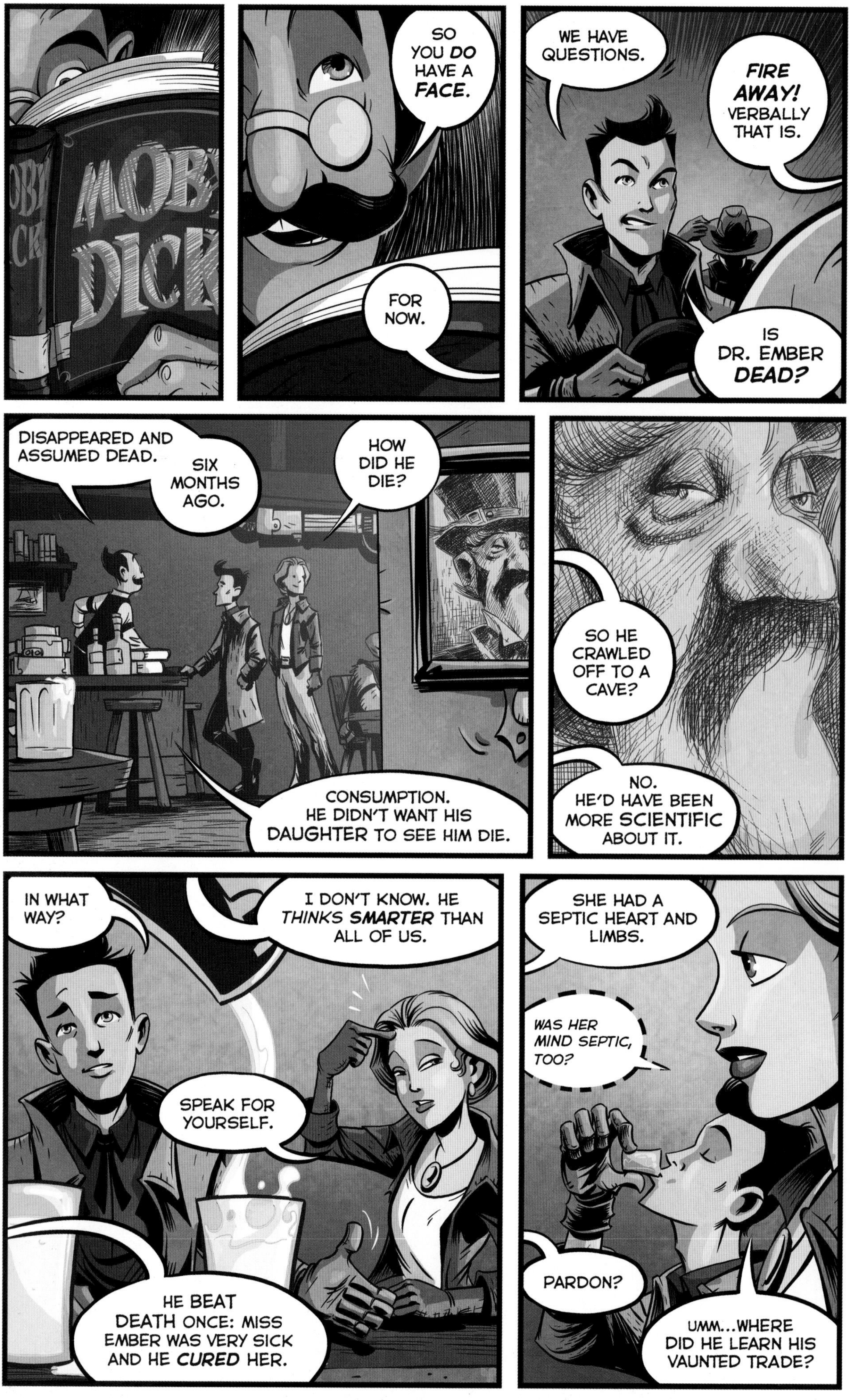

MOBY DICK
SO YOU DO HAVE A FACE.
FOR NOW.
WE HAVE QUESTIONS.
FIRE AWAY! VERBALLY THAT IS.
IS DR. EMBER DEAD?
DISAPPEARED AND ASSUMED DEAD.
SIX MONTHS AGO.
HOW DID HE DIE?
CONSUMPTION. HE DIDN'T WANT HIS DAUGHTER TO SEE HIM DIE.
SO HE CRAWLED OFF TO A CAVE?
NO. HE'D HAVE BEEN MORE SCIENTIFIC ABOUT IT.
IN WHAT WAY?
I DON'T KNOW. HE THINKS SMARTER THAN ALL OF US.
SPEAK FOR YOURSELF.
HE BEAT DEATH ONCE: MISS EMBER WAS VERY SICK AND HE CURED HER.
SHE HAD A SEPTIC HEART AND LIMBS.
WAS HER MIND SEPTIC, TOO?
PARDON?
UMM...WHERE DID HE LEARN HIS VAUNTED TRADE?

FORGIVE THE MELODRAMA-- ON A DARK AND STORMY NIGHT HE TOLD ME HIS TALE.

A MAN WITH A MIND LIKE HIS IS VERY VALUABLE TO THOSE WHO MAKE WAR.

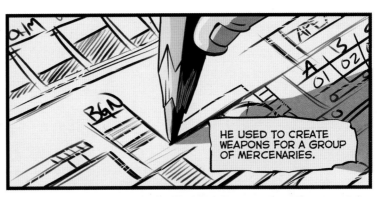

HE USED TO CREATE WEAPONS FOR A GROUP OF MERCENARIES.

VAST SUMS OF MONEY WERE INVOLVED.

HE CREATED SO VERY MANY DESTRUCTIVE DEVICES FOR THEM.

AND THEY USED THOSE DEVICES.

IN MEXICO. CHINA. JAPAN. ANYWHERE SHIPS COULD SAIL.

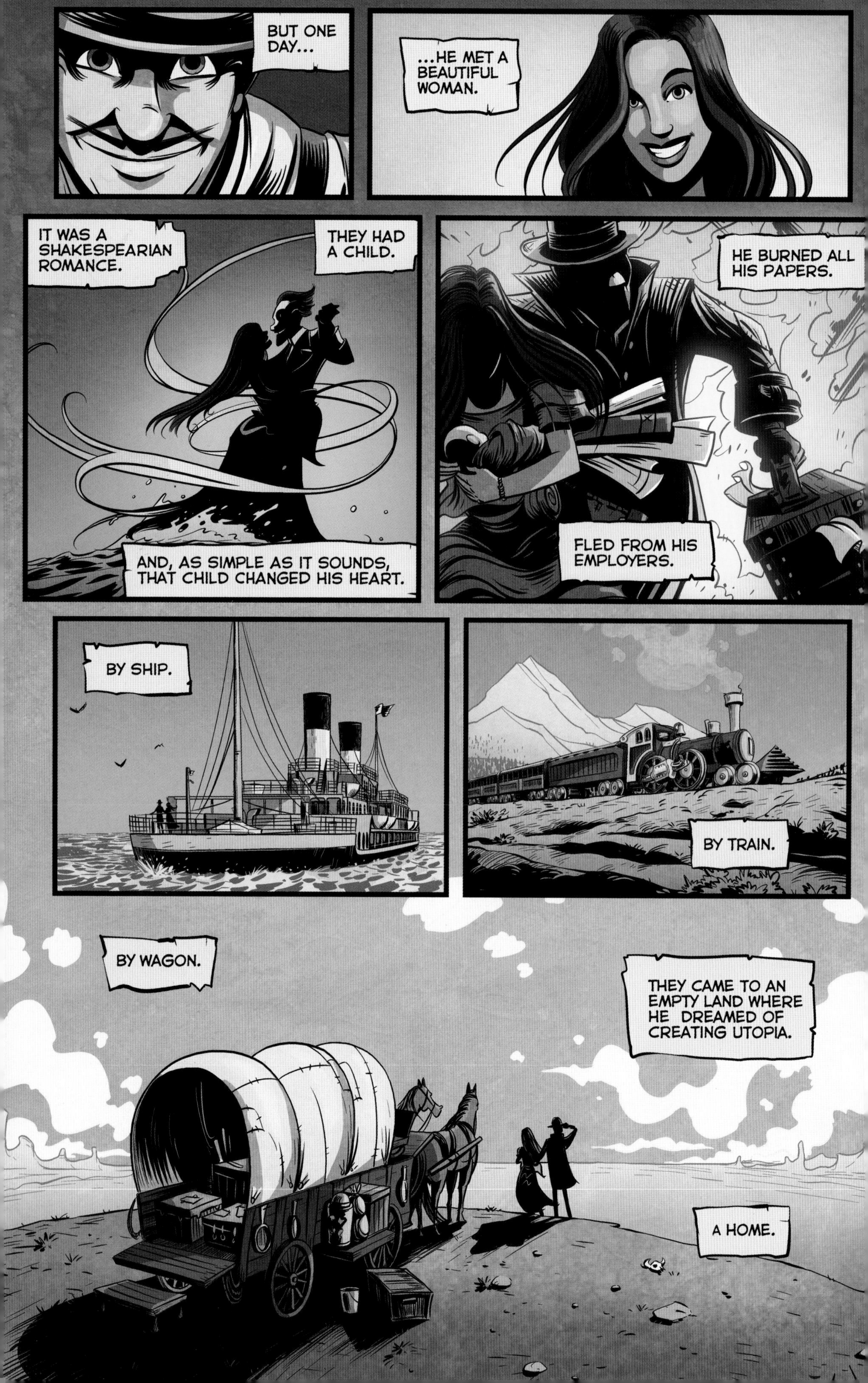
BUT ONE DAY...
...HE MET A BEAUTIFUL WOMAN.
IT WAS A SHAKESPEARIAN ROMANCE.
THEY HAD A CHILD.
AND, AS SIMPLE AS IT SOUNDS, THAT CHILD CHANGED HIS HEART.
HE BURNED ALL HIS PAPERS.
FLED FROM HIS EMPLOYERS.
BY SHIP.
BY TRAIN.
BY WAGON.
THEY CAME TO AN EMPTY LAND WHERE HE DREAMED OF CREATING UTOPIA.
A HOME.

WHY DID THE MERCENARIES FOLLOW HIM FOR ALL THESE YEARS?

REVENGE?

NO. THEY WANTED THAT MAGNIFICENT DEVICE.

IT'S A WEAPON.

BOYS LIKE *WEAPONS*. AND THEY THINK THAT *KEY* WILL *UNLOCK IT*.

ZOUNDS! YOU'RE THINKING LOGICALLY, TAVIA. *CONGRATS!*

STICK THIS *LOGIC* IN YOUR BRAINBOX, MODO. WE HAVE TO *HUNT THEM DOWN*.

WHERE MIGHT THEY BE HOLED UP?

THUCK!

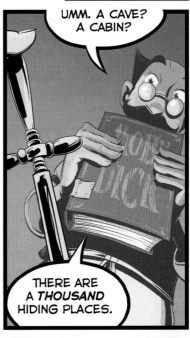

UMM. A CAVE? A CABIN?

THERE ARE A *THOUSAND* HIDING PLACES.

WHERE AND HOW DID THE SHERIFF DIE?

FELL OFF HIS HORSE AND BROKE HIS NECK IN THE ALOCA HILLS.

THEN THAT'S WHERE WE'LL START.

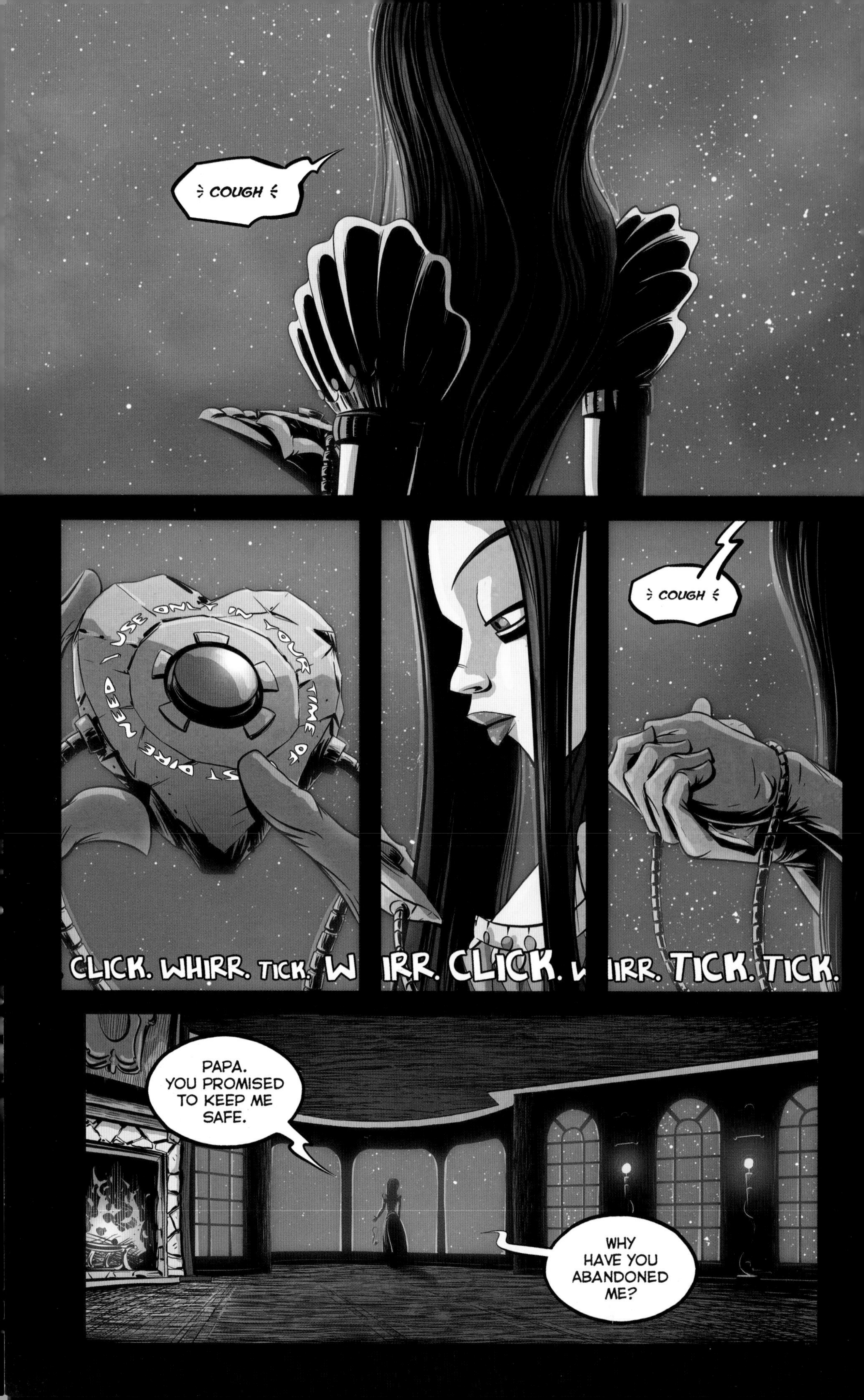
COUGH
USE ONLY IN YOUR TIME OF ... DIRE NEED
COUGH
CLICK. WHIRR. TICK. W IRR. CLICK. W IRR. TICK. TICK.
PAPA. YOU PROMISED TO KEEP ME SAFE.
WHY HAVE YOU ABANDONED ME?

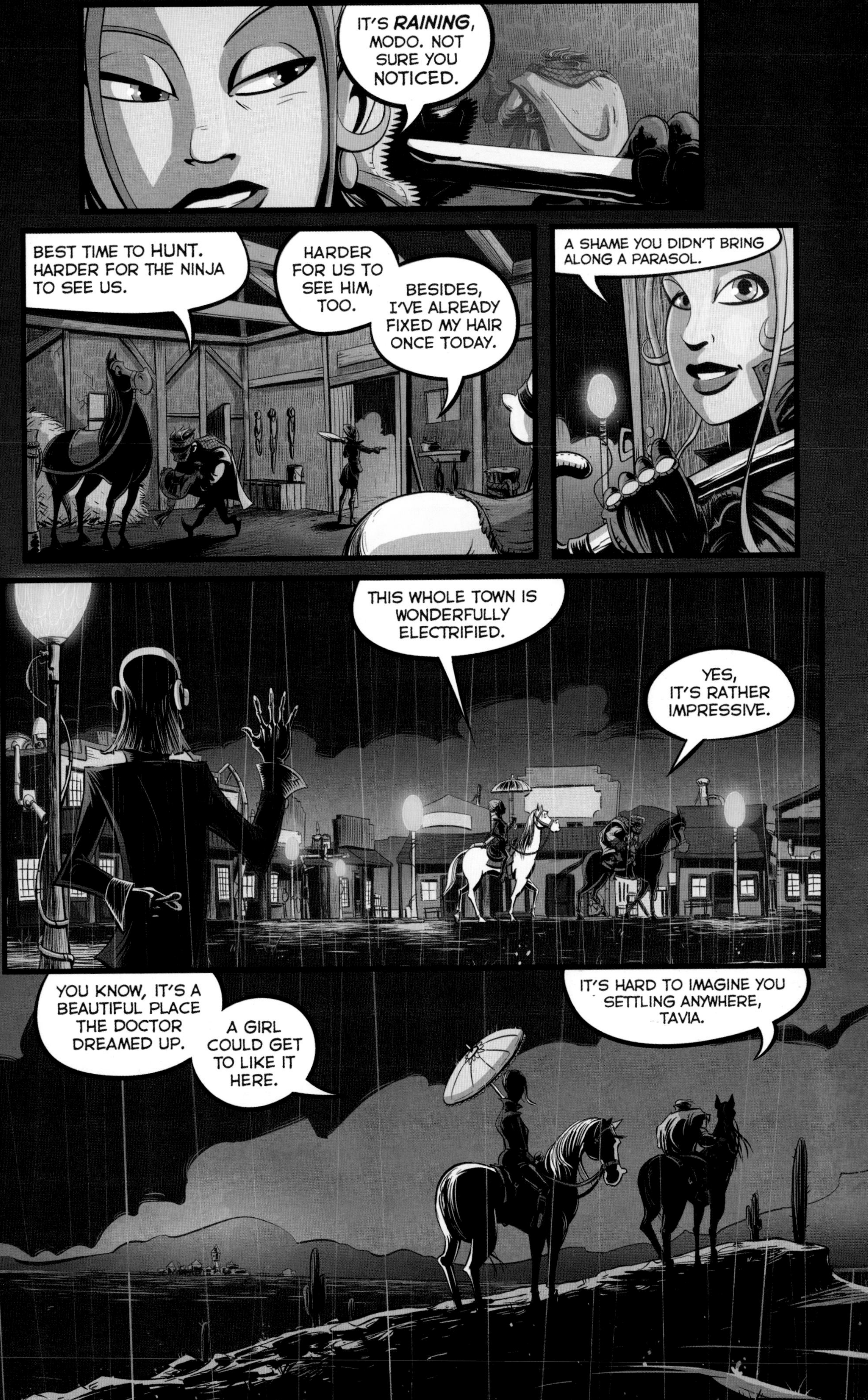
IT'S RAINING, MODO. NOT SURE YOU NOTICED.
BEST TIME TO HUNT. HARDER FOR THE NINJA TO SEE US.
HARDER FOR US TO SEE HIM, TOO.
BESIDES, I'VE ALREADY FIXED MY HAIR ONCE TODAY.
A SHAME YOU DIDN'T BRING ALONG A PARASOL.
THIS WHOLE TOWN IS WONDERFULLY ELECTRIFIED.
YES, IT'S RATHER IMPRESSIVE.
YOU KNOW, IT'S A BEAUTIFUL PLACE THE DOCTOR DREAMED UP.
A GIRL COULD GET TO LIKE IT HERE.
IT'S HARD TO IMAGINE YOU SETTLING ANYWHERE, TAVIA.

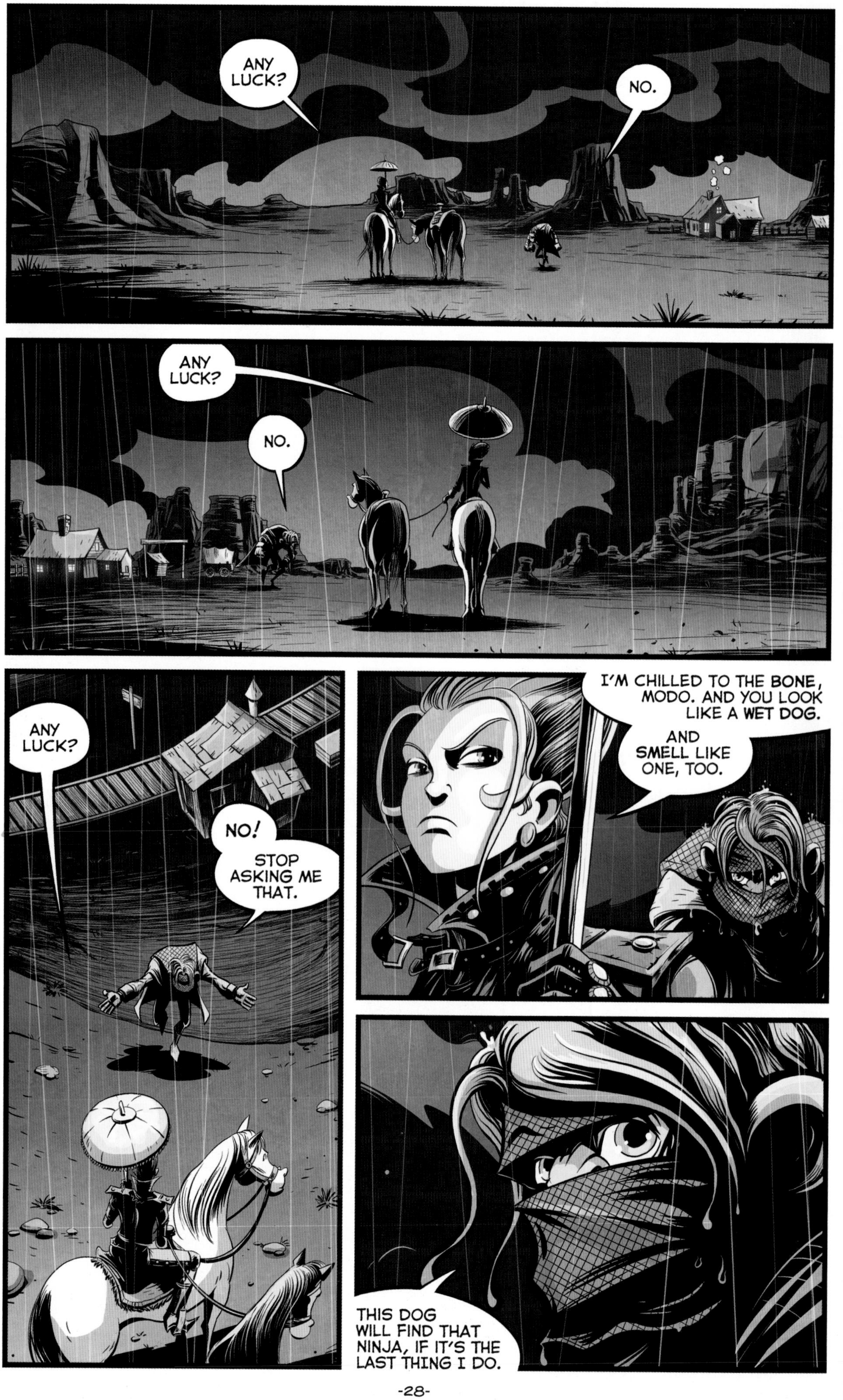
ANY LUCK?
NO.
ANY LUCK?
NO.
ANY LUCK?
NO! STOP ASKING ME THAT.
I'M CHILLED TO THE BONE, MODO. AND YOU LOOK LIKE A WET DOG.
AND SMELL LIKE ONE, TOO.
THIS DOG WILL FIND THAT NINJA, IF IT'S THE LAST THING I DO.

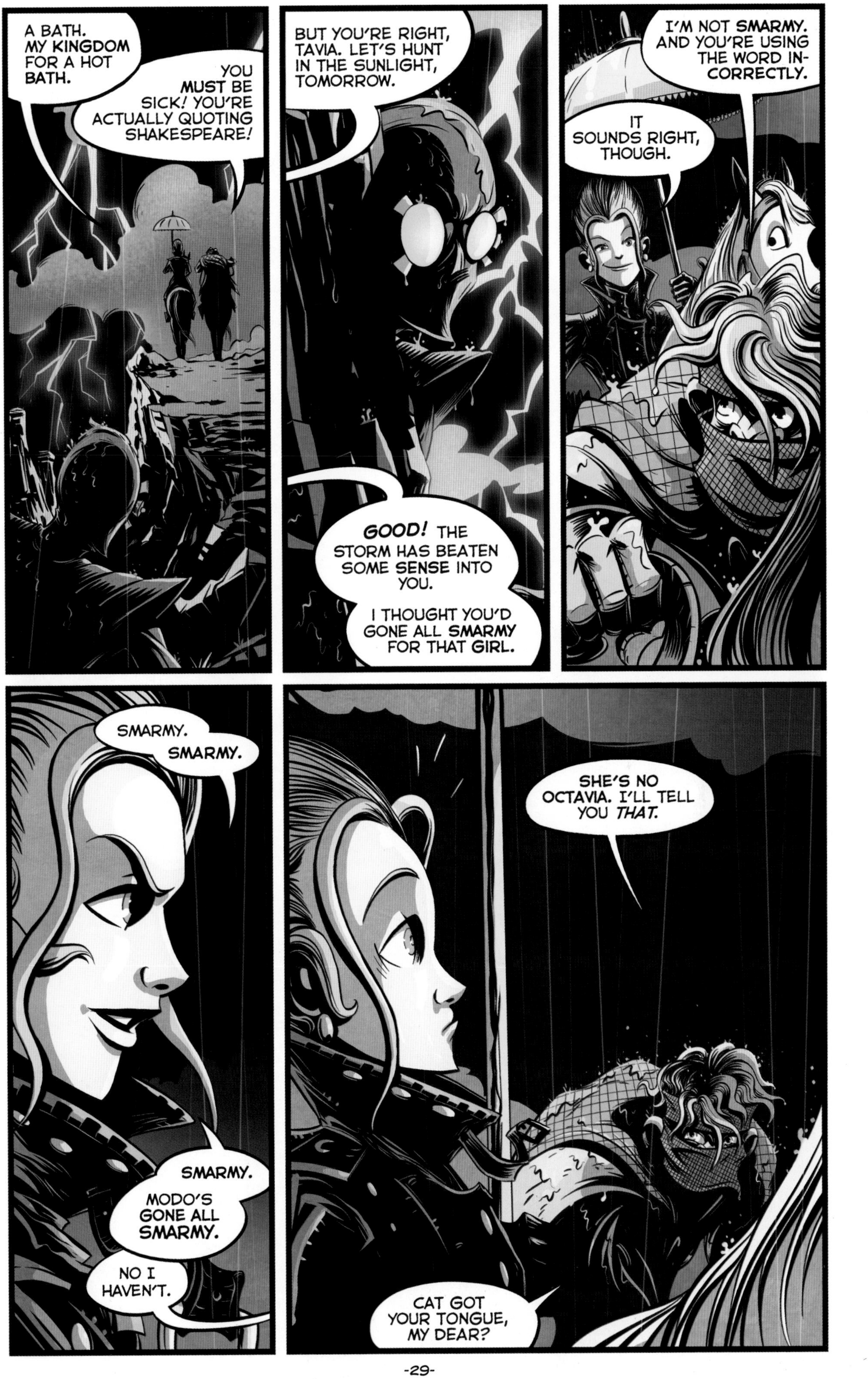
A BATH. MY KINGDOM FOR A HOT BATH.
YOU MUST BE SICK! YOU'RE ACTUALLY QUOTING SHAKESPEARE!
BUT YOU'RE RIGHT, TAVIA. LET'S HUNT IN THE SUNLIGHT, TOMORROW.
GOOD! THE STORM HAS BEATEN SOME SENSE INTO YOU.
I THOUGHT YOU'D GONE ALL SMARMY FOR THAT GIRL.
I'M NOT SMARMY. AND YOU'RE USING THE WORD INCORRECTLY.
IT SOUNDS RIGHT, THOUGH.
SMARMY.
SMARMY.
SMARMY.
MODO'S GONE ALL SMARMY.
NO I HAVEN'T.
SHE'S NO OCTAVIA. I'LL TELL YOU THAT.
CAT GOT YOUR TONGUE, MY DEAR?

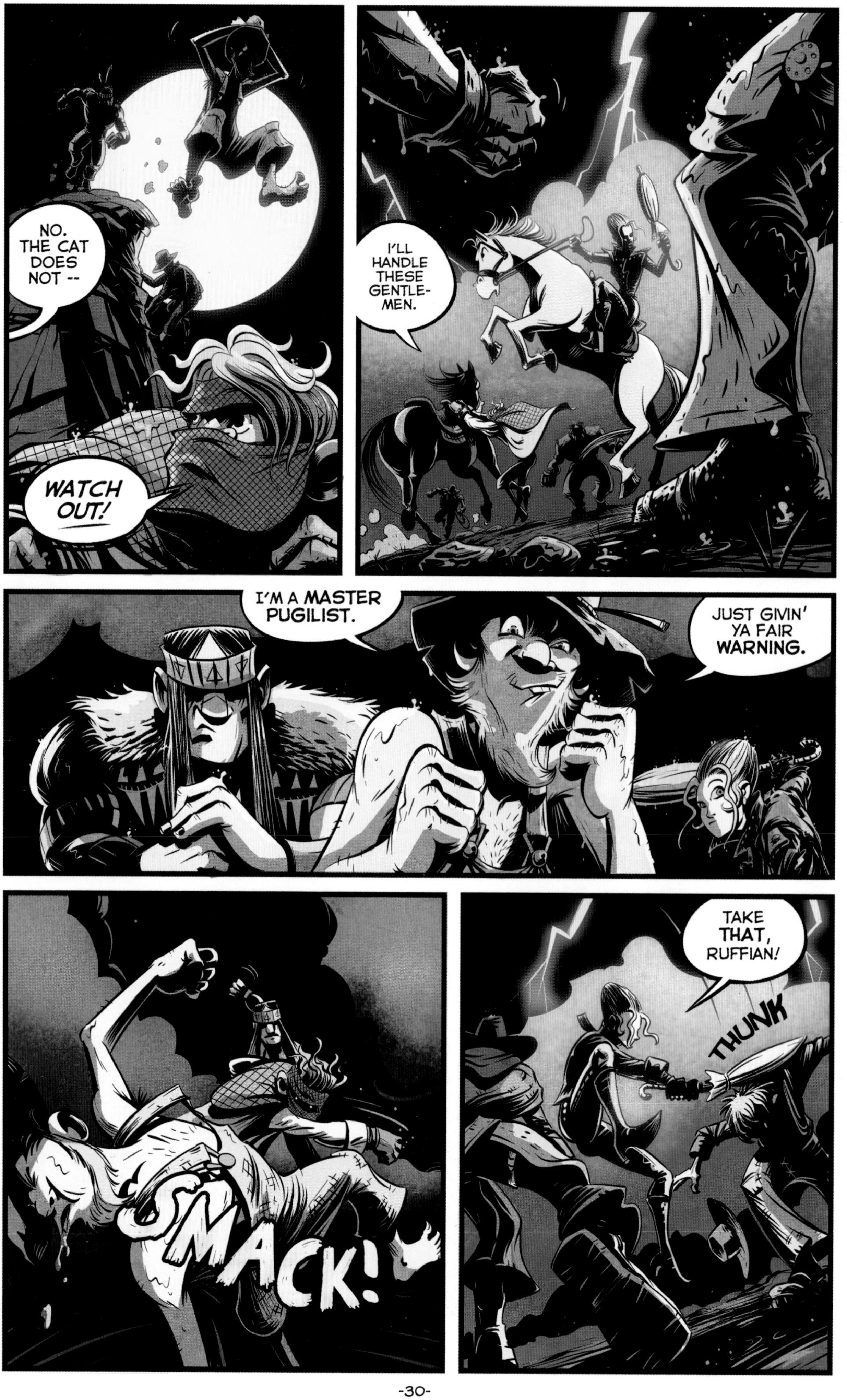
NO. THE CAT DOES NOT --
WATCH OUT!
I'LL HANDLE THESE GENTLE-MEN.
I'M A MASTER PUGILIST.
JUST GIVIN' YA FAIR WARNING.
SMACK!
TAKE THAT, RUFFIAN!
THUNK

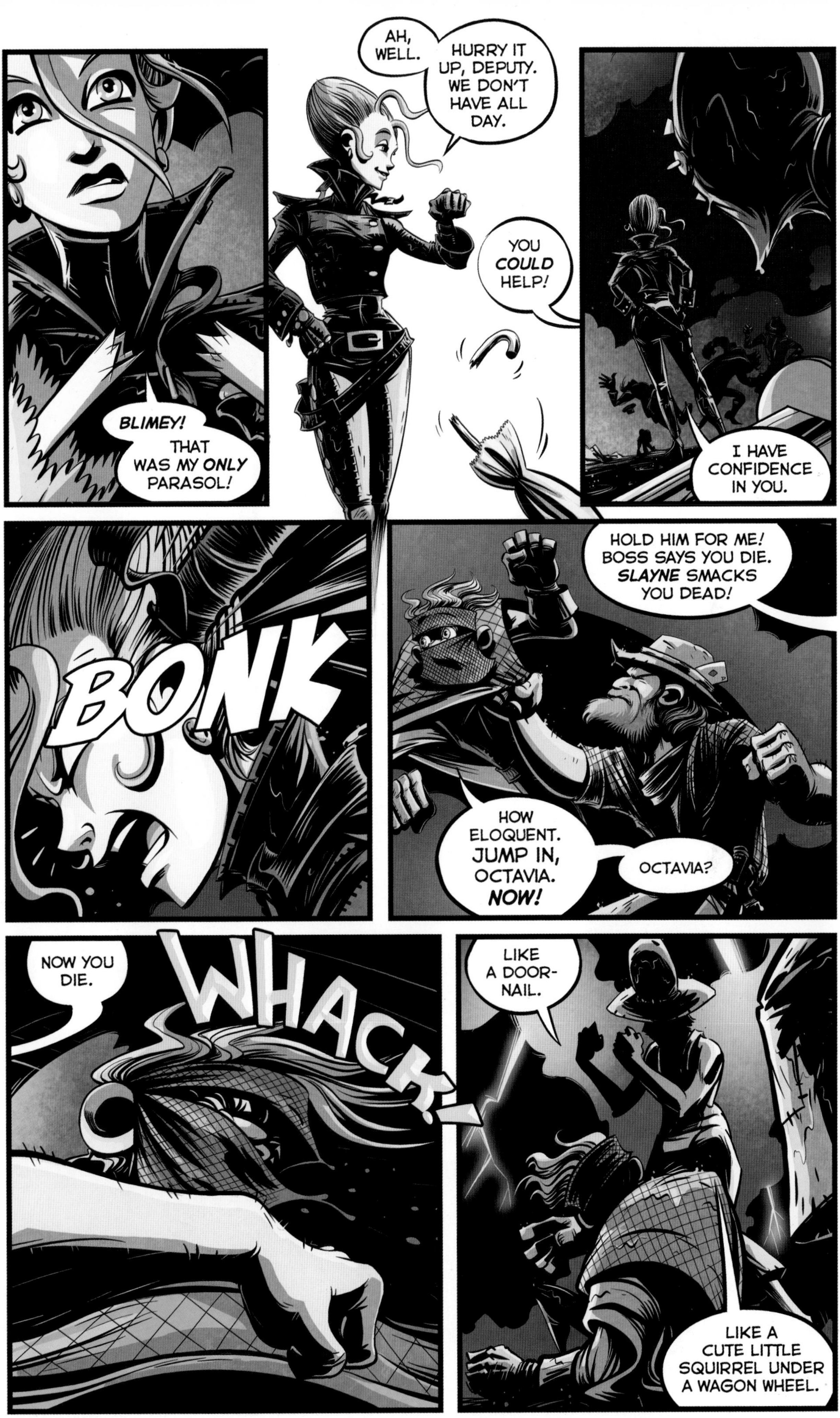
BLIMEY! THAT WAS MY ONLY PARASOL!
AH, WELL.
HURRY IT UP, DEPUTY. WE DON'T HAVE ALL DAY.
YOU COULD HELP!
I HAVE CONFIDENCE IN YOU.
BONK
HOLD HIM FOR ME! BOSS SAYS YOU DIE. SLAYNE SMACKS YOU DEAD!
HOW ELOQUENT. JUMP IN, OCTAVIA. NOW!
OCTAVIA?
NOW YOU DIE.
WHACK!
LIKE A DOOR-NAIL.
LIKE A CUTE LITTLE SQUIRREL UNDER A WAGON WHEEL.

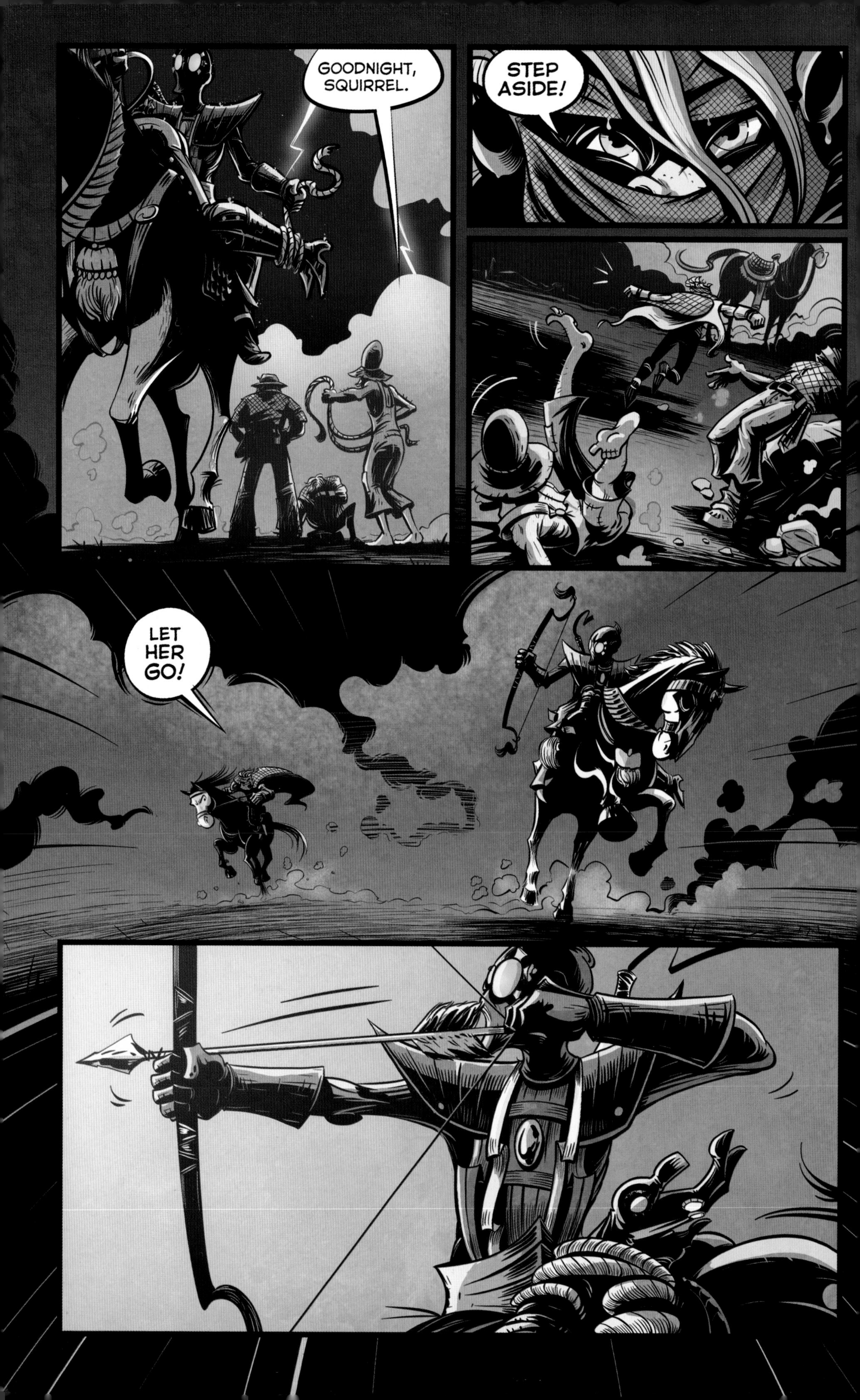
GOODNIGHT, SQUIRREL.
STEP ASIDE!
LET HER GO!

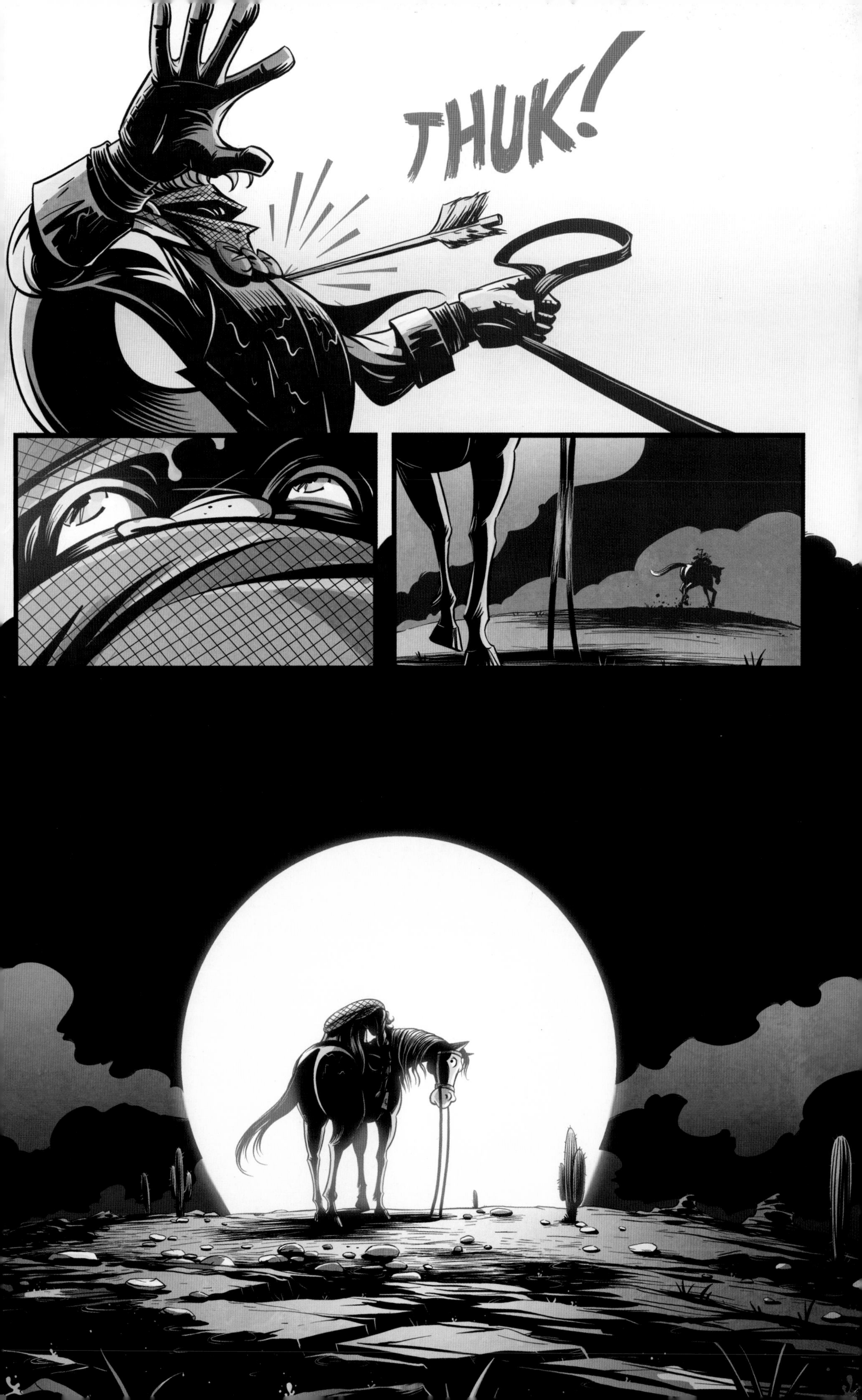
THUK!

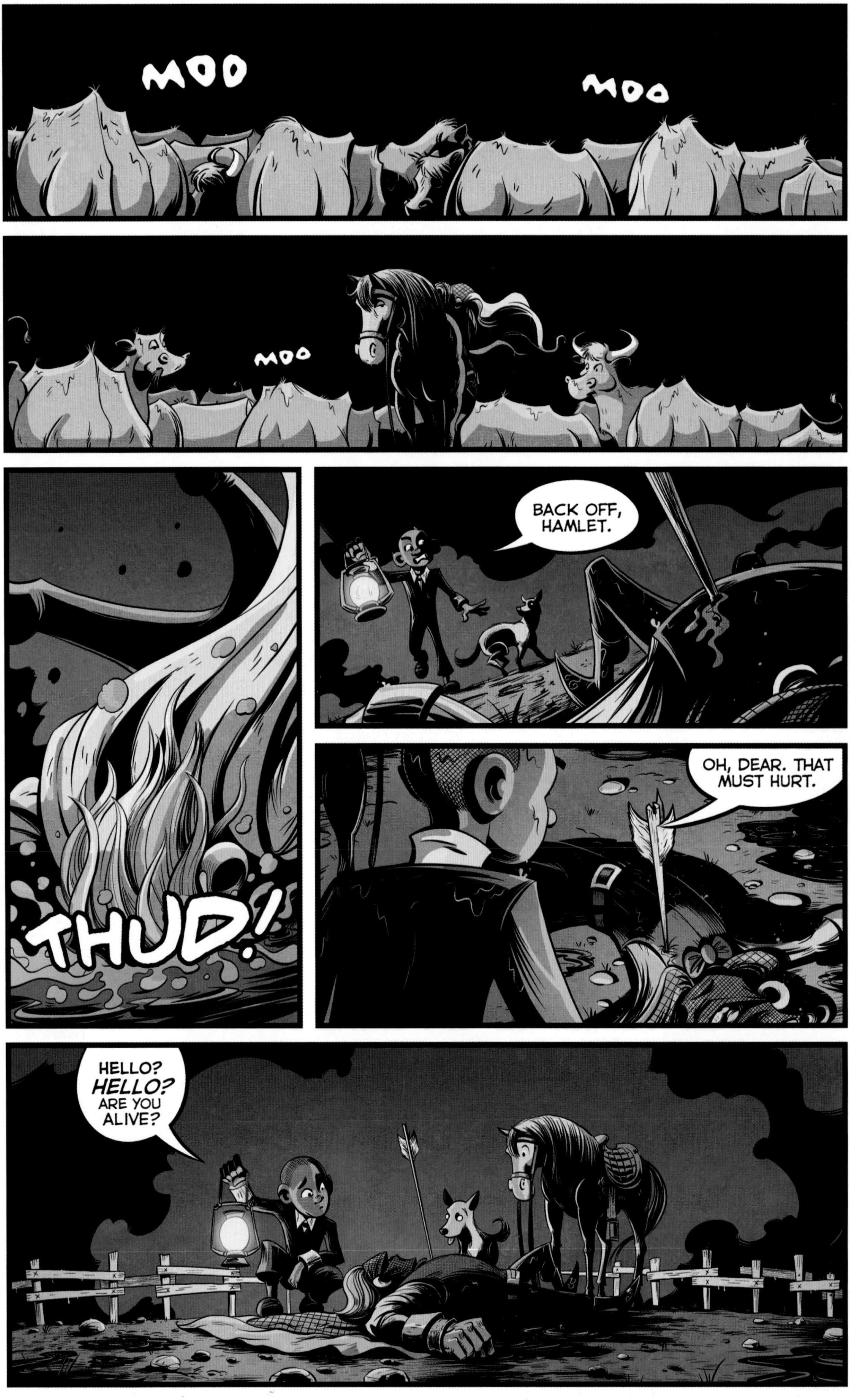
MOO
MOO
MOO
THUD!
BACK OFF, HAMLET.
OH, DEAR. THAT MUST HURT.
HELLO? *HELLO?* ARE YOU ALIVE?

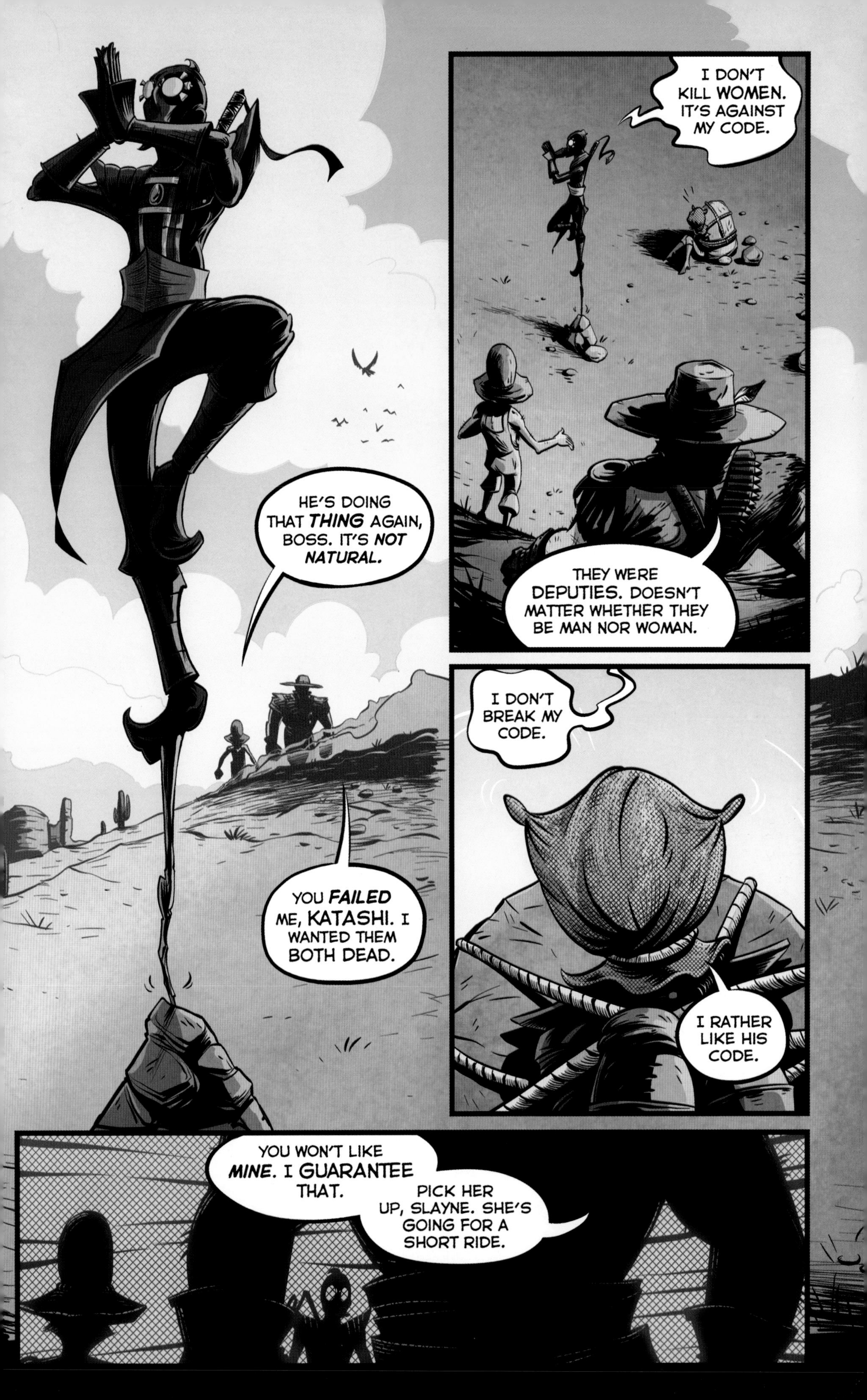
HE'S DOING THAT THING AGAIN, BOSS. IT'S NOT NATURAL.
YOU FAILED ME, KATASHI. I WANTED THEM BOTH DEAD.
I DON'T KILL WOMEN. IT'S AGAINST MY CODE.
THEY WERE DEPUTIES. DOESN'T MATTER WHETHER THEY BE MAN NOR WOMAN.
I DON'T BREAK MY CODE.
I RATHER LIKE HIS CODE.
YOU WON'T LIKE MINE. I GUARANTEE THAT.
PICK HER UP, SLAYNE. SHE'S GOING FOR A SHORT RIDE.

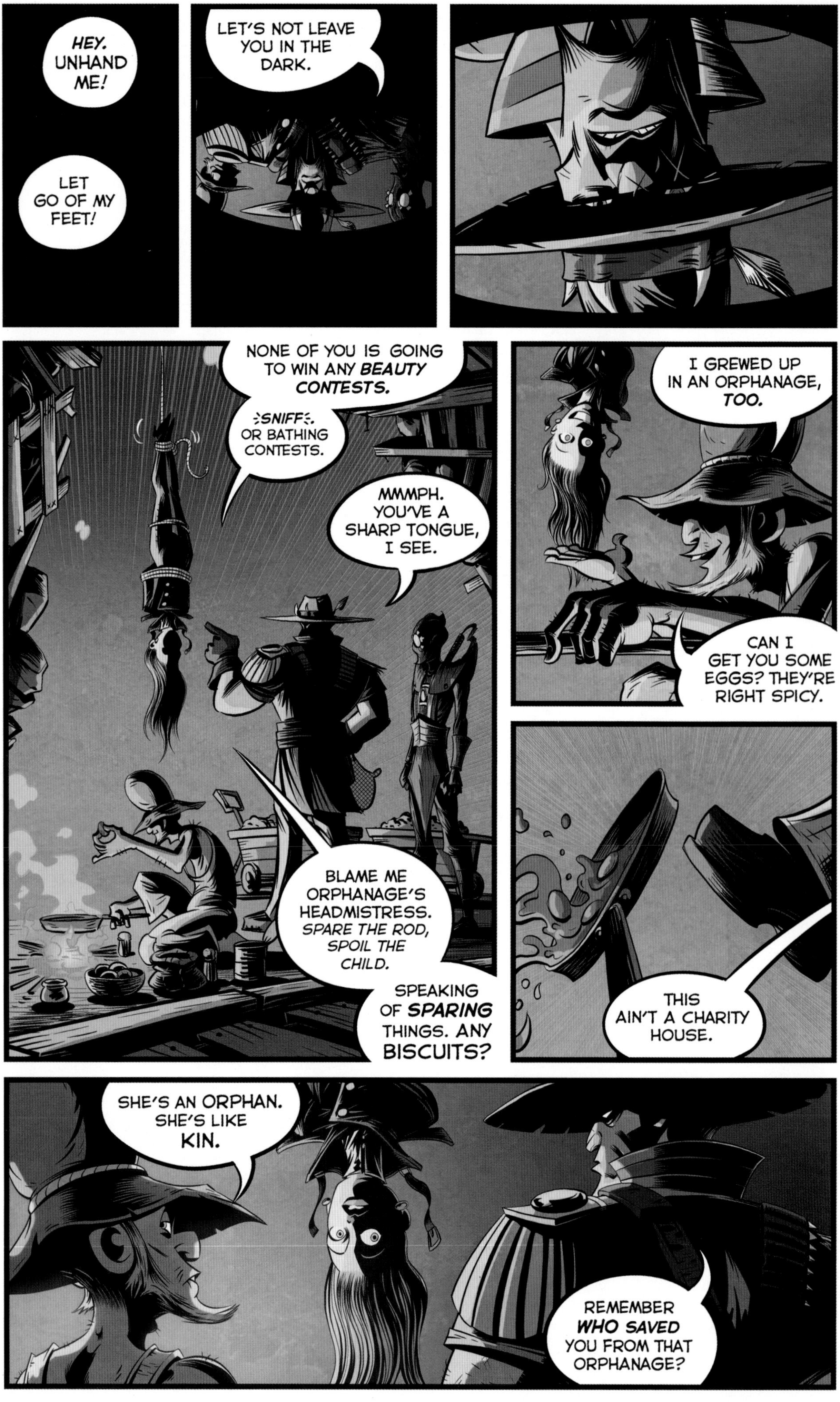
HEY. UNHAND ME!
LET GO OF MY FEET!
LET'S NOT LEAVE YOU IN THE DARK.
NONE OF YOU IS GOING TO WIN ANY BEAUTY CONTESTS.
SNIFF. OR BATHING CONTESTS.
MMMPH. YOU'VE A SHARP TONGUE, I SEE.
BLAME ME ORPHANAGE'S HEADMISTRESS. SPARE THE ROD, SPOIL THE CHILD.
SPEAKING OF SPARING THINGS. ANY BISCUITS?
I GREWED UP IN AN ORPHANAGE, TOO.
CAN I GET YOU SOME EGGS? THEY'RE RIGHT SPICY.
THIS AIN'T A CHARITY HOUSE.
SHE'S AN ORPHAN. SHE'S LIKE KIN.
REMEMBER WHO SAVED YOU FROM THAT ORPHANAGE?

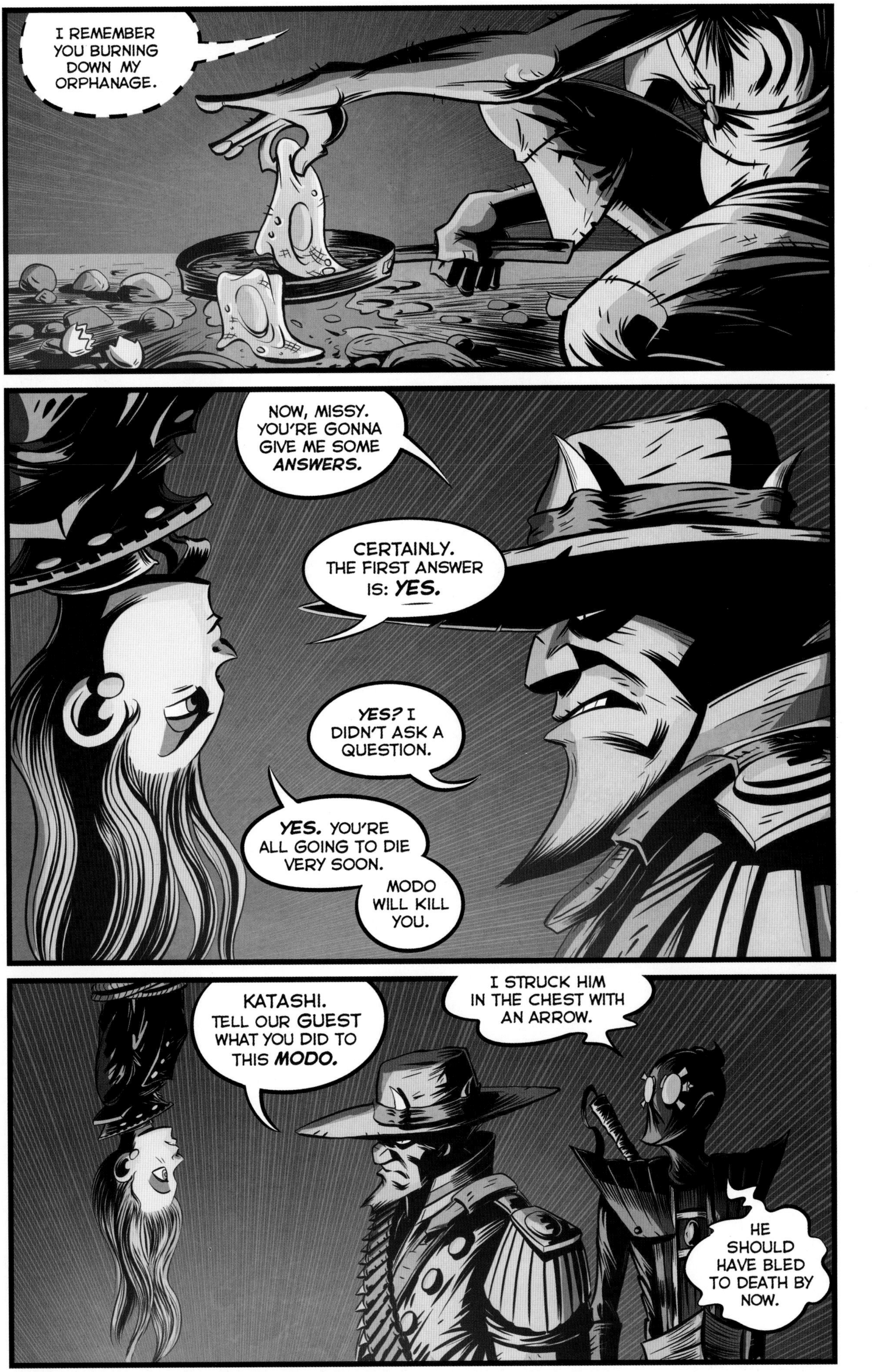
I REMEMBER YOU BURNING DOWN MY ORPHANAGE.
NOW, MISSY. YOU'RE GONNA GIVE ME SOME ANSWERS.
CERTAINLY. THE FIRST ANSWER IS: YES.
YES? I DIDN'T ASK A QUESTION.
YES. YOU'RE ALL GOING TO DIE VERY SOON.
MODO WILL KILL YOU.
KATASHI. TELL OUR GUEST WHAT YOU DID TO THIS MODO.
I STRUCK HIM IN THE CHEST WITH AN ARROW.
HE SHOULD HAVE BLED TO DEATH BY NOW.

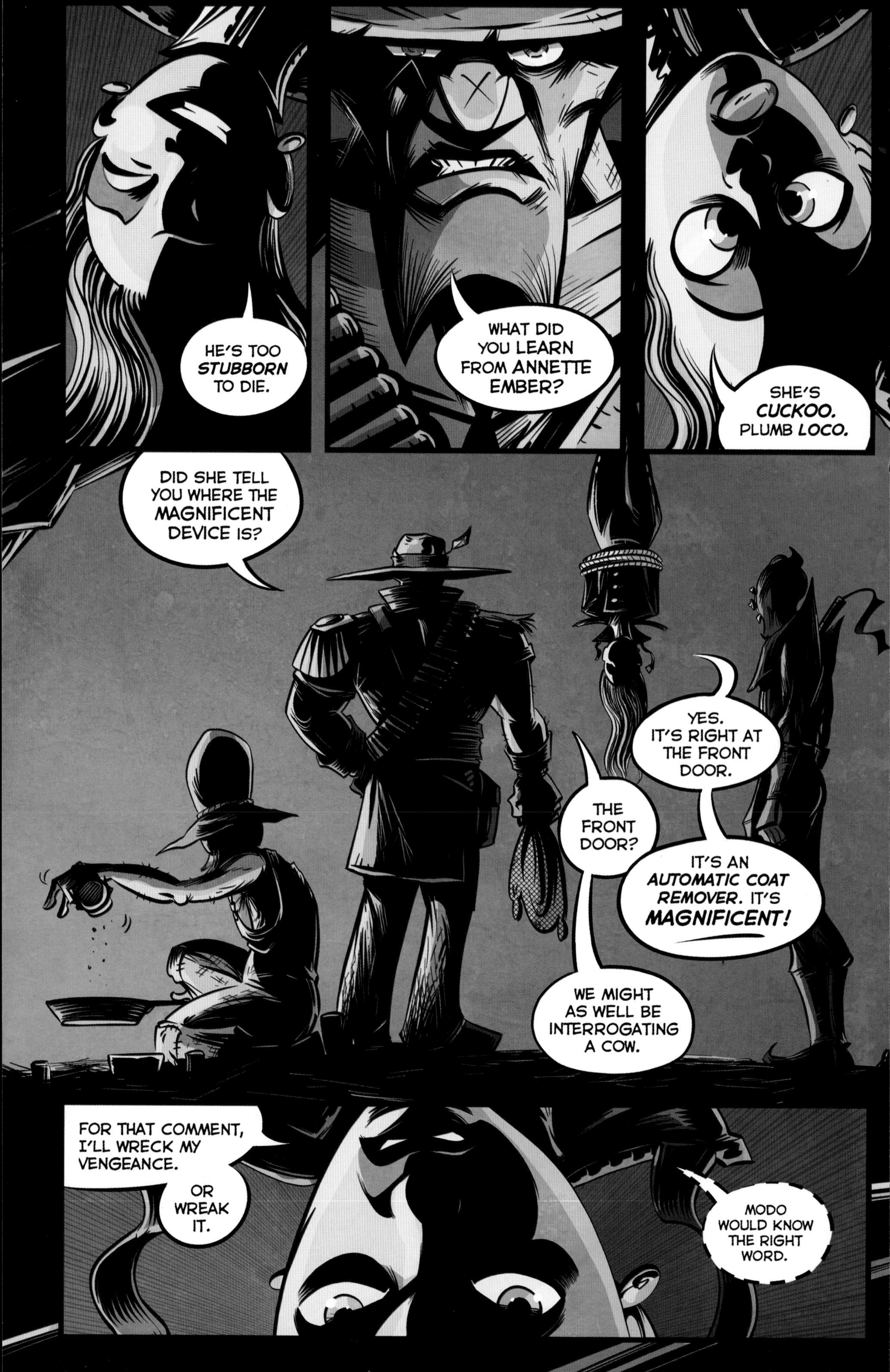
HE'S TOO STUBBORN TO DIE.
WHAT DID YOU LEARN FROM ANNETTE EMBER?
SHE'S CUCKOO. PLUMB LOCO.
DID SHE TELL YOU WHERE THE MAGNIFICENT DEVICE IS?
YES. IT'S RIGHT AT THE FRONT DOOR.
THE FRONT DOOR?
IT'S AN AUTOMATIC COAT REMOVER. IT'S MAGNIFICENT!
WE MIGHT AS WELL BE INTERROGATING A COW.
FOR THAT COMMENT, I'LL WRECK MY VENGEANCE.
OR WREAK IT.
MODO WOULD KNOW THE RIGHT WORD.

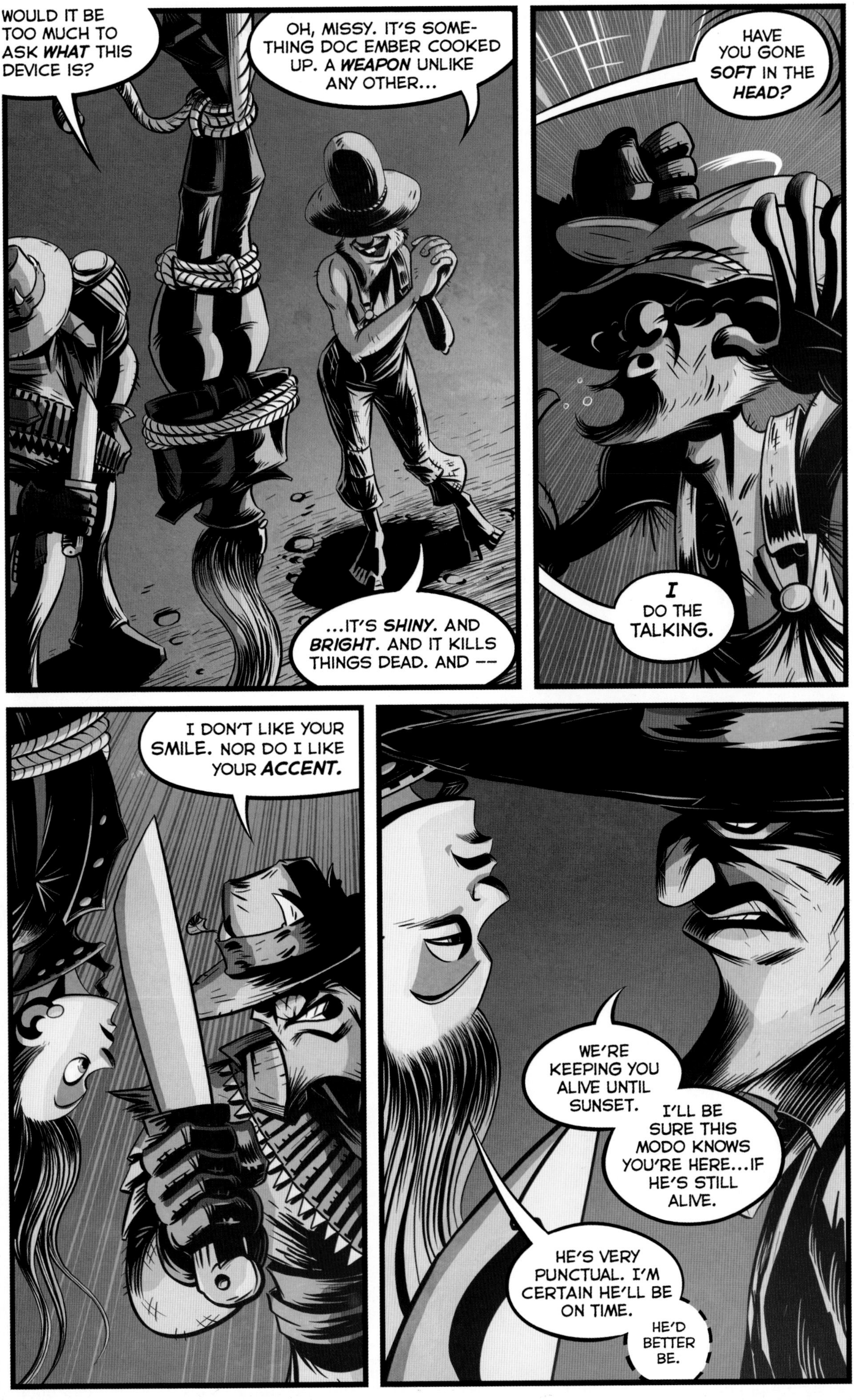
WOULD IT BE TOO MUCH TO ASK *WHAT* THIS DEVICE IS?
OH, MISSY. IT'S SOMETHING DOC EMBER COOKED UP. A *WEAPON* UNLIKE ANY OTHER...
...IT'S *SHINY*. AND *BRIGHT*. AND IT KILLS THINGS DEAD. AND --
HAVE YOU GONE *SOFT* IN THE *HEAD?*
I DO THE TALKING.
I DON'T LIKE YOUR SMILE. NOR DO I LIKE YOUR *ACCENT.*
WE'RE KEEPING YOU ALIVE UNTIL SUNSET.
I'LL BE SURE THIS MODO KNOWS YOU'RE HERE...IF HE'S STILL ALIVE.
HE'S VERY PUNCTUAL. I'M CERTAIN HE'LL BE ON TIME.
HE'D BETTER BE.

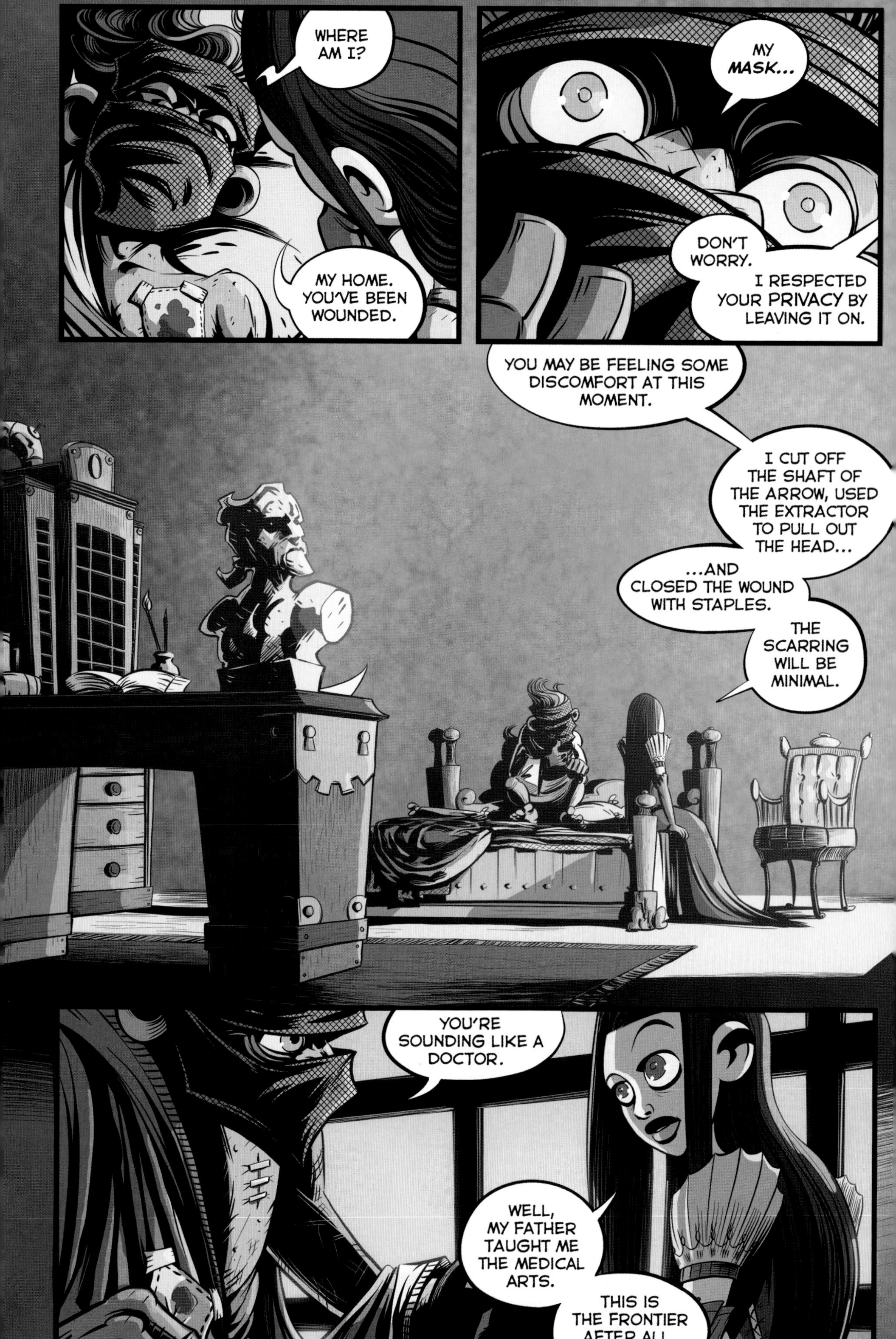
WHERE AM I?
MY HOME. YOU'VE BEEN WOUNDED.
MY MASK...
DON'T WORRY.
I RESPECTED YOUR PRIVACY BY LEAVING IT ON.
YOU MAY BE FEELING SOME DISCOMFORT AT THIS MOMENT.
I CUT OFF THE SHAFT OF THE ARROW, USED THE EXTRACTOR TO PULL OUT THE HEAD...
...AND CLOSED THE WOUND WITH STAPLES.
THE SCARRING WILL BE MINIMAL.
YOU'RE SOUNDING LIKE A DOCTOR.
WELL, MY FATHER TAUGHT ME THE MEDICAL ARTS.
THIS IS THE FRONTIER AFTER ALL.

UGH!

THAT DOES HURT.

IT'S A *WOUND.* WOUNDS HURT.

BUT I HAVE TO GO. THEY HAVE OCTAVIA.

I SUGGEST YOU STAY STILL.

YOU RISK REOPENING YOUR WOUND.

DID ONE OF HER CAPTORS HAVE A SCARRED FACE?

I DON'T KNOW.

IT WAS DARK. I COULDN'T SEE THEIR FACES ALL THAT WELL. WHY?

MY FATHER WAS CERTAIN THAT MY *UNCLE,* AN EXTREMELY VIOLENT MAN, IS SEARCHING FOR US.

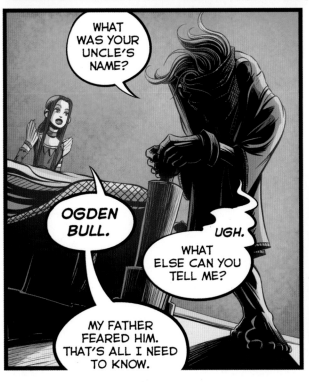

WHAT WAS YOUR UNCLE'S NAME?

OGDEN BULL.

UGH.

WHAT ELSE CAN YOU TELL ME?

MY FATHER FEARED HIM. THAT'S ALL I NEED TO KNOW.

LOOK, IF YOU INSIST ON GETTING UP, YOU'LL NEED SOME CLOTHES. YOURS WERE BLOODIED.

YOU CAN WEAR MY FATHER'S.

GET DRESSED. I'LL TURN MY BACK.

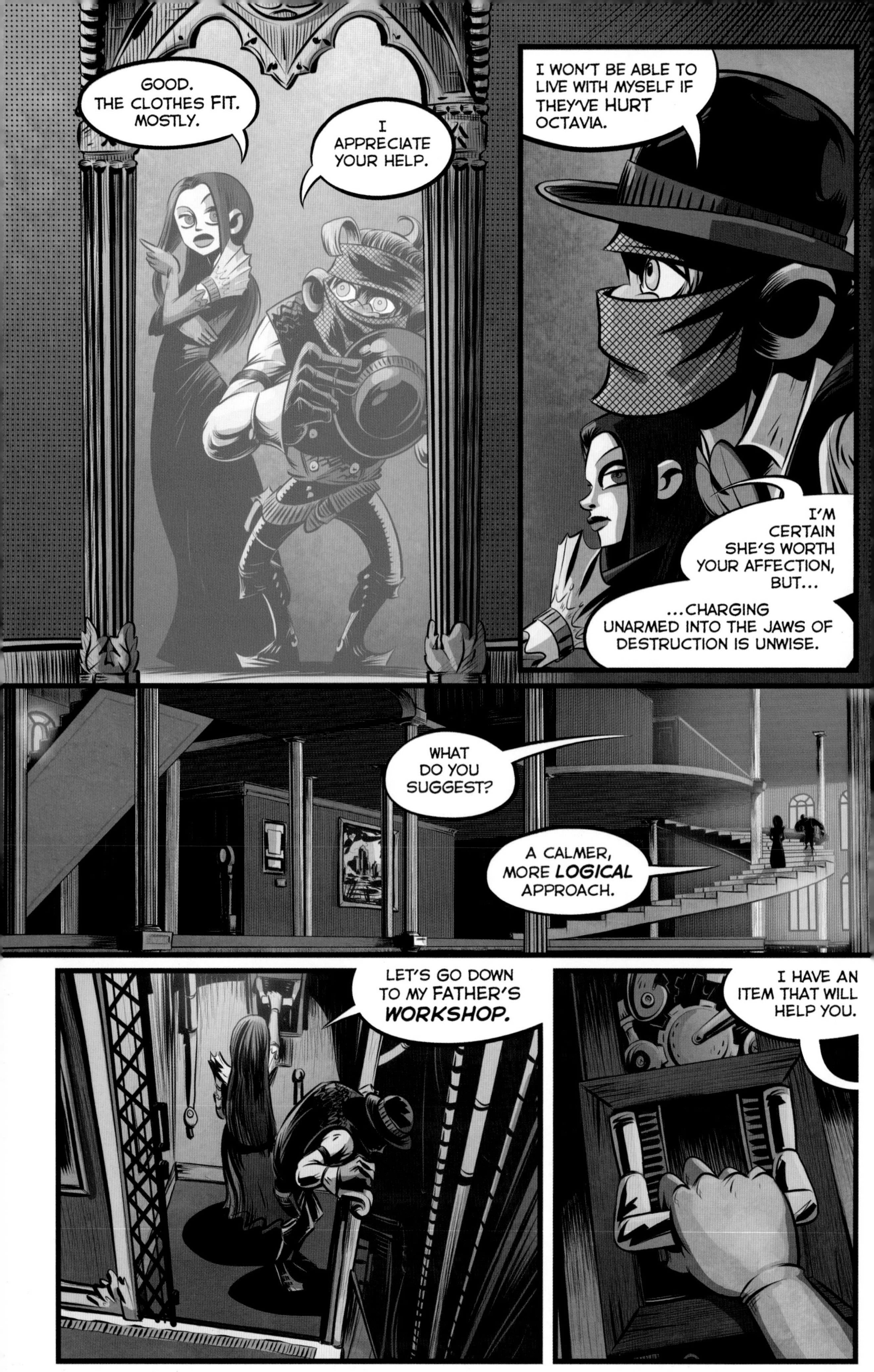
GOOD. THE CLOTHES FIT. MOSTLY.
I APPRECIATE YOUR HELP.
I WON'T BE ABLE TO LIVE WITH MYSELF IF THEY'VE HURT OCTAVIA.
I'M CERTAIN SHE'S WORTH YOUR AFFECTION, BUT...
...CHARGING UNARMED INTO THE JAWS OF DESTRUCTION IS UNWISE.
WHAT DO YOU SUGGEST?
A CALMER, MORE *LOGICAL* APPROACH.
LET'S GO DOWN TO MY FATHER'S *WORKSHOP.*
I HAVE AN ITEM THAT WILL HELP YOU.

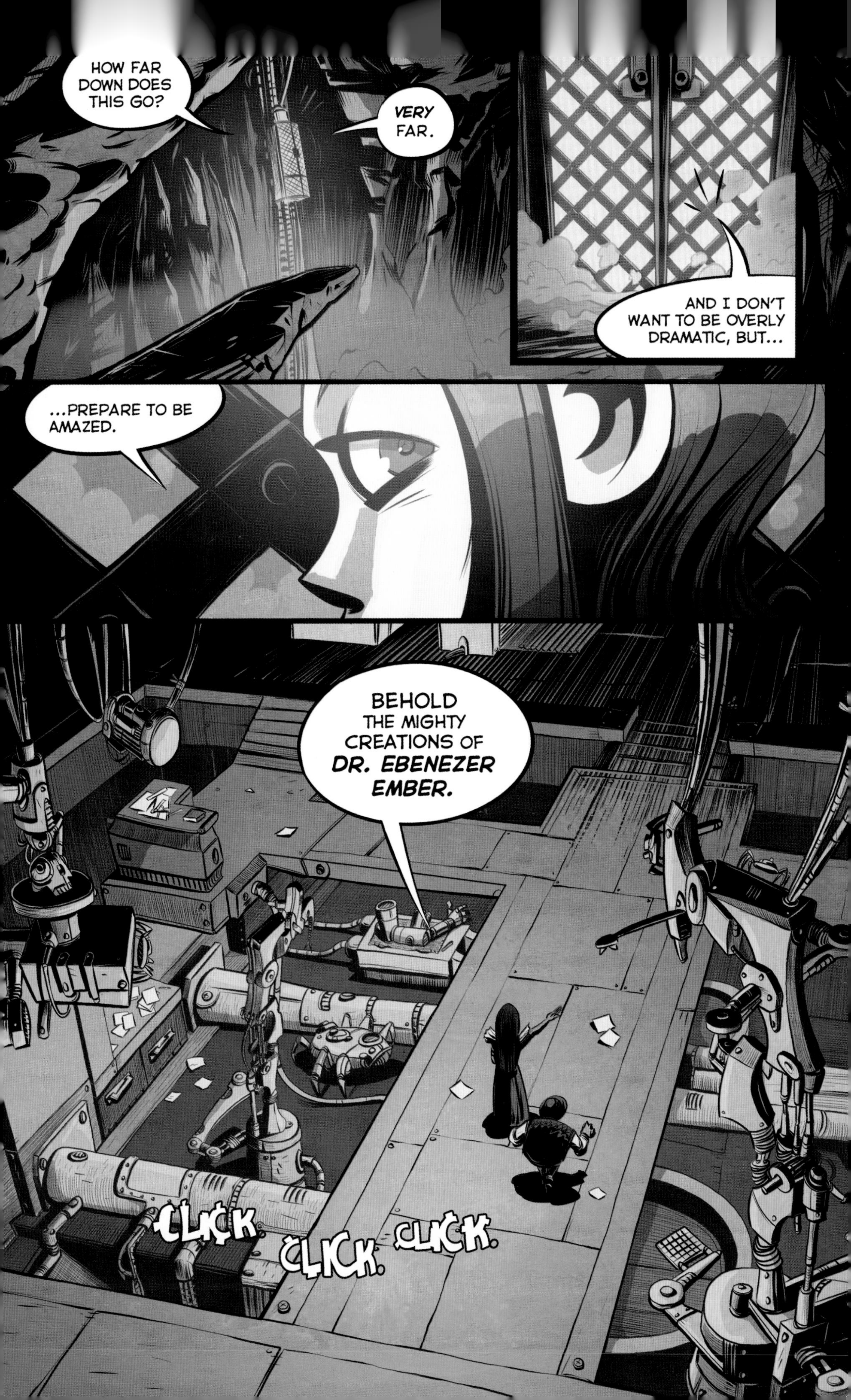
HOW FAR DOWN DOES THIS GO?
VERY FAR.
AND I DON'T WANT TO BE OVERLY DRAMATIC, BUT...
...PREPARE TO BE AMAZED.
BEHOLD THE MIGHTY CREATIONS OF DR. EBENEZER EMBER.
CLICK. CLICK. CLICK.

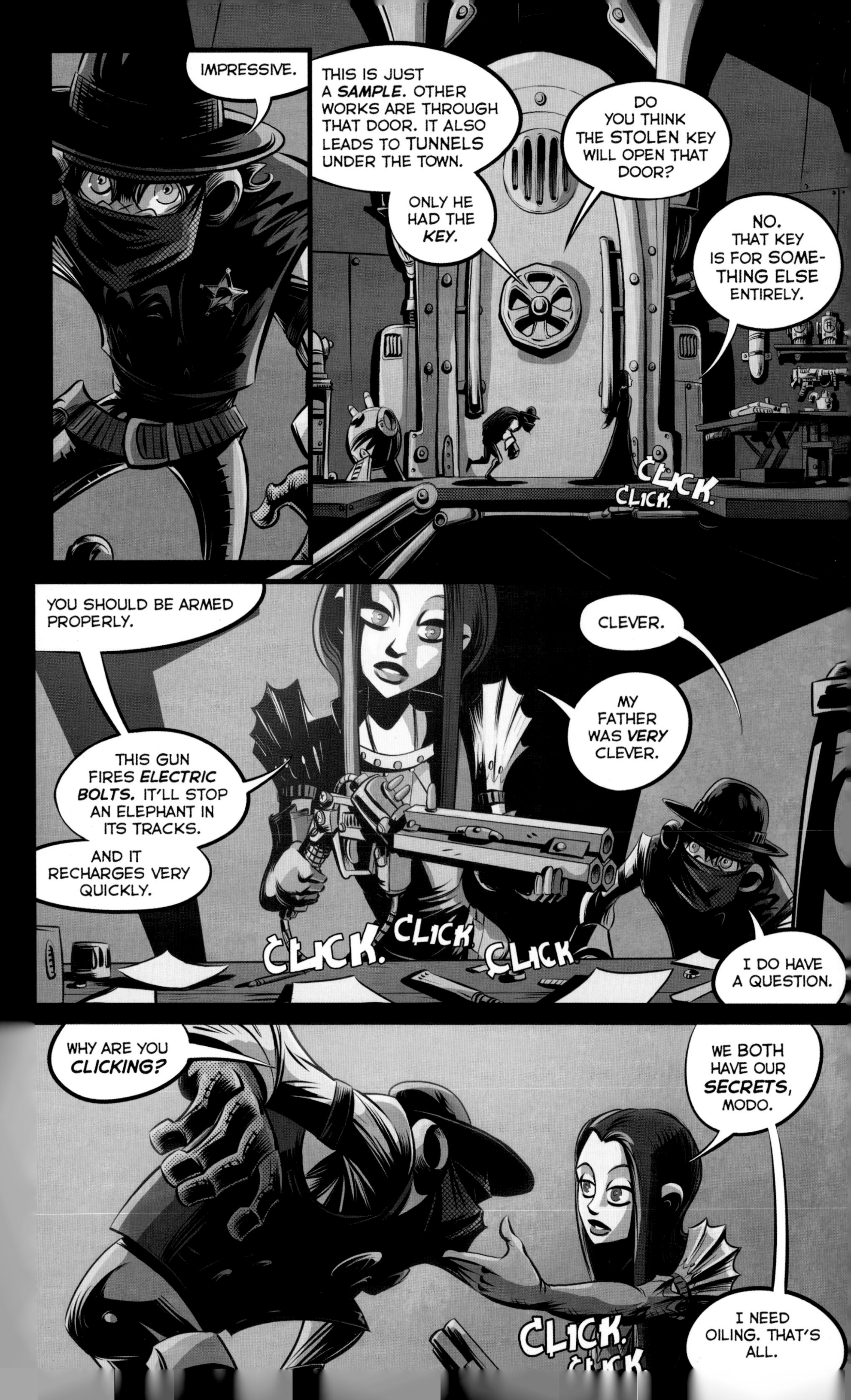
IMPRESSIVE.
THIS IS JUST A SAMPLE. OTHER WORKS ARE THROUGH THAT DOOR. IT ALSO LEADS TO TUNNELS UNDER THE TOWN.
ONLY HE HAD THE KEY.
DO YOU THINK THE STOLEN KEY WILL OPEN THAT DOOR?
NO. THAT KEY IS FOR SOMETHING ELSE ENTIRELY.
CLICK. CLICK.
YOU SHOULD BE ARMED PROPERLY.
THIS GUN FIRES ELECTRIC BOLTS. IT'LL STOP AN ELEPHANT IN ITS TRACKS.
AND IT RECHARGES VERY QUICKLY.
CLEVER.
MY FATHER WAS VERY CLEVER.
CLICK. CLICK CLICK
I DO HAVE A QUESTION.
WHY ARE YOU CLICKING?
WE BOTH HAVE OUR SECRETS, MODO.
I NEED OILING. THAT'S ALL.
CLICK.

I BECAME SEPTIC WHEN I WAS FIFTEEN. MY LIMBS GREW WEAK.

MY HEART *FAILED.*

FAILED?

YES. MY FATHER REPLACED MY BEATING HEART WITH ONE OF CLOCKWORK.

HE TURNED THE KEY. ONCE. TEN TIMES. TWENTY. I LOST COUNT.

EVERY TURN WAS A *YEAR* OF LIFE.

SO YOU DON'T KNOW HOW LONG YOU'LL LIVE?

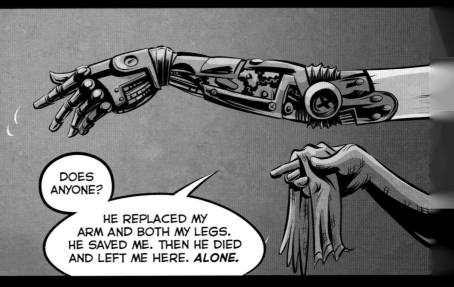

DOES ANYONE?

HE REPLACED MY ARM AND BOTH MY LEGS. HE SAVED ME. THEN HE DIED AND LEFT ME HERE. *ALONE.*

HE'D PROMISED TO ALWAYS PROTECT ME.

THE STOLEN KEY IS FOR MY *HEART.* I DIDN'T FEEL I COULD TELL YOU THAT BEFORE. I NEED TO WIND IT ONCE A WEEK.

I'LL FIND IT AND RETURN IT. I PROMISE.

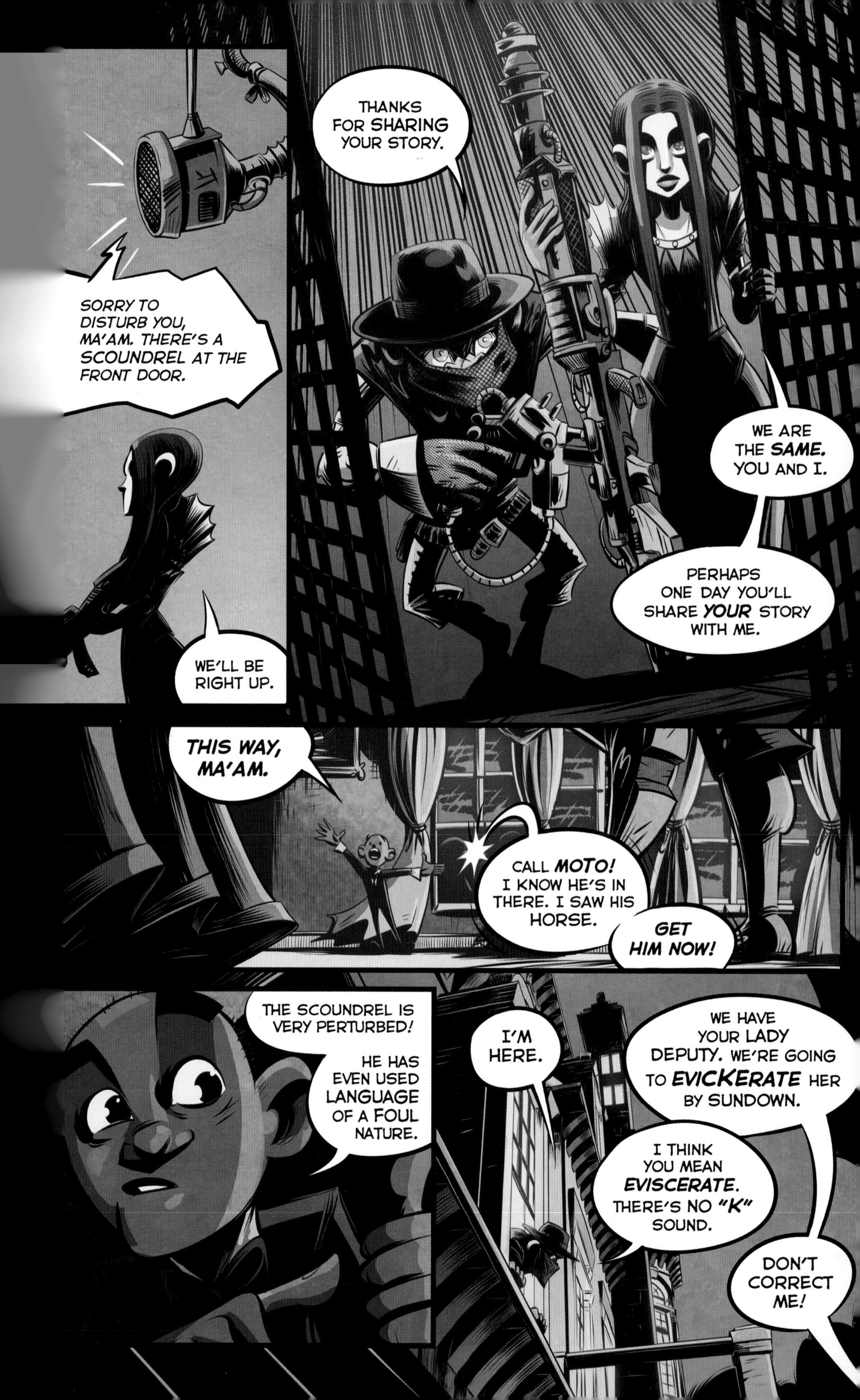

SORRY TO DISTURB YOU, MA'AM. THERE'S A SCOUNDREL AT THE FRONT DOOR.
WE'LL BE RIGHT UP.
THANKS FOR SHARING YOUR STORY.
WE ARE THE SAME. YOU AND I.
PERHAPS ONE DAY YOU'LL SHARE YOUR STORY WITH ME.
THIS WAY, MA'AM.
CALL MOTO! I KNOW HE'S IN THERE. I SAW HIS HORSE.
GET HIM NOW!
THE SCOUNDREL IS VERY PERTURBED!
HE HAS EVEN USED LANGUAGE OF A FOUL NATURE.
I'M HERE.
WE HAVE YOUR LADY DEPUTY. WE'RE GOING TO EVICKERATE HER BY SUNDOWN.
I THINK YOU MEAN EVISCERATE. THERE'S NO "K" SOUND.
DON'T CORRECT ME!

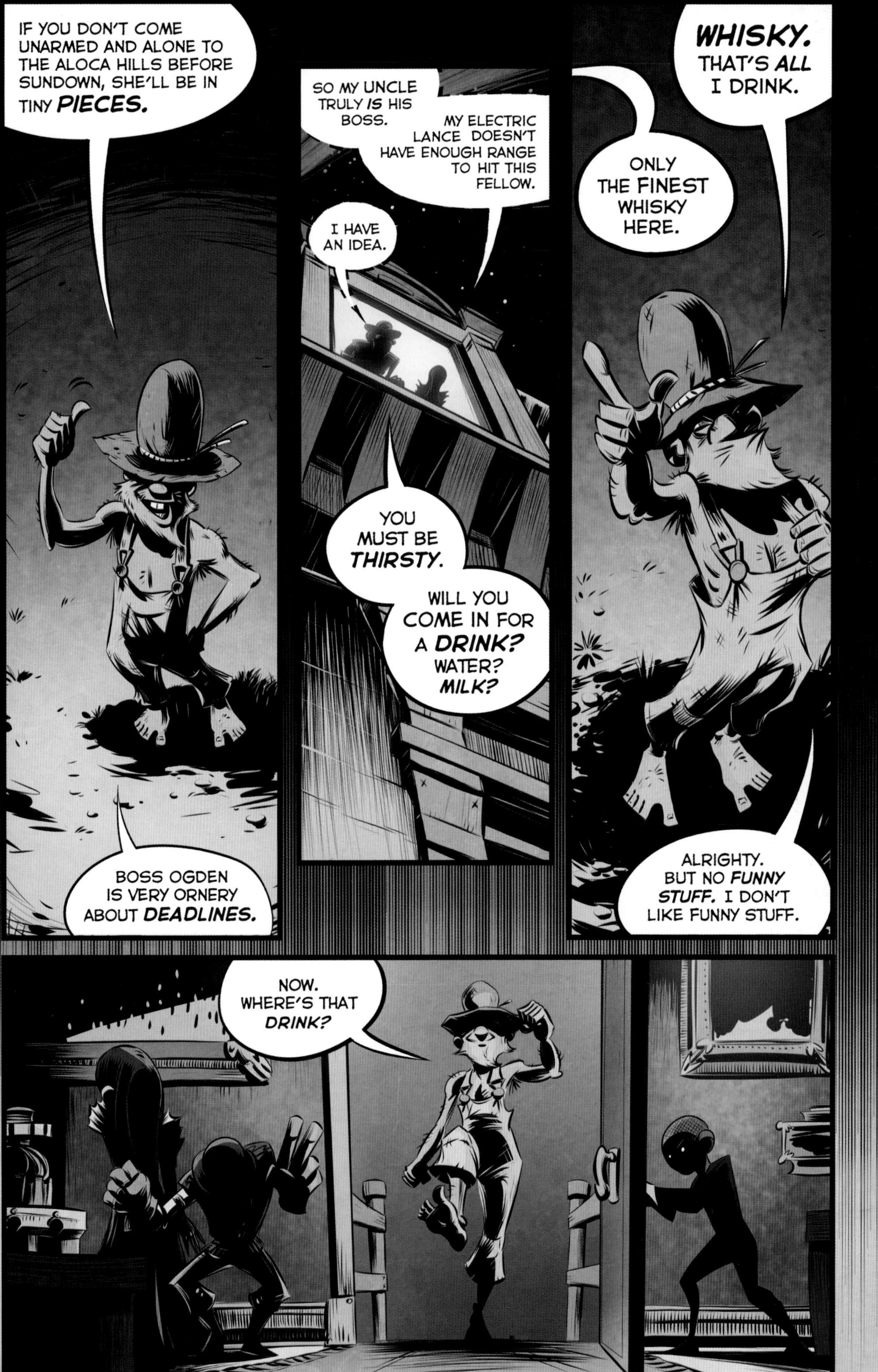
IF YOU DON'T COME UNARMED AND ALONE TO THE ALOCA HILLS BEFORE SUNDOWN, SHE'LL BE IN TINY *PIECES.*
BOSS OGDEN IS VERY ORNERY ABOUT *DEADLINES.*
SO MY UNCLE TRULY *IS* HIS BOSS.
MY ELECTRIC LANCE DOESN'T HAVE ENOUGH RANGE TO HIT THIS FELLOW.
I HAVE AN IDEA.
YOU MUST BE *THIRSTY.*
WILL YOU COME IN FOR A *DRINK?* WATER? *MILK?*
WHISKY. THAT'S *ALL* I DRINK.
ONLY THE FINEST WHISKY HERE.
ALRIGHTY. BUT NO *FUNNY STUFF.* I DON'T LIKE FUNNY STUFF.
NOW. WHERE'S THAT *DRINK?*

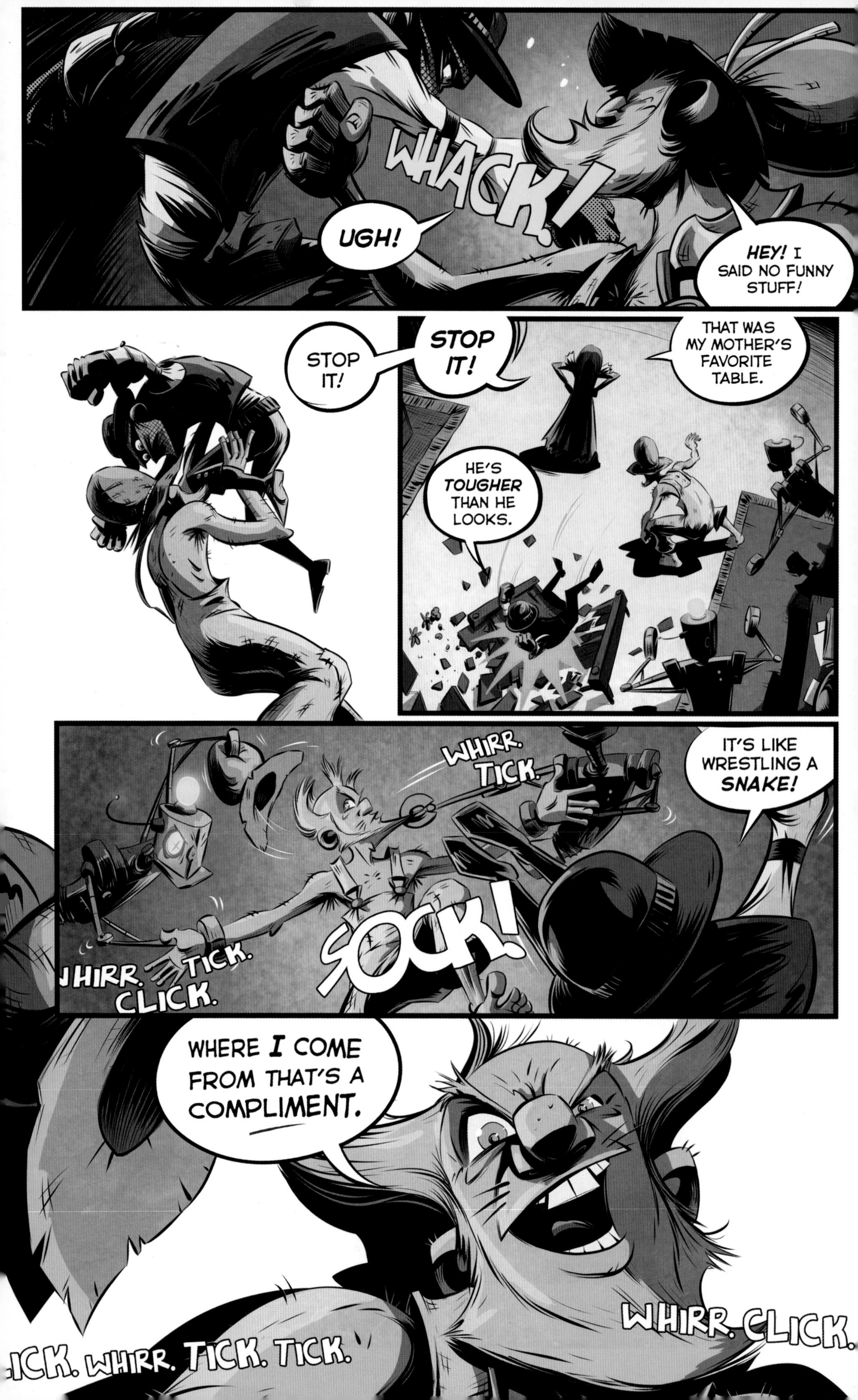
WHACK!
UGH!
HEY! I SAID NO FUNNY STUFF!
STOP IT!
STOP IT!
THAT WAS MY MOTHER'S FAVORITE TABLE.
HE'S TOUGHER THAN HE LOOKS.
WHIRR. TICK.
IT'S LIKE WRESTLING A SNAKE!
SOCK!
WHIRR. TICK. CLICK.
WHERE I COME FROM THAT'S A COMPLIMENT.
WHIRR. CLICK.
ICK. WHIRR. TICK. TICK.

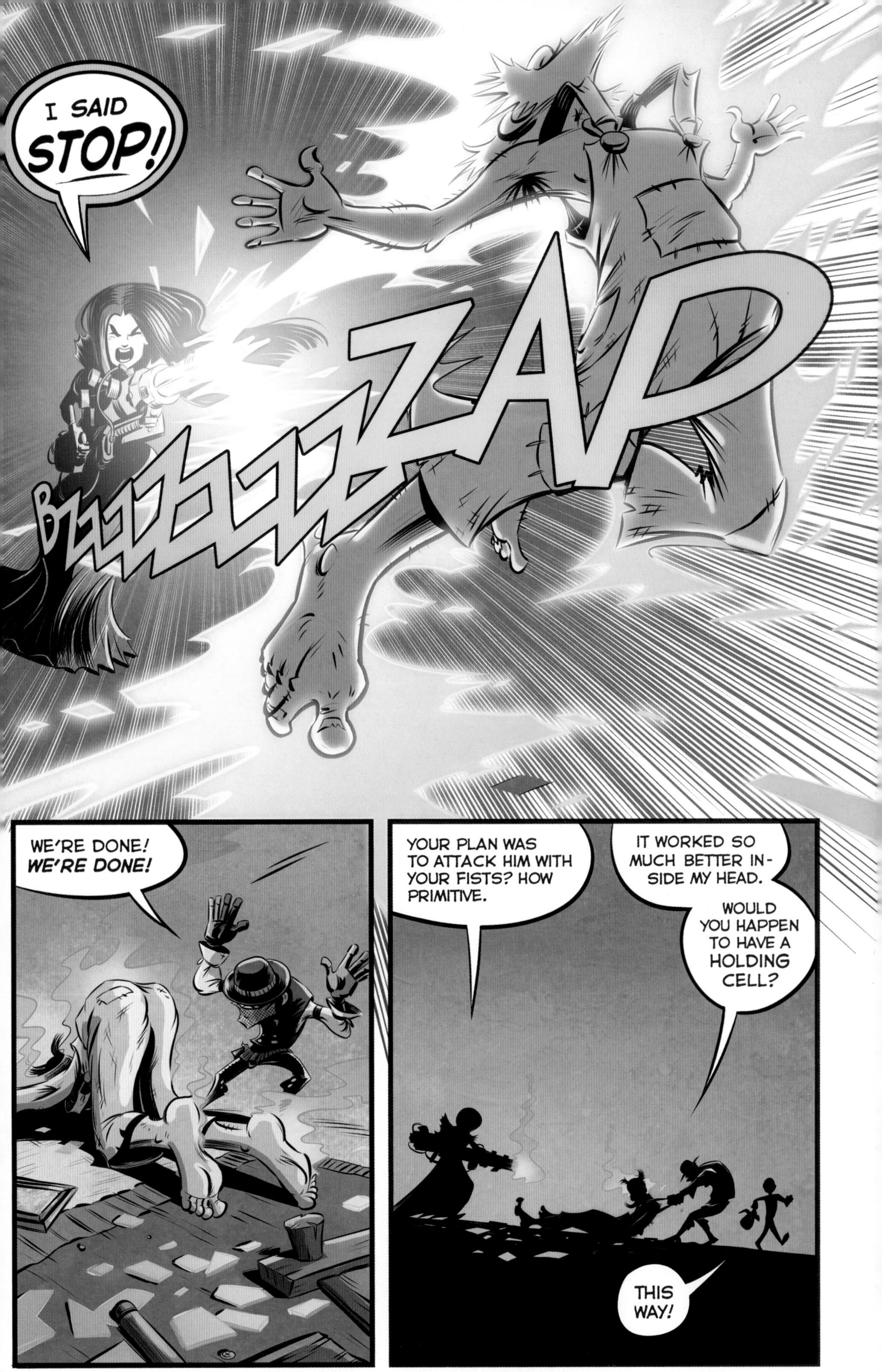
I SAID STOP!
BZZZZZZZZAP
WE'RE DONE! WE'RE DONE!
YOUR PLAN WAS TO ATTACK HIM WITH YOUR FISTS? HOW PRIMITIVE.
IT WORKED SO MUCH BETTER IN-SIDE MY HEAD.
WOULD YOU HAPPEN TO HAVE A HOLDING CELL?
THIS WAY!

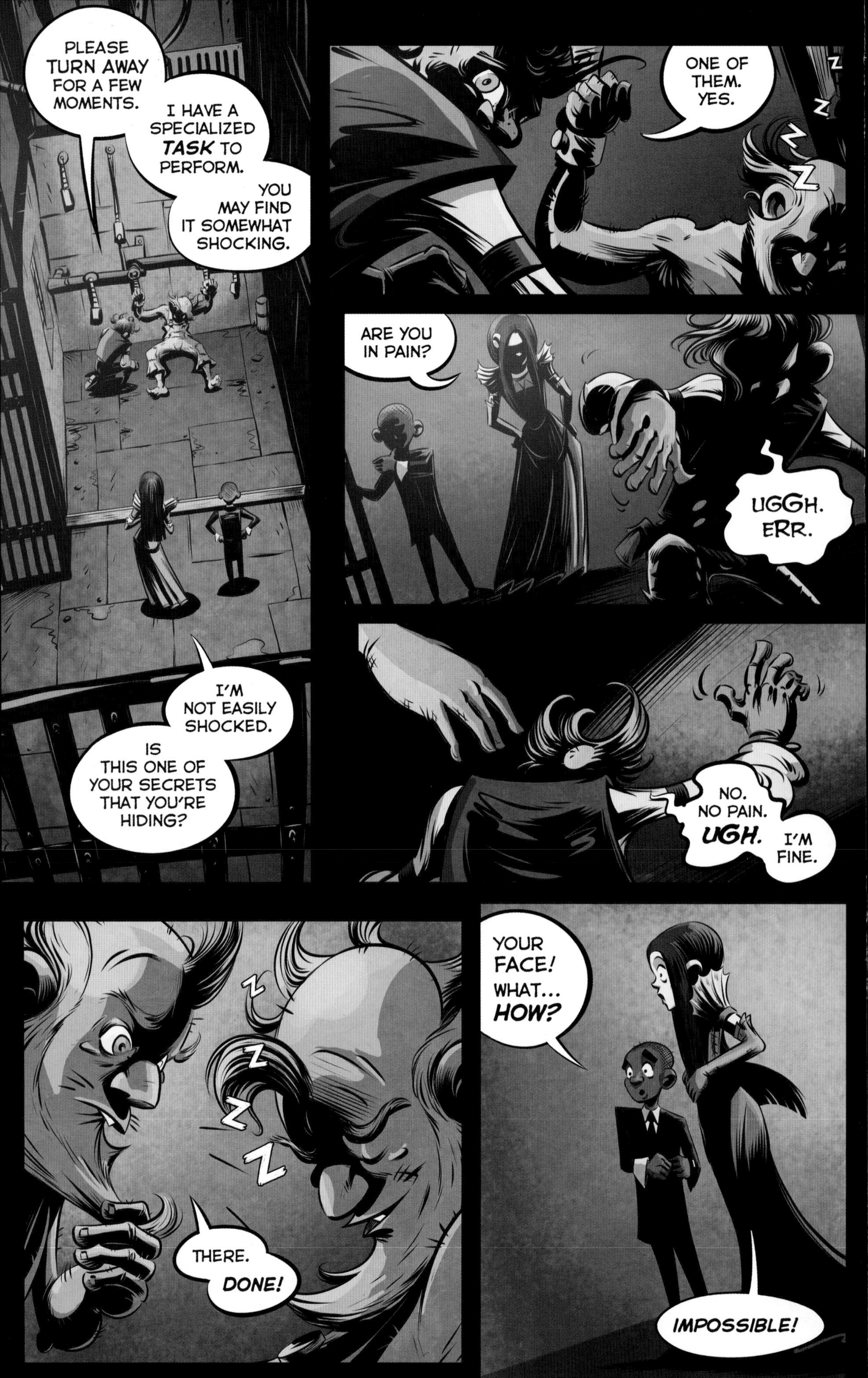
PLEASE TURN AWAY FOR A FEW MOMENTS.
I HAVE A SPECIALIZED TASK TO PERFORM.
YOU MAY FIND IT SOMEWHAT SHOCKING.
I'M NOT EASILY SHOCKED.
IS THIS ONE OF YOUR SECRETS THAT YOU'RE HIDING?
ONE OF THEM. YES.
Z
Z
Z
Z
ARE YOU IN PAIN?
UGGH. ERR.
NO. NO PAIN. UGH.
I'M FINE.
Z
Z
Z
Z
THERE. DONE!
YOUR FACE! WHAT... HOW?
IMPOSSIBLE!

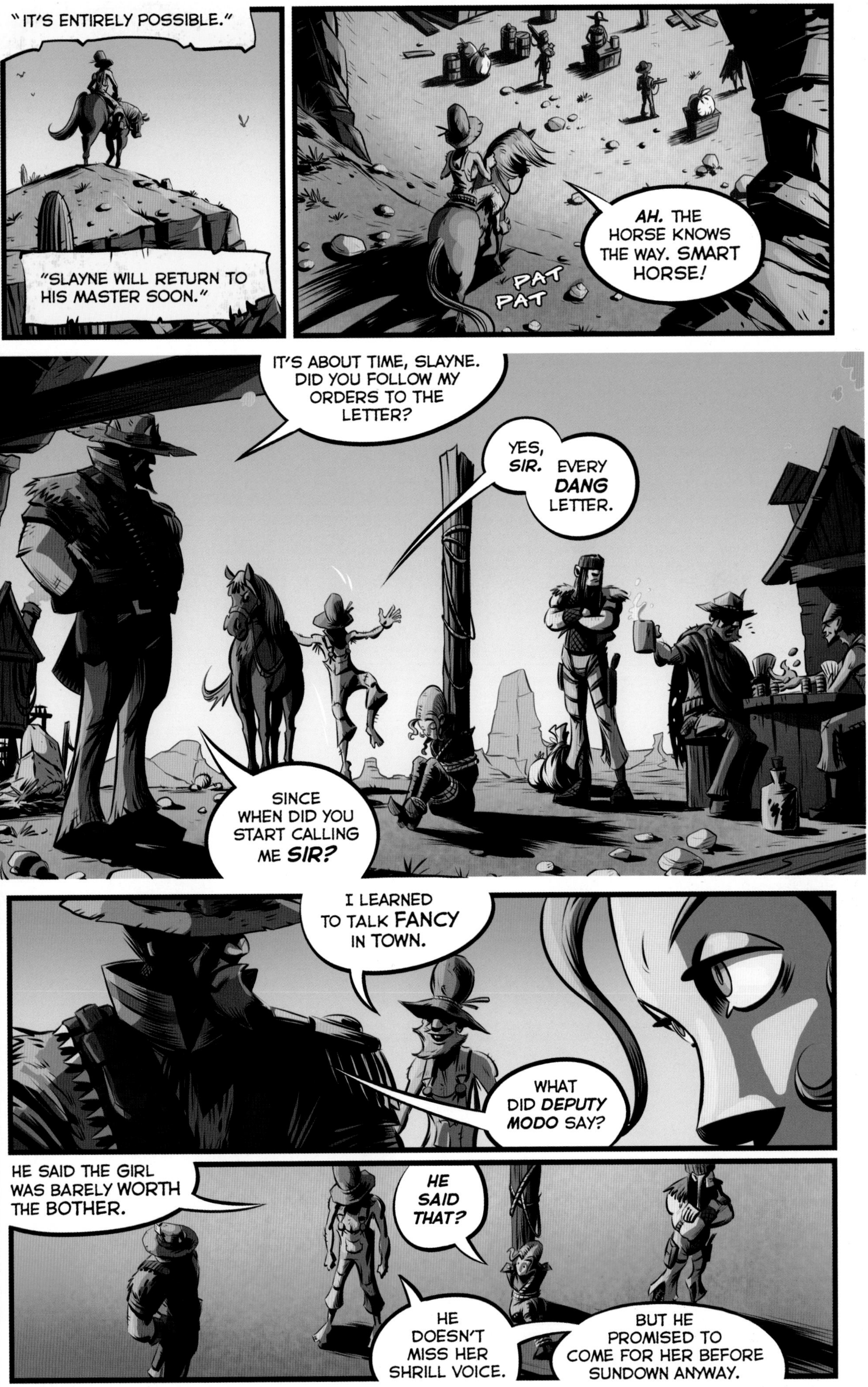
"IT'S ENTIRELY POSSIBLE."
"SLAYNE WILL RETURN TO HIS MASTER SOON."
AH. THE HORSE KNOWS THE WAY. SMART HORSE!
PAT PAT
IT'S ABOUT TIME, SLAYNE. DID YOU FOLLOW MY ORDERS TO THE LETTER?
YES, SIR. EVERY DANG LETTER.
SINCE WHEN DID YOU START CALLING ME SIR?
I LEARNED TO TALK FANCY IN TOWN.
WHAT DID DEPUTY MODO SAY?
HE SAID THE GIRL WAS BARELY WORTH THE BOTHER.
HE SAID THAT?
HE DOESN'T MISS HER SHRILL VOICE.
BUT HE PROMISED TO COME FOR HER BEFORE SUNDOWN ANYWAY.

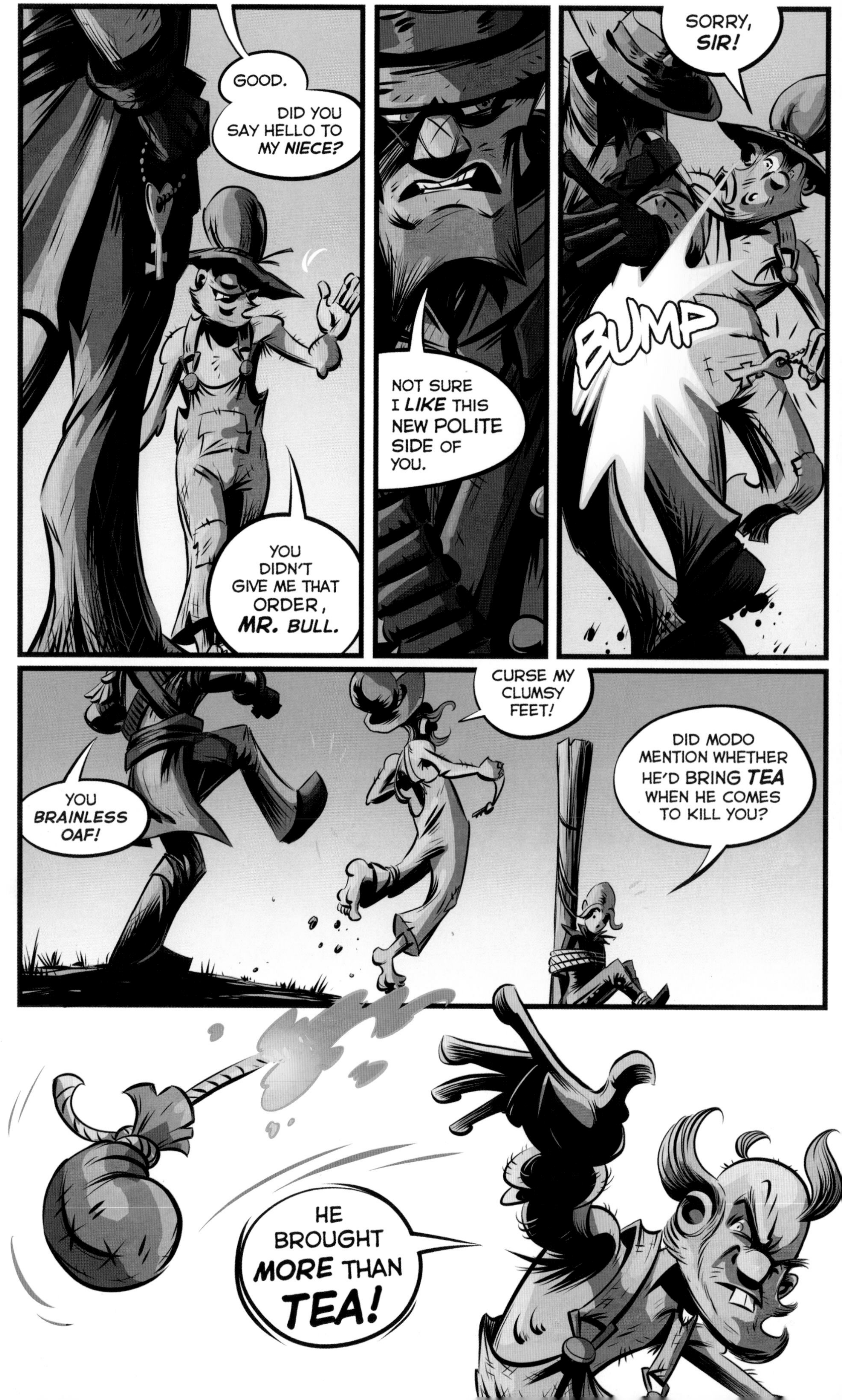
GOOD.
DID YOU SAY HELLO TO MY NIECE?
YOU DIDN'T GIVE ME THAT ORDER, MR. BULL.
NOT SURE I LIKE THIS NEW POLITE SIDE OF YOU.
SORRY, SIR!
BUMP
CURSE MY CLUMSY FEET!
YOU BRAINLESS OAF!
DID MODO MENTION WHETHER HE'D BRING TEA WHEN HE COMES TO KILL YOU?
HE BROUGHT MORE THAN TEA!

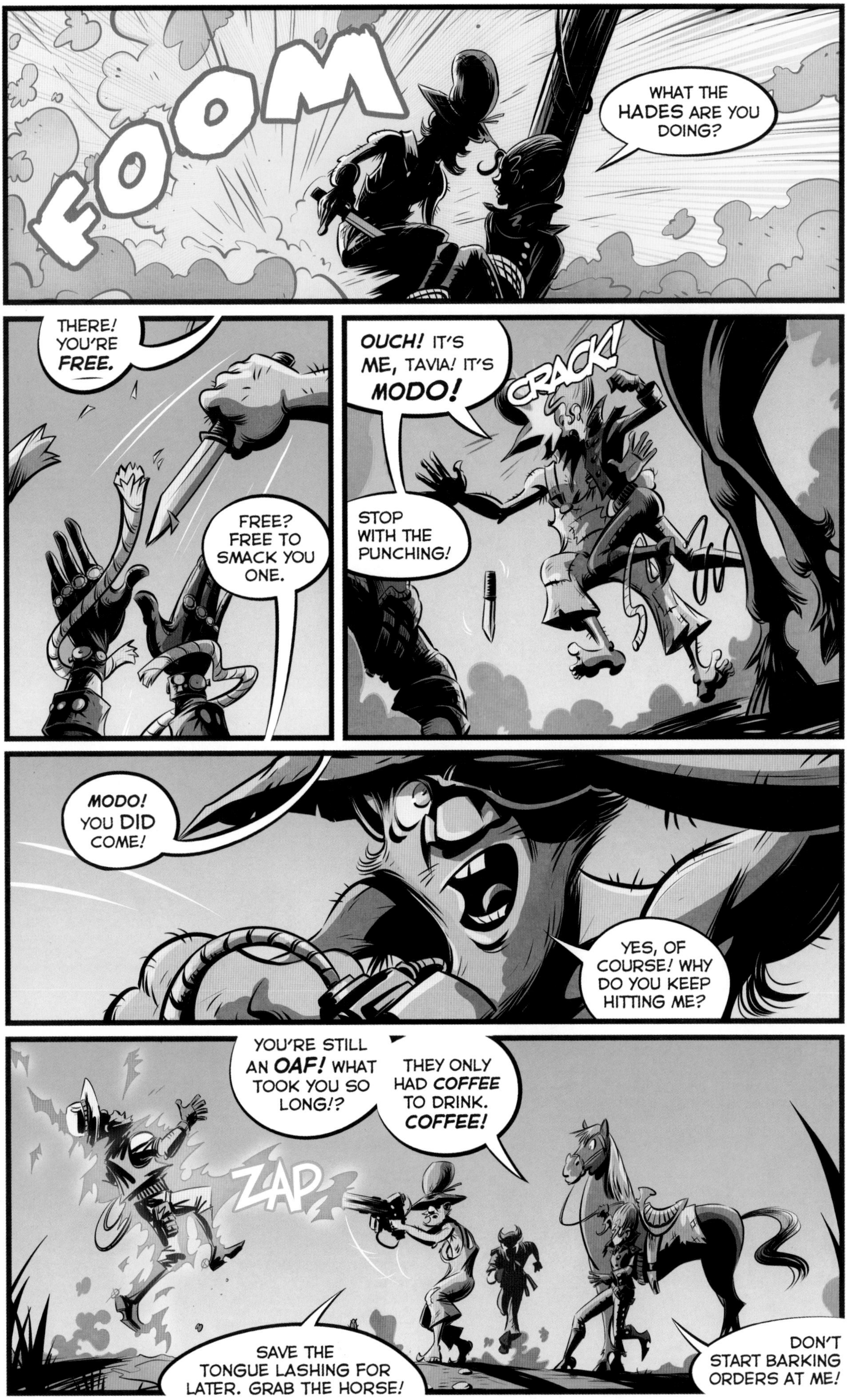
FOOM
WHAT THE HADES ARE YOU DOING?
THERE! YOU'RE FREE.
FREE? FREE TO SMACK YOU ONE.
OUCH! IT'S ME, TAVIA! IT'S MODO!
CRACK!
STOP WITH THE PUNCHING!
MODO! YOU DID COME!
YES, OF COURSE! WHY DO YOU KEEP HITTING ME?
YOU'RE STILL AN OAF! WHAT TOOK YOU SO LONG!?
THEY ONLY HAD COFFEE TO DRINK. COFFEE!
ZAP
SAVE THE TONGUE LASHING FOR LATER. GRAB THE HORSE!
DON'T START BARKING ORDERS AT ME!

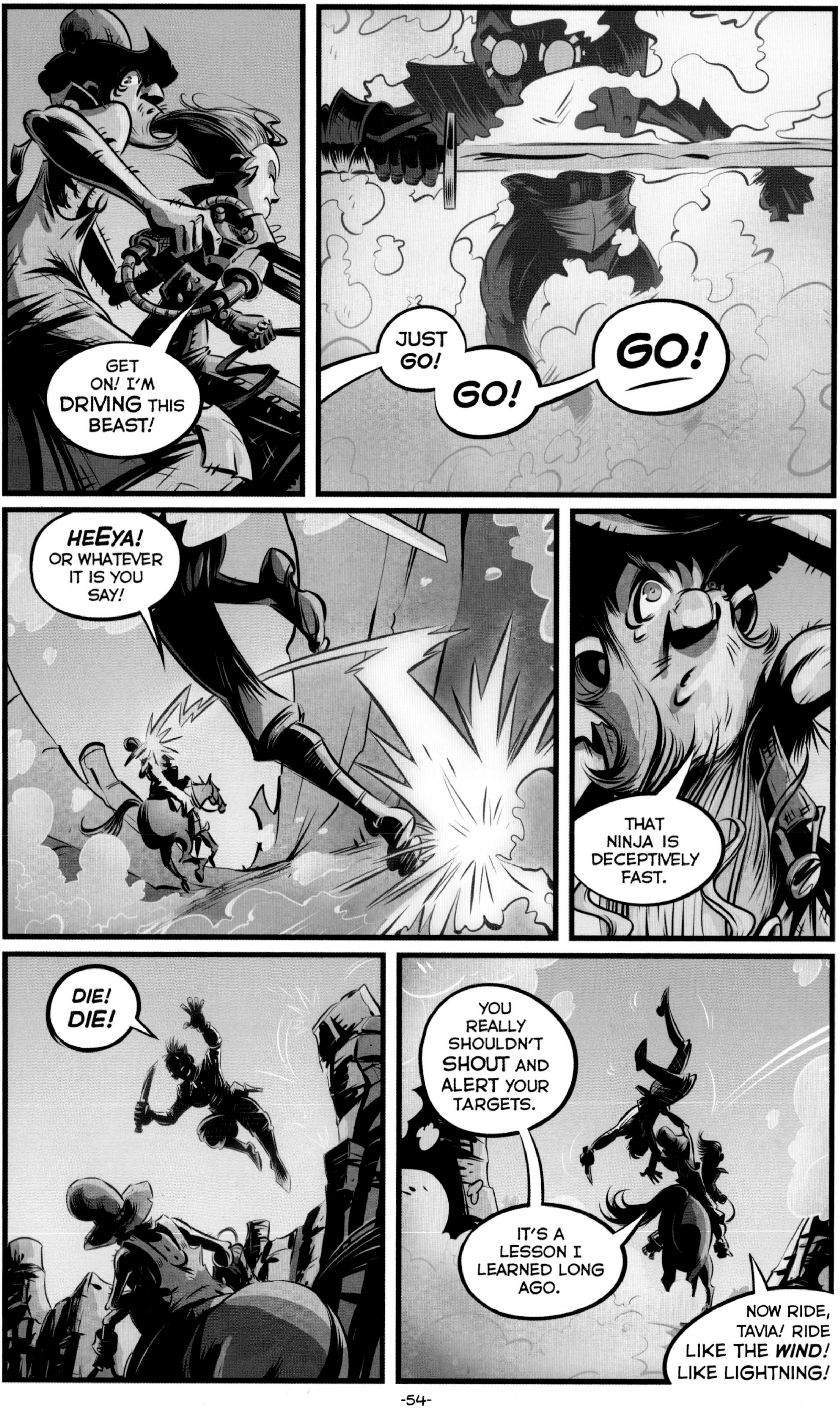
GET ON! I'M DRIVING THIS BEAST!
JUST GO!
GO!
GO!
HEEYA! OR WHATEVER IT IS YOU SAY!
THAT NINJA IS DECEPTIVELY FAST.
DIE! DIE!
YOU REALLY SHOULDN'T SHOUT AND ALERT YOUR TARGETS.
IT'S A LESSON I LEARNED LONG AGO.
NOW RIDE, TAVIA! RIDE LIKE THE WIND! LIKE LIGHTNING!

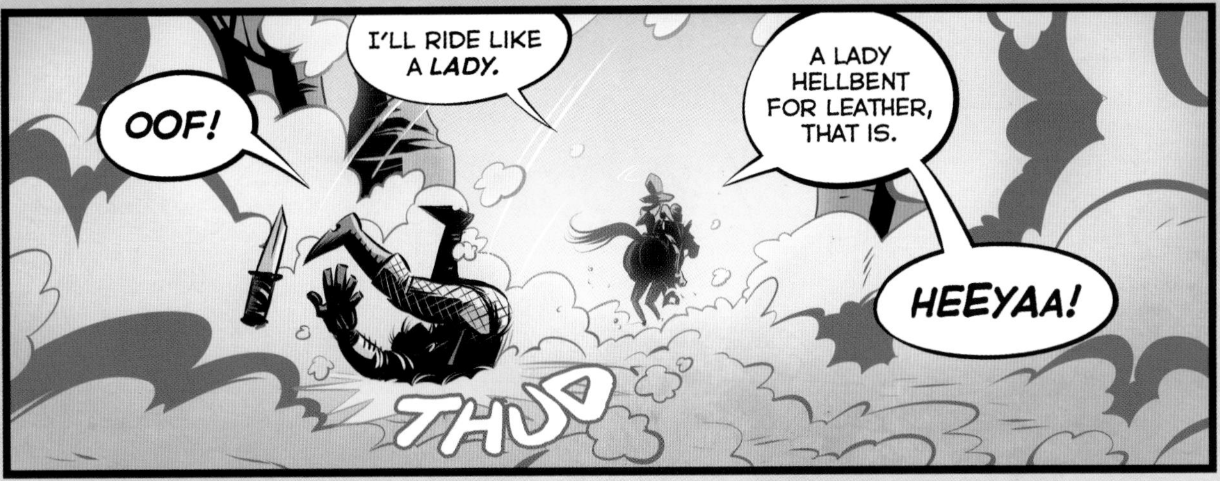
OOF!
I'LL RIDE LIKE A *LADY.*
A LADY HELLBENT FOR LEATHER, THAT IS.
HEEYAA!
THUD

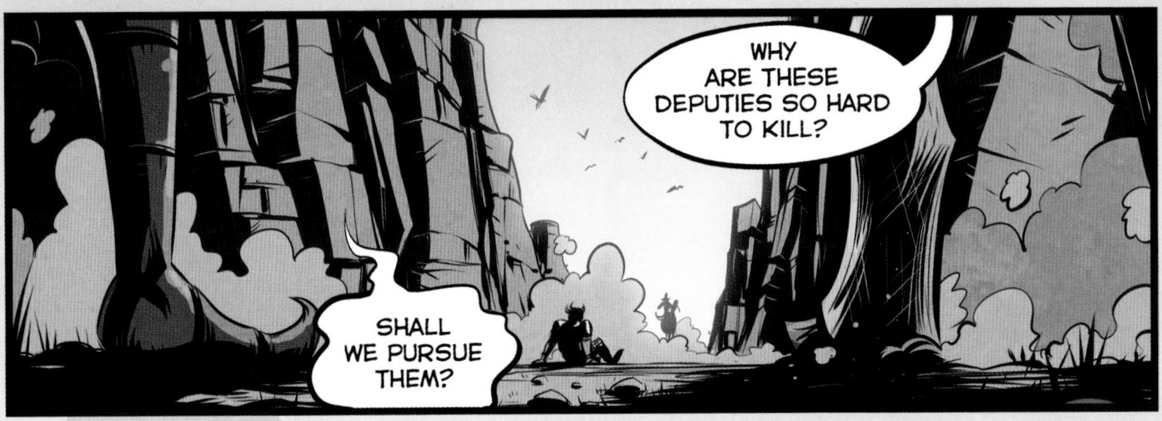
WHY ARE THESE DEPUTIES SO HARD TO KILL?
SHALL WE PURSUE THEM?

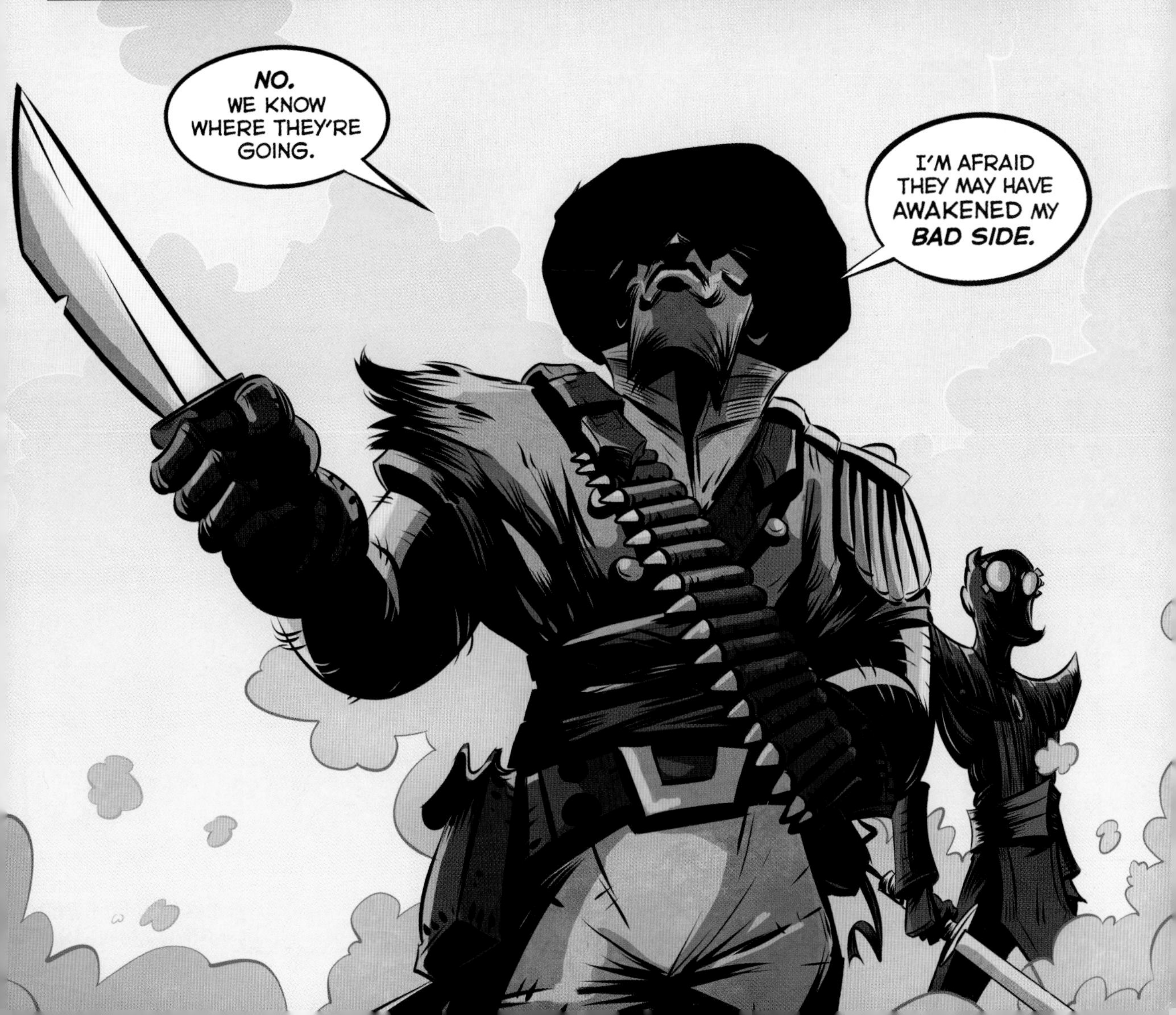
NO. WE KNOW WHERE THEY'RE GOING.
I'M AFRAID THEY MAY HAVE AWAKENED MY *BAD SIDE.*

AW, YOU CAME BACK FOR ME.

I MISSED OUR CLEVER REPARTEE.

I STILL—

≷UGH≷

-- I'M TOO *TIRED* TO HOLD SLAYNE'S *SHAPE.*

≷ARGH≷

YOUR BAD DRIVING IS GOING TO WRECK MISS EMBER'S SURGICAL HANDIWORK.

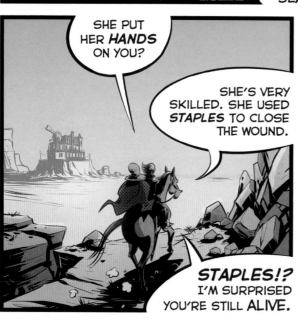

SHE PUT HER *HANDS* ON YOU?

SHE'S VERY SKILLED. SHE USED *STAPLES* TO CLOSE THE WOUND.

STAPLES!? I'M SURPRISED YOU'RE STILL ALIVE.

I PROBABLY SHOULDN'T MENTION THAT SHE DRESSED ME IN HER FATHER'S CLOTHES.

THAT'S A THOUSAND SHADES OF *ODD.*

HEY. STOP HERE.

UGH. WE MUST TELL ANNETTE WHAT HAPPENED.

OH. SHE'S *ANNETTE* TO YOU NOW.

SHE'S A BIG GIRL. SHE'LL BE FINE. I'M TAKING YOU TO THE TOWN DOCTOR.

ASSUMING THERE IS ONE.

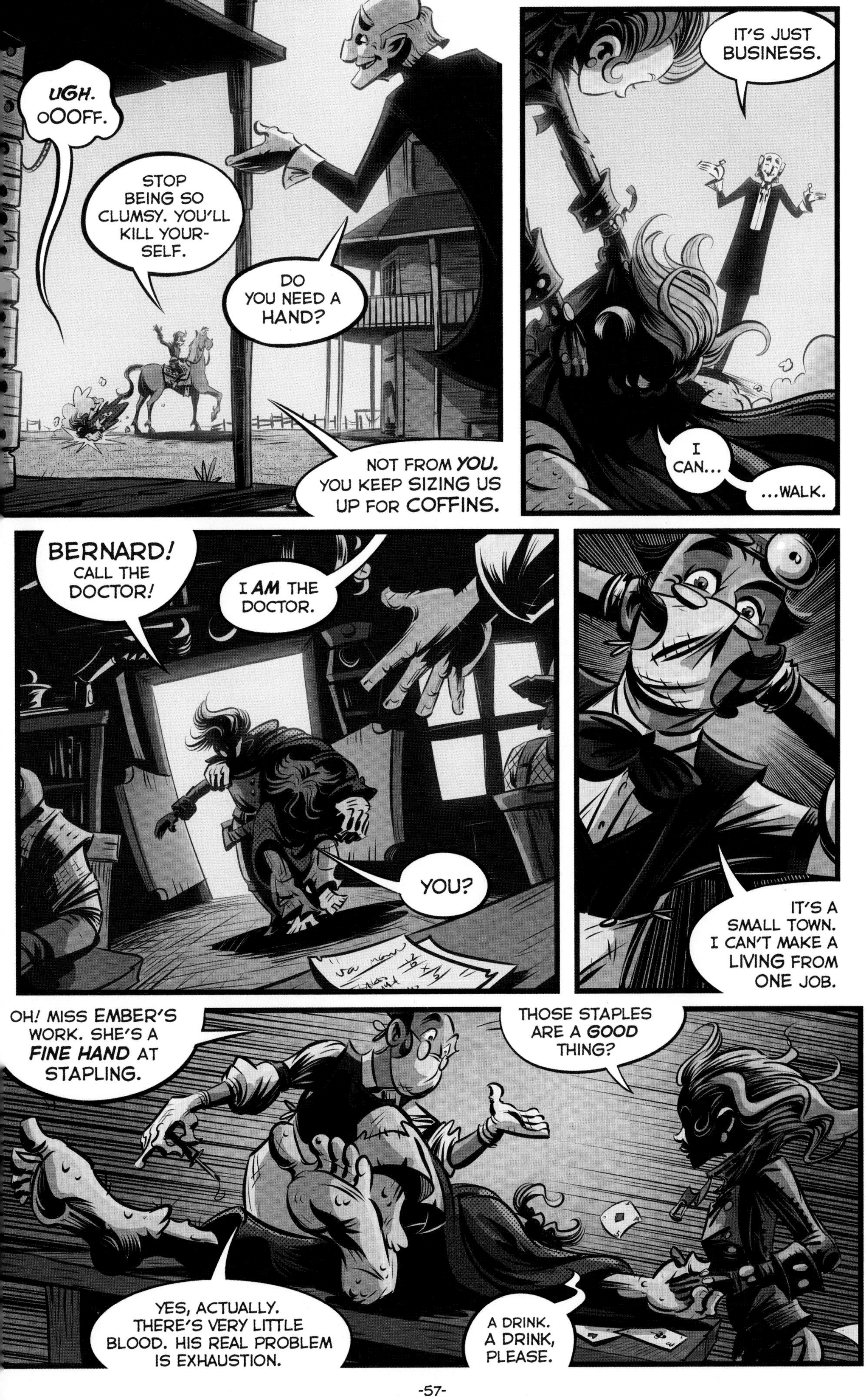
UGH. oOOFF.
STOP BEING SO CLUMSY. YOU'LL KILL YOUR-SELF.
DO YOU NEED A HAND?
NOT FROM YOU. YOU KEEP SIZING US UP FOR COFFINS.
IT'S JUST BUSINESS.
I CAN...
...WALK.
BERNARD! CALL THE DOCTOR!
I AM THE DOCTOR.
YOU?
IT'S A SMALL TOWN. I CAN'T MAKE A LIVING FROM ONE JOB.
OH! MISS EMBER'S WORK. SHE'S A FINE HAND AT STAPLING.
THOSE STAPLES ARE A GOOD THING?
YES, ACTUALLY. THERE'S VERY LITTLE BLOOD. HIS REAL PROBLEM IS EXHAUSTION.
A DRINK. A DRINK, PLEASE.

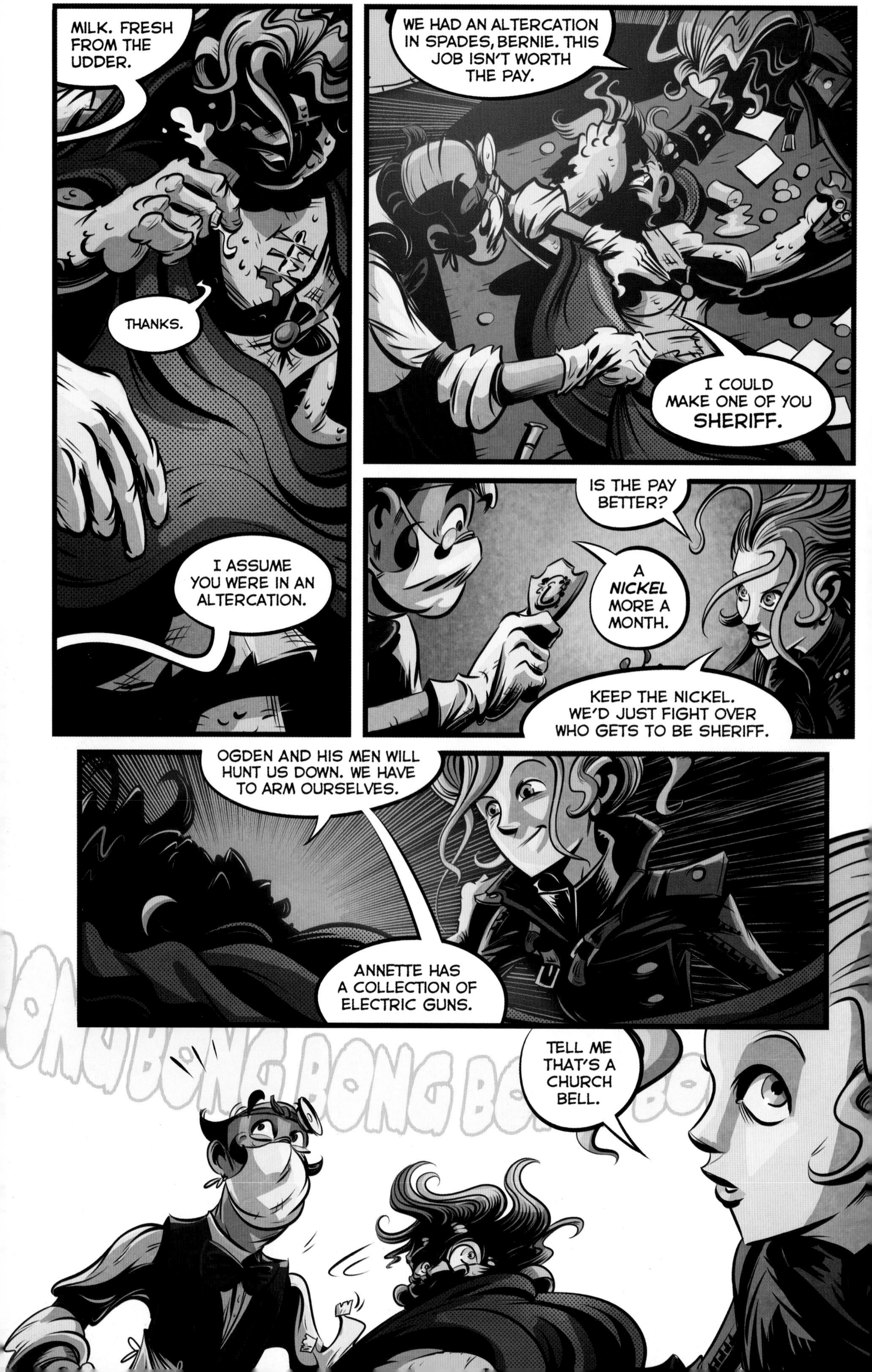
MILK. FRESH FROM THE UDDER.
THANKS.
I ASSUME YOU WERE IN AN ALTERCATION.
WE HAD AN ALTERCATION IN SPADES, BERNIE. THIS JOB ISN'T WORTH THE PAY.
I COULD MAKE ONE OF YOU SHERIFF.
IS THE PAY BETTER?
A NICKEL MORE A MONTH.
KEEP THE NICKEL. WE'D JUST FIGHT OVER WHO GETS TO BE SHERIFF.
OGDEN AND HIS MEN WILL HUNT US DOWN. WE HAVE TO ARM OURSELVES.
ANNETTE HAS A COLLECTION OF ELECTRIC GUNS.
BONG BONG BONG BONG BO
TELL ME THAT'S A CHURCH BELL.

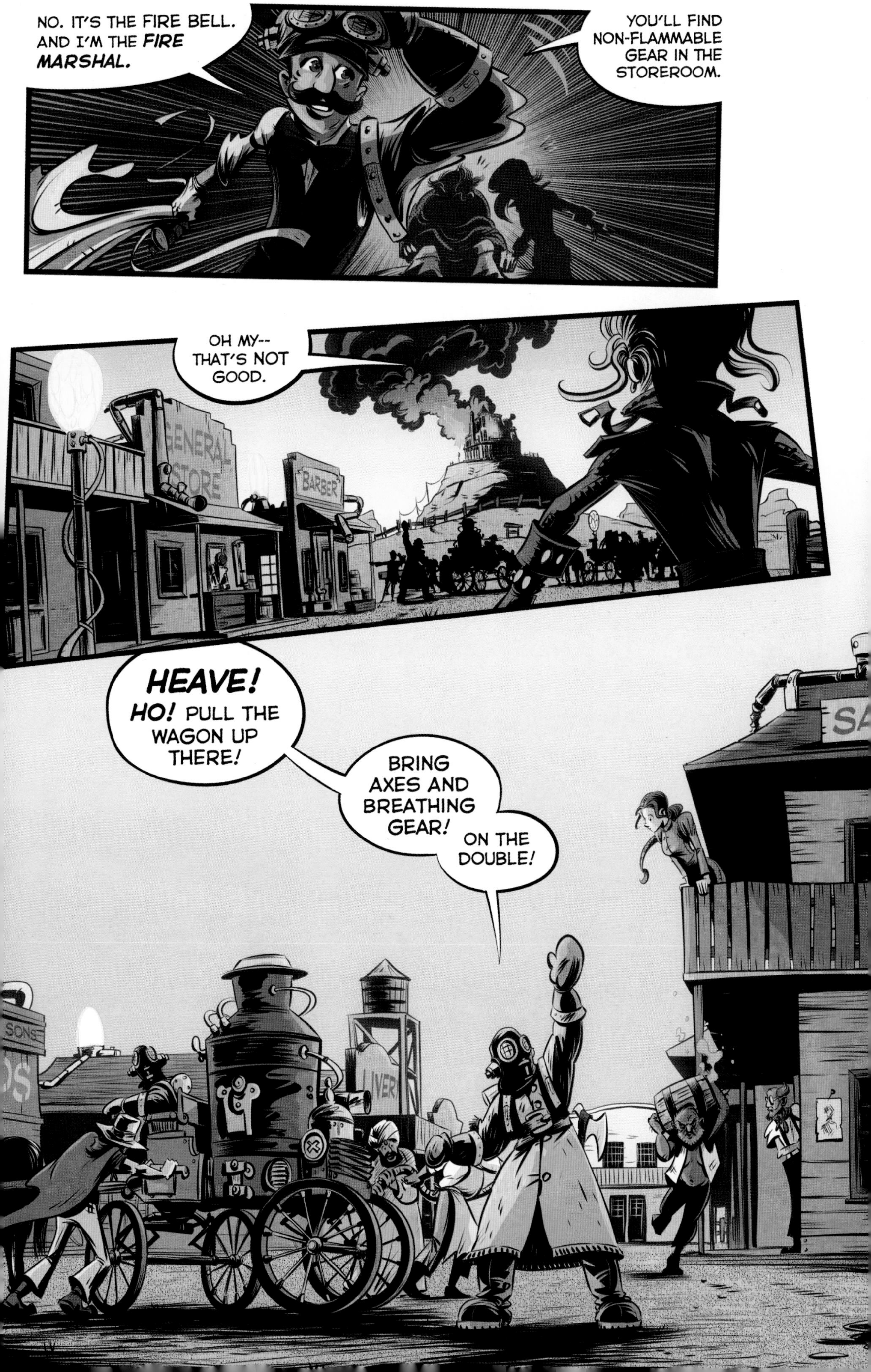
NO. IT'S THE FIRE BELL. AND I'M THE *FIRE MARSHAL.*
YOU'LL FIND NON-FLAMMABLE GEAR IN THE STOREROOM.
OH MY-- THAT'S NOT GOOD.
GENERAL STORE
BARBER
HEAVE! HO! PULL THE WAGON UP THERE!
BRING AXES AND BREATHING GEAR!
ON THE DOUBLE!

MR. MODO. THEY... IT'S *HORRIBLE.*

GET A LADDER UP TO THOSE WINDOWS. KEEP THE WATER PRESSURE HIGH!

WHAT HAPPENED?

DO YOU SEE *ANNETTE?*

DON'T GET YOUR KNICKERS IN A KNOT. WE'LL FIND HER.

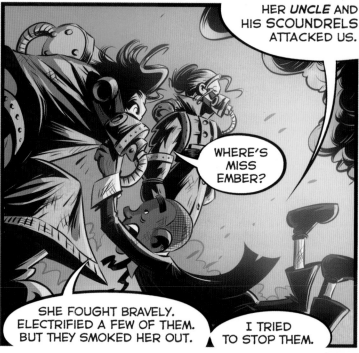

HER *UNCLE* AND HIS SCOUNDRELS ATTACKED US.

WHERE'S MISS EMBER?

SHE FOUGHT BRAVELY. ELECTRIFIED A FEW OF THEM. BUT THEY SMOKED HER OUT.

I TRIED TO STOP THEM.

YOU DID YOUR BEST, ALEC.

THEY SAID THEY'D BE BACK AT HIGH NOON TO TRADE *HER* FOR THE *KEY.*

IF YOU'RE NOT THERE THEY'LL BURN THE WHOLE TOWN DOWN.

SILLY MEN AND THEIR CHILDISH NEED TO BURN THINGS.

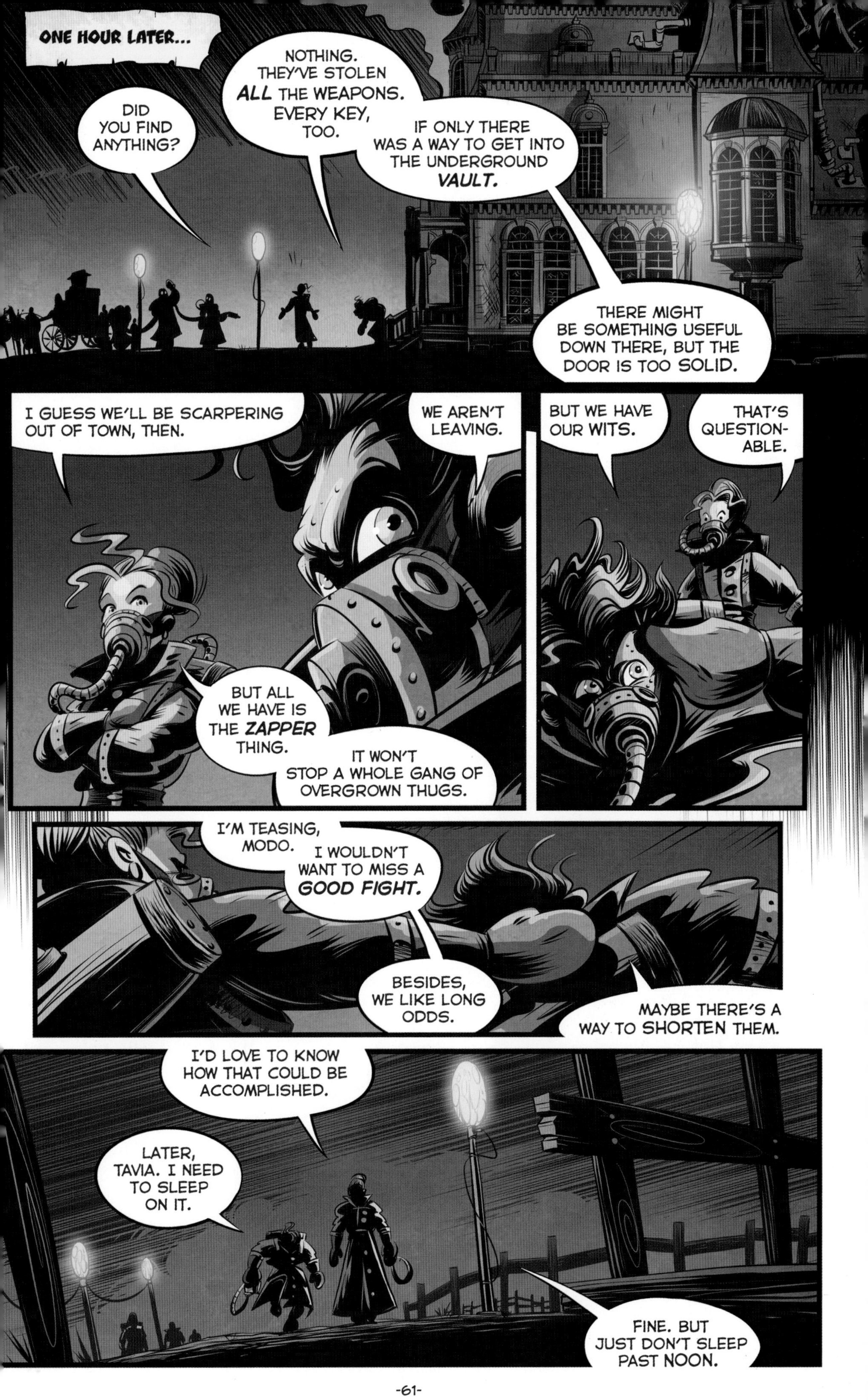
ONE HOUR LATER...
DID YOU FIND ANYTHING?
NOTHING. THEY'VE STOLEN ALL THE WEAPONS. EVERY KEY, TOO.
IF ONLY THERE WAS A WAY TO GET INTO THE UNDERGROUND VAULT.
THERE MIGHT BE SOMETHING USEFUL DOWN THERE, BUT THE DOOR IS TOO SOLID.
I GUESS WE'LL BE SCARPERING OUT OF TOWN, THEN.
WE AREN'T LEAVING.
BUT ALL WE HAVE IS THE ZAPPER THING.
IT WON'T STOP A WHOLE GANG OF OVERGROWN THUGS.
BUT WE HAVE OUR WITS.
THAT'S QUESTION-ABLE.
I'M TEASING, MODO.
I WOULDN'T WANT TO MISS A GOOD FIGHT.
BESIDES, WE LIKE LONG ODDS.
MAYBE THERE'S A WAY TO SHORTEN THEM.
I'D LOVE TO KNOW HOW THAT COULD BE ACCOMPLISHED.
LATER, TAVIA. I NEED TO SLEEP ON IT.
FINE. BUT JUST DON'T SLEEP PAST NOON.

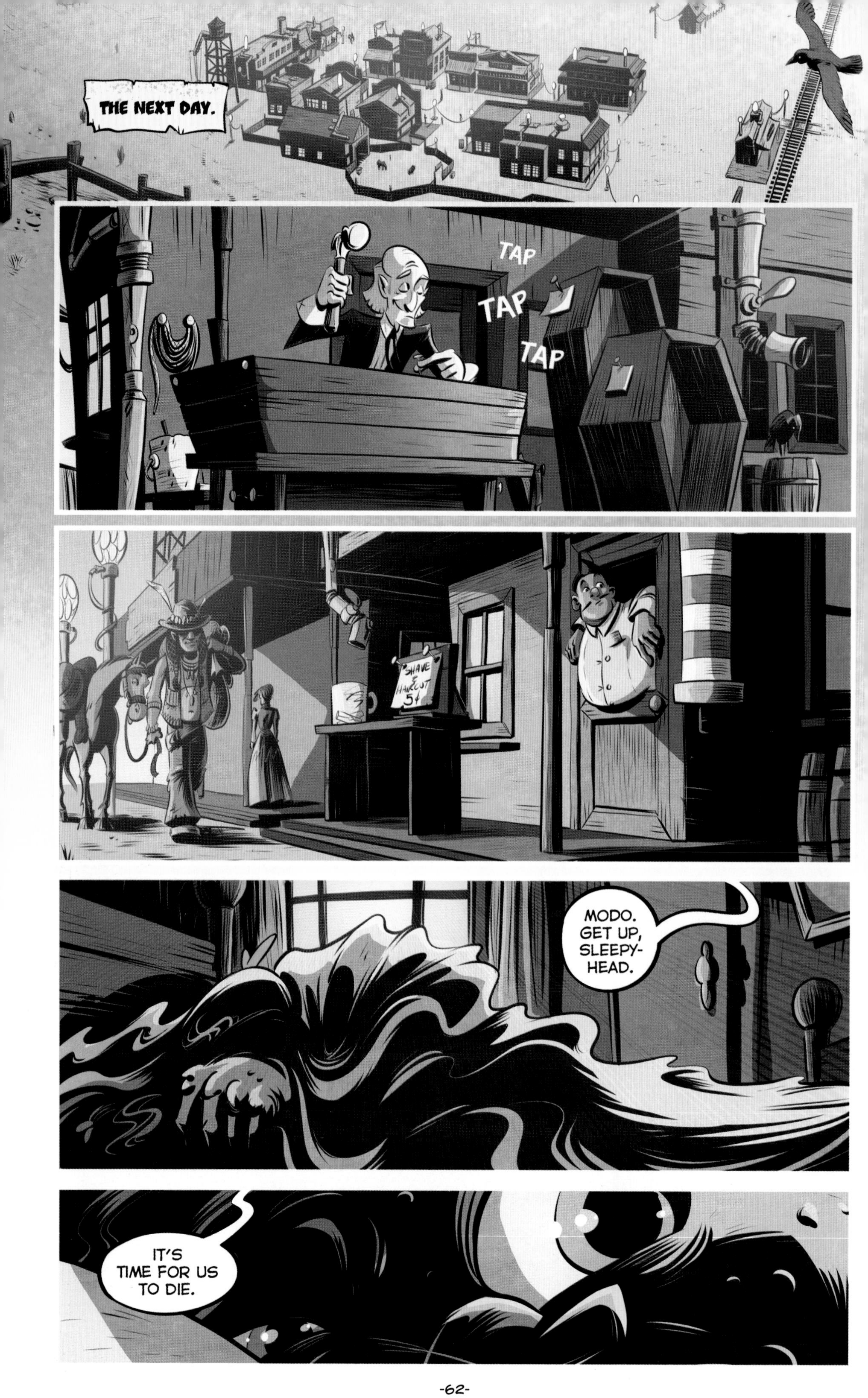
THE NEXT DAY.
TAP
TAP
TAP
SHAVE & HAIRCUT 5¢
MODO. GET UP, SLEEPY-HEAD.
IT'S TIME FOR US TO DIE.

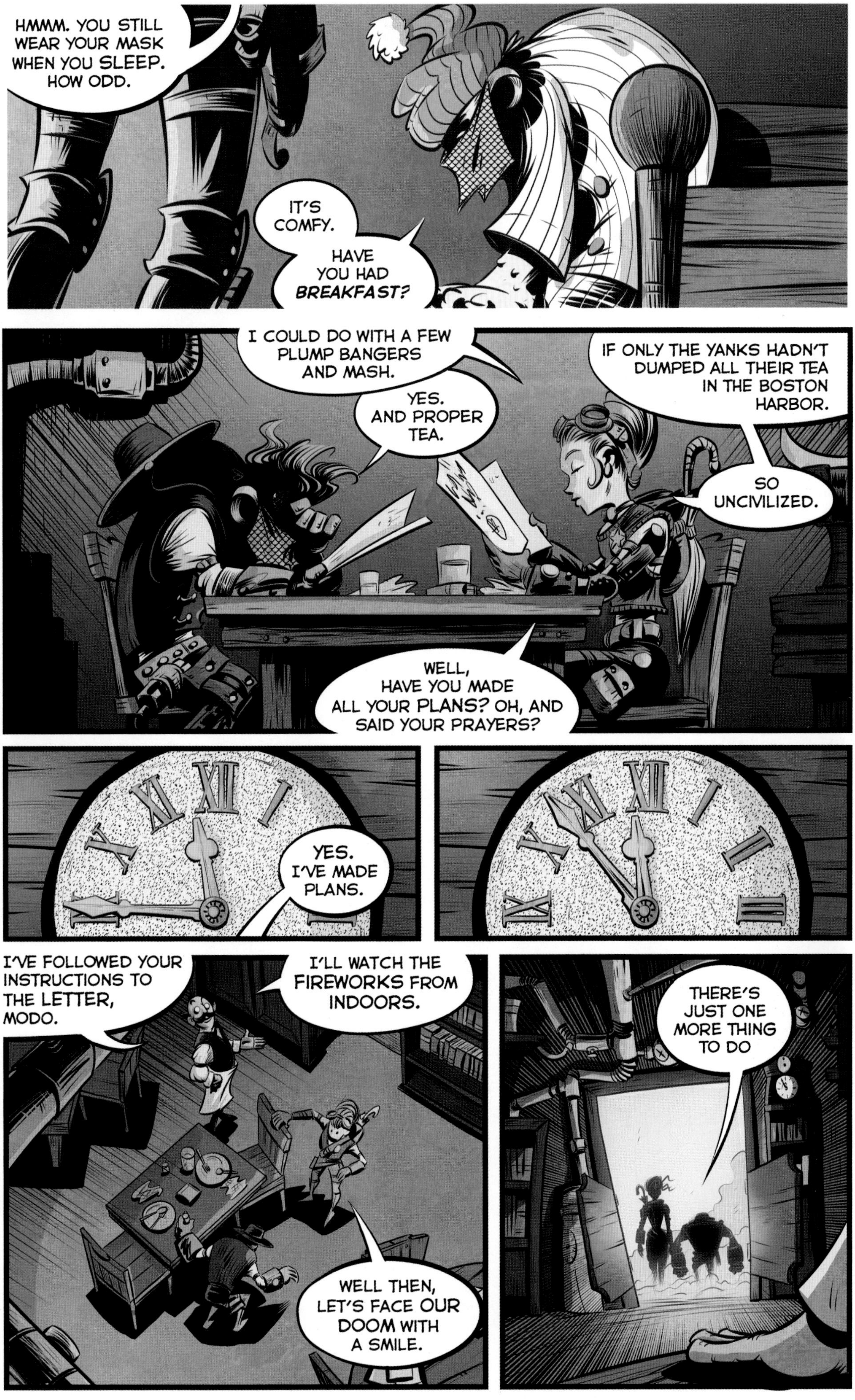
HMMM. YOU STILL WEAR YOUR MASK WHEN YOU SLEEP. HOW ODD.
IT'S COMFY.
HAVE YOU HAD *BREAKFAST?*
I COULD DO WITH A FEW PLUMP BANGERS AND MASH.
YES. AND PROPER TEA.
IF ONLY THE YANKS HADN'T DUMPED ALL THEIR TEA IN THE BOSTON HARBOR.
SO UNCIVILIZED.
WELL, HAVE YOU MADE ALL YOUR PLANS? OH, AND SAID YOUR PRAYERS?
YES. I'VE MADE PLANS.
I'VE FOLLOWED YOUR INSTRUCTIONS TO THE LETTER, MODO.
I'LL WATCH THE FIREWORKS FROM INDOORS.
WELL THEN, LET'S FACE OUR DOOM WITH A SMILE.
THERE'S JUST ONE MORE THING TO DO

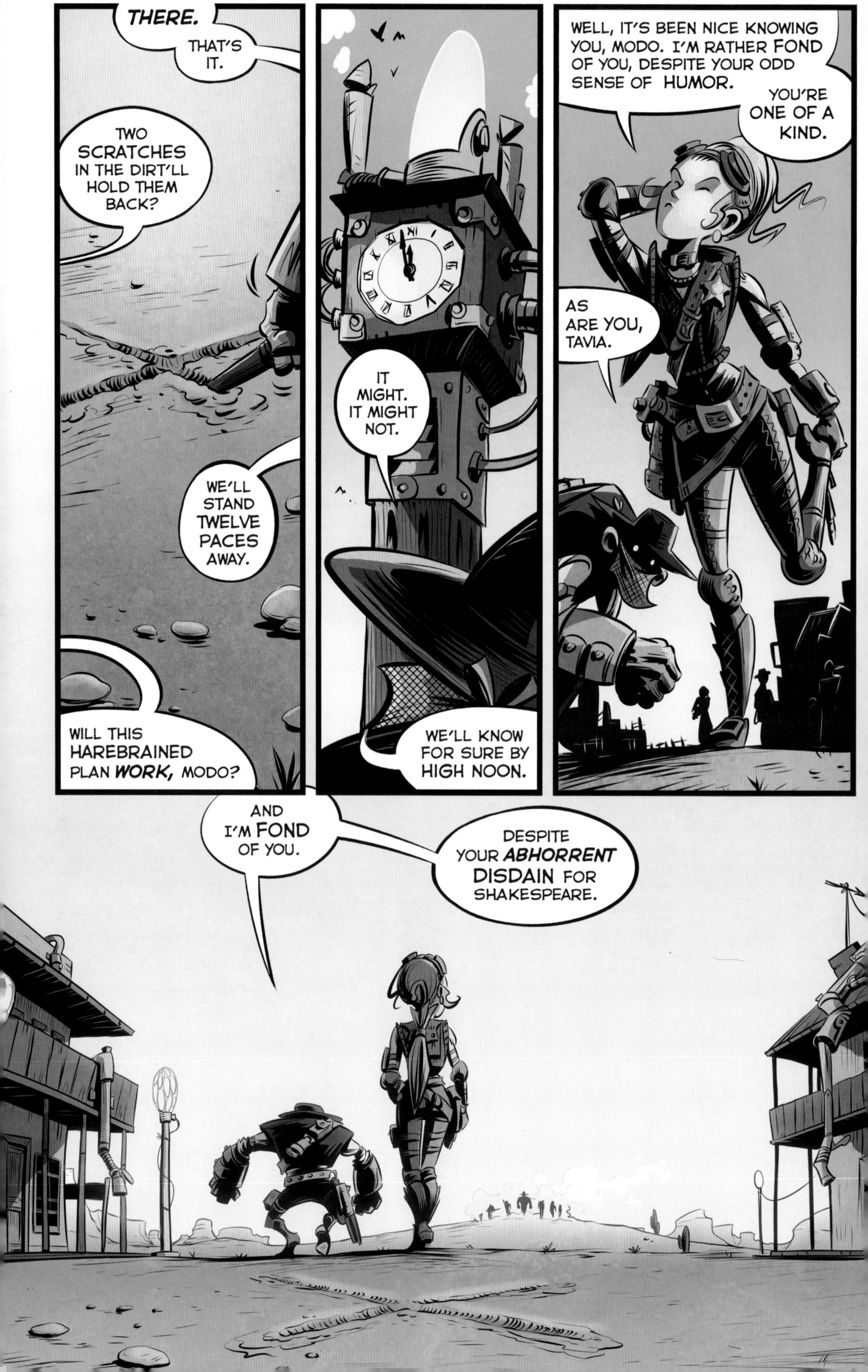
THERE.
THAT'S IT.
TWO SCRATCHES IN THE DIRT'LL HOLD THEM BACK?
WE'LL STAND TWELVE PACES AWAY.
WILL THIS HAREBRAINED PLAN WORK, MODO?
IT MIGHT. IT MIGHT NOT.
WE'LL KNOW FOR SURE BY HIGH NOON.
WELL, IT'S BEEN NICE KNOWING YOU, MODO. I'M RATHER FOND OF YOU, DESPITE YOUR ODD SENSE OF HUMOR.
YOU'RE ONE OF A KIND.
AS ARE YOU, TAVIA.
AND I'M FOND OF YOU.
DESPITE YOUR ABHORRENT DISDAIN FOR SHAKESPEARE.

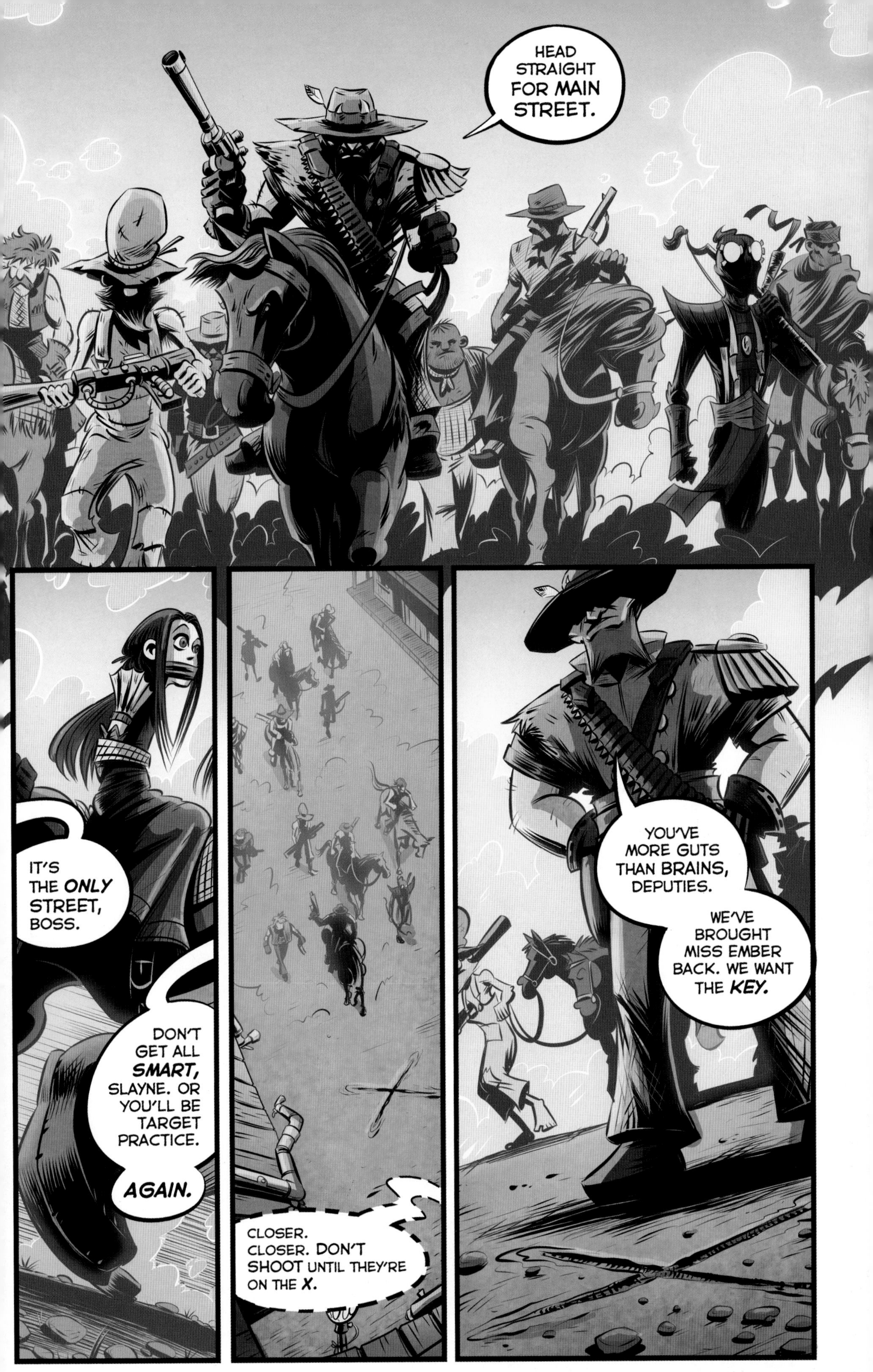

HEAD STRAIGHT FOR MAIN STREET.
IT'S THE ONLY STREET, BOSS.
DON'T GET ALL SMART, SLAYNE. OR YOU'LL BE TARGET PRACTICE.
AGAIN.
CLOSER. CLOSER. DON'T SHOOT UNTIL THEY'RE ON THE X.
YOU'VE MORE GUTS THAN BRAINS, DEPUTIES.
WE'VE BROUGHT MISS EMBER BACK. WE WANT THE KEY.

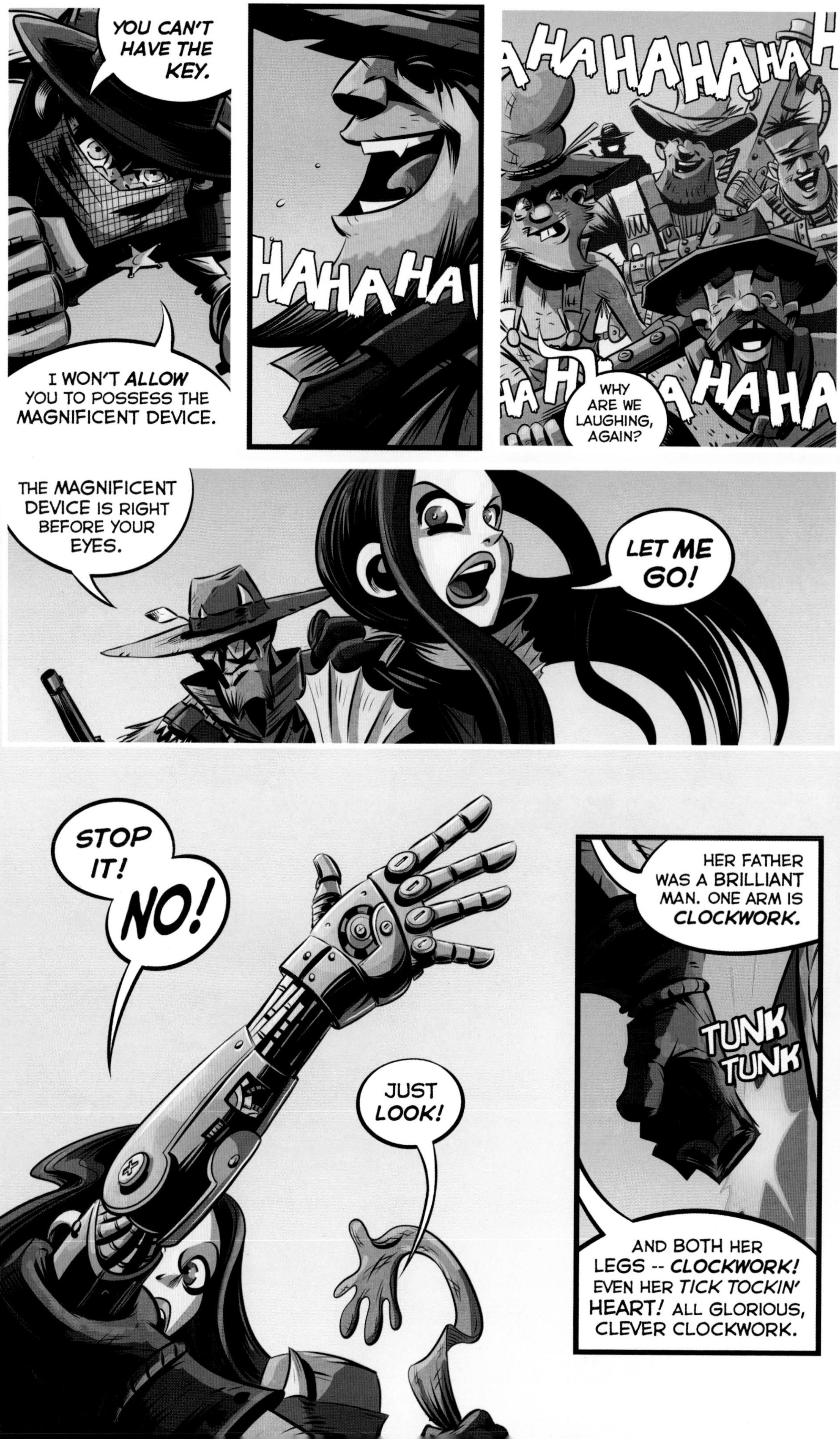
YOU CAN'T HAVE THE KEY.
I WON'T ALLOW YOU TO POSSESS THE MAGNIFICENT DEVICE.
HAHAHAHA
HAHAHAHAHA
WHY ARE WE LAUGHING, AGAIN?
HAHAHA
THE MAGNIFICENT DEVICE IS RIGHT BEFORE YOUR EYES.
LET ME GO!
STOP IT! NO!
JUST LOOK!
HER FATHER WAS A BRILLIANT MAN. ONE ARM IS CLOCKWORK.
TUNK TUNK
AND BOTH HER LEGS -- CLOCKWORK! EVEN HER TICK TOCKIN' HEART! ALL GLORIOUS, CLEVER CLOCKWORK.

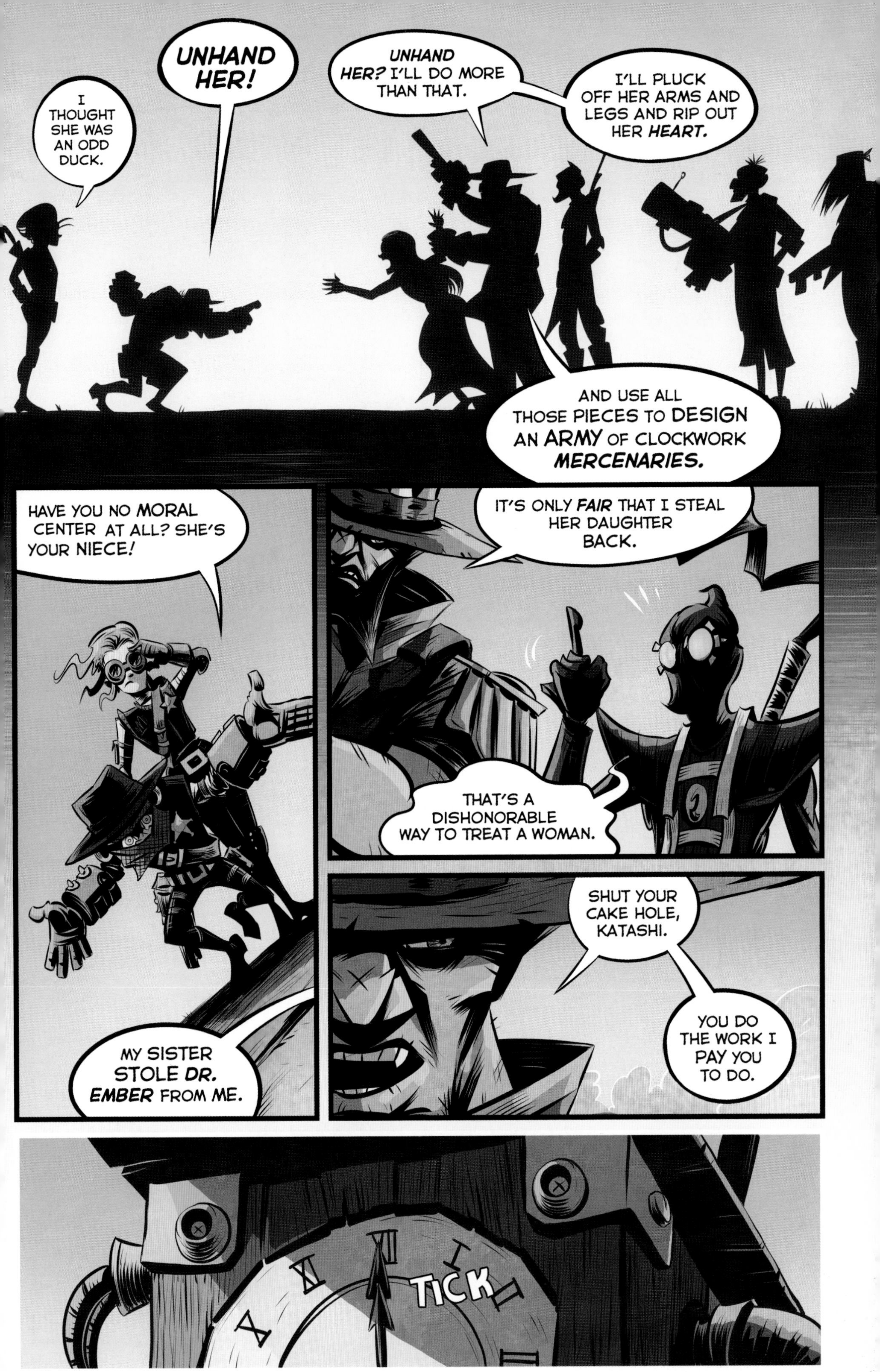

I THOUGHT SHE WAS AN ODD DUCK.
UNHAND HER!
UNHAND HER? I'LL DO MORE THAN THAT.
I'LL PLUCK OFF HER ARMS AND LEGS AND RIP OUT HER HEART.
AND USE ALL THOSE PIECES TO DESIGN AN ARMY OF CLOCKWORK MERCENARIES.
HAVE YOU NO MORAL CENTER AT ALL? SHE'S YOUR NIECE!
MY SISTER STOLE DR. EMBER FROM ME.
IT'S ONLY FAIR THAT I STEAL HER DAUGHTER BACK.
THAT'S A DISHONORABLE WAY TO TREAT A WOMAN.
SHUT YOUR CAKE HOLE, KATASHI.
YOU DO THE WORK I PAY YOU TO DO.
TICK

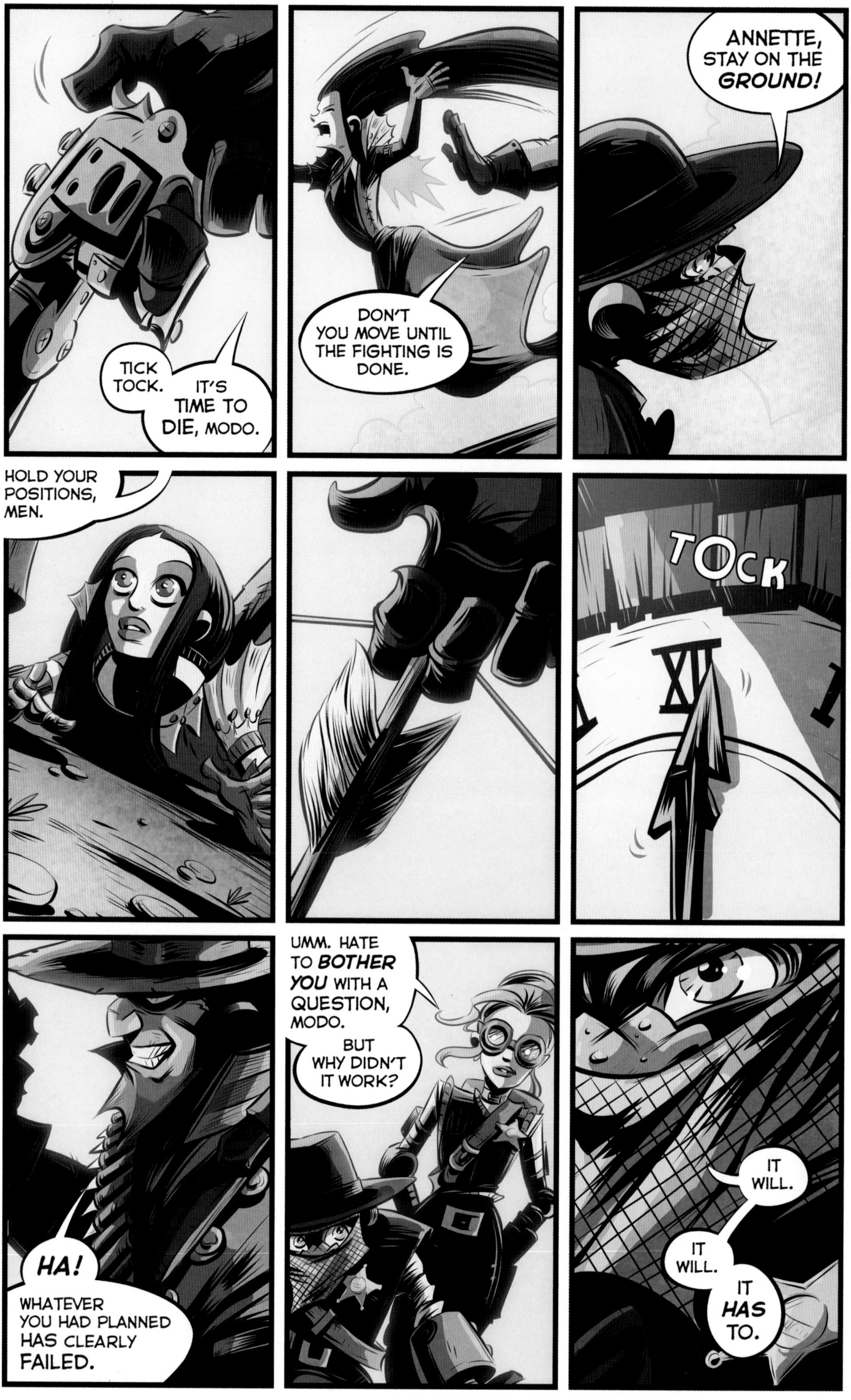
TICK TOCK. IT'S TIME TO DIE, MODO.
DON'T YOU MOVE UNTIL THE FIGHTING IS DONE.
ANNETTE, STAY ON THE GROUND!
HOLD YOUR POSITIONS, MEN.
TOCK
HA! WHATEVER YOU HAD PLANNED HAS CLEARLY FAILED.
UMM. HATE TO BOTHER YOU WITH A QUESTION, MODO.
BUT WHY DIDN'T IT WORK?
IT WILL.
IT WILL.
IT HAS TO.

RATTLE
RATTLE
RATTLE
FOOSH
FOOSH
FOOSH
BONK
WHACK
WHAT THE—
KONK
BONK

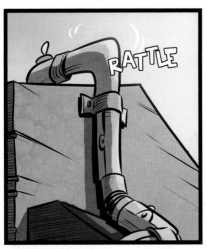

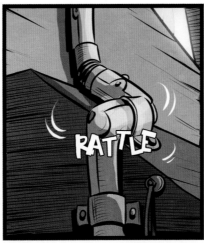

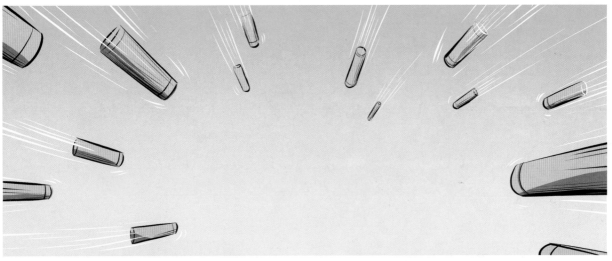

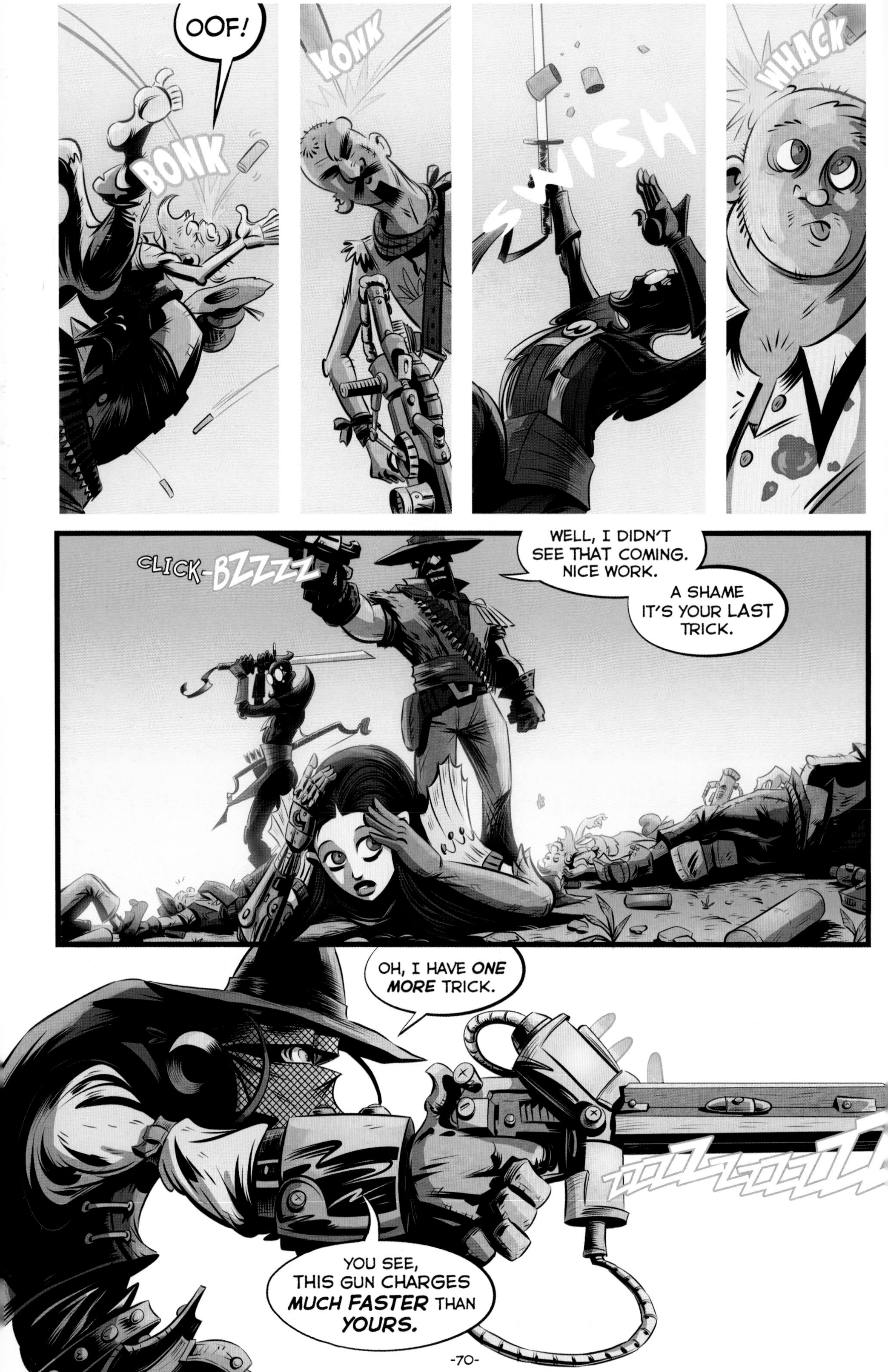
OOF!
BONK
KONK
SWISH
WHACK
CLICK-BZZZZ
WELL, I DIDN'T SEE THAT COMING. NICE WORK.
A SHAME IT'S YOUR LAST TRICK.
OH, I HAVE *ONE MORE* TRICK.
YOU SEE, THIS GUN CHARGES *MUCH FASTER* THAN *YOURS.*

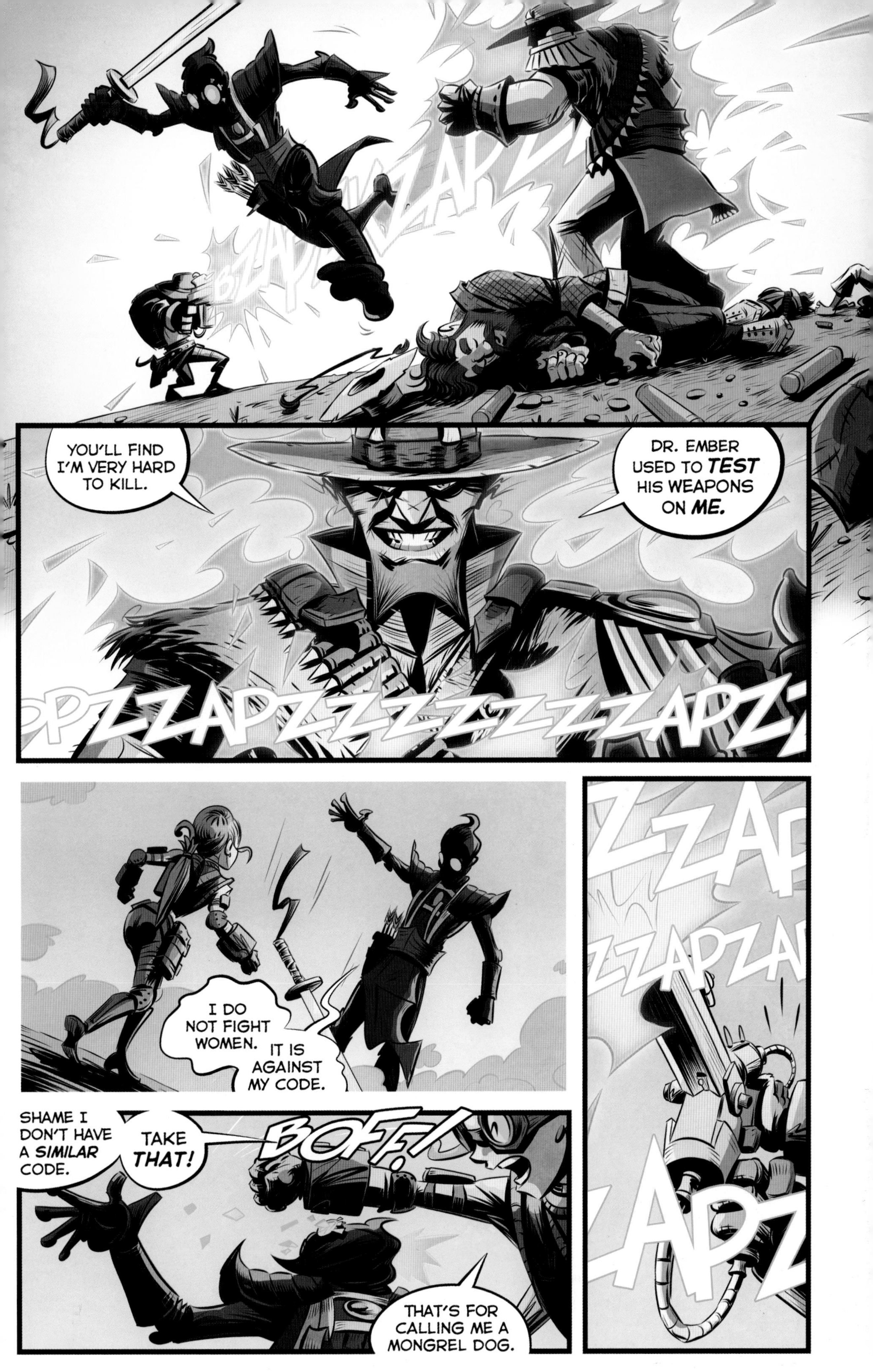
BZAP
ZZAPZ
YOU'LL FIND I'M VERY HARD TO KILL.
DR. EMBER USED TO TEST HIS WEAPONS ON ME.
PZZAPZZZZZZZZZAPZ
I DO NOT FIGHT WOMEN.
IT IS AGAINST MY CODE.
ZZAP
ZZAPZA
SHAME I DON'T HAVE A SIMILAR CODE.
TAKE THAT!
BOFF!
THAT'S FOR CALLING ME A MONGREL DOG.
ZAPZ

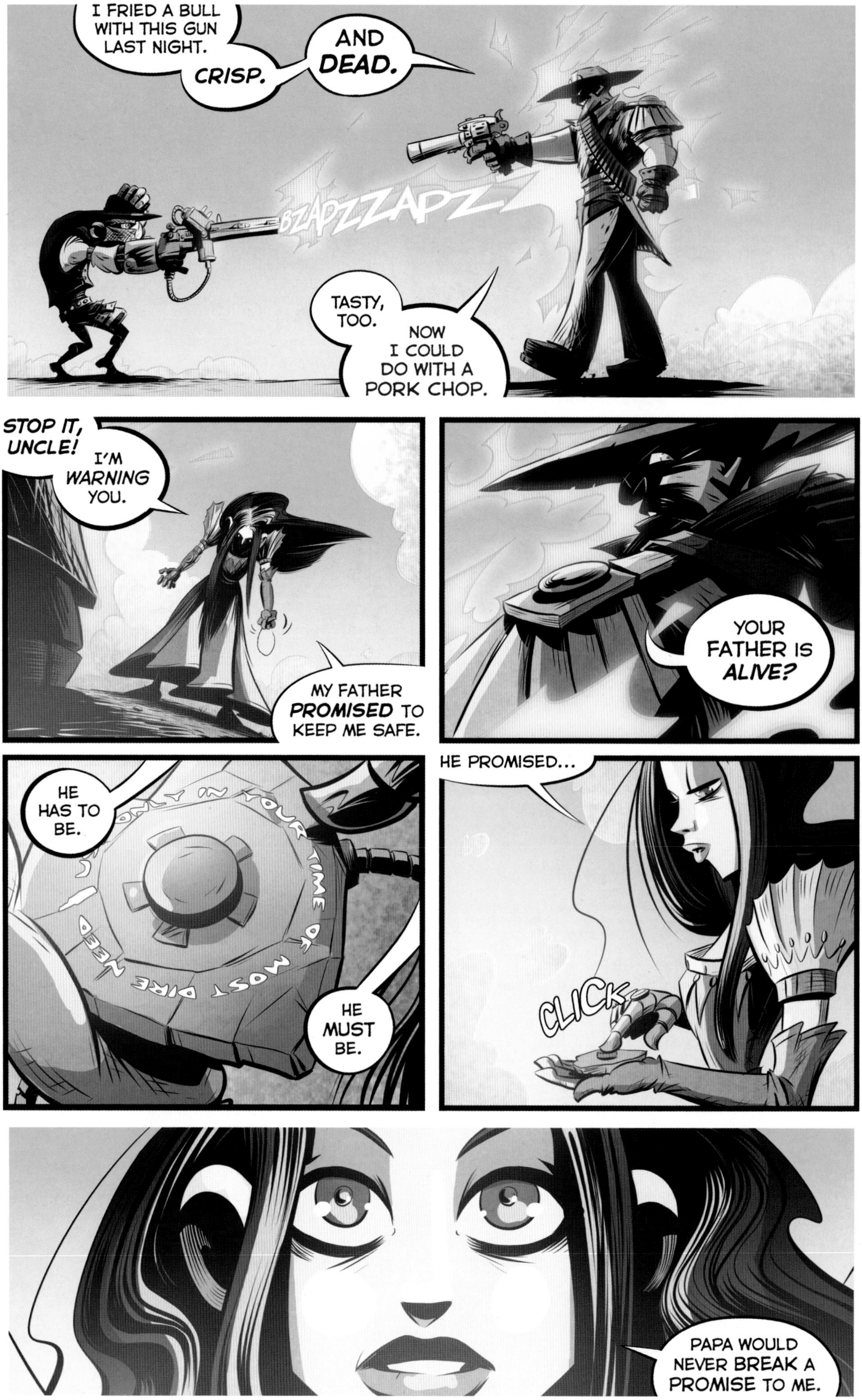
I FRIED A BULL WITH THIS GUN LAST NIGHT.
CRISP.
AND DEAD.
BZAPZZZAPZ
TASTY, TOO.
NOW I COULD DO WITH A PORK CHOP.
STOP IT, UNCLE!
I'M WARNING YOU.
MY FATHER PROMISED TO KEEP ME SAFE.
YOUR FATHER IS ALIVE?
HE HAS TO BE.
ONLY IN YOUR TIME OF MOST DIRE NEED
HE MUST BE.
HE PROMISED...
CLICK
PAPA WOULD NEVER BREAK A PROMISE TO ME.

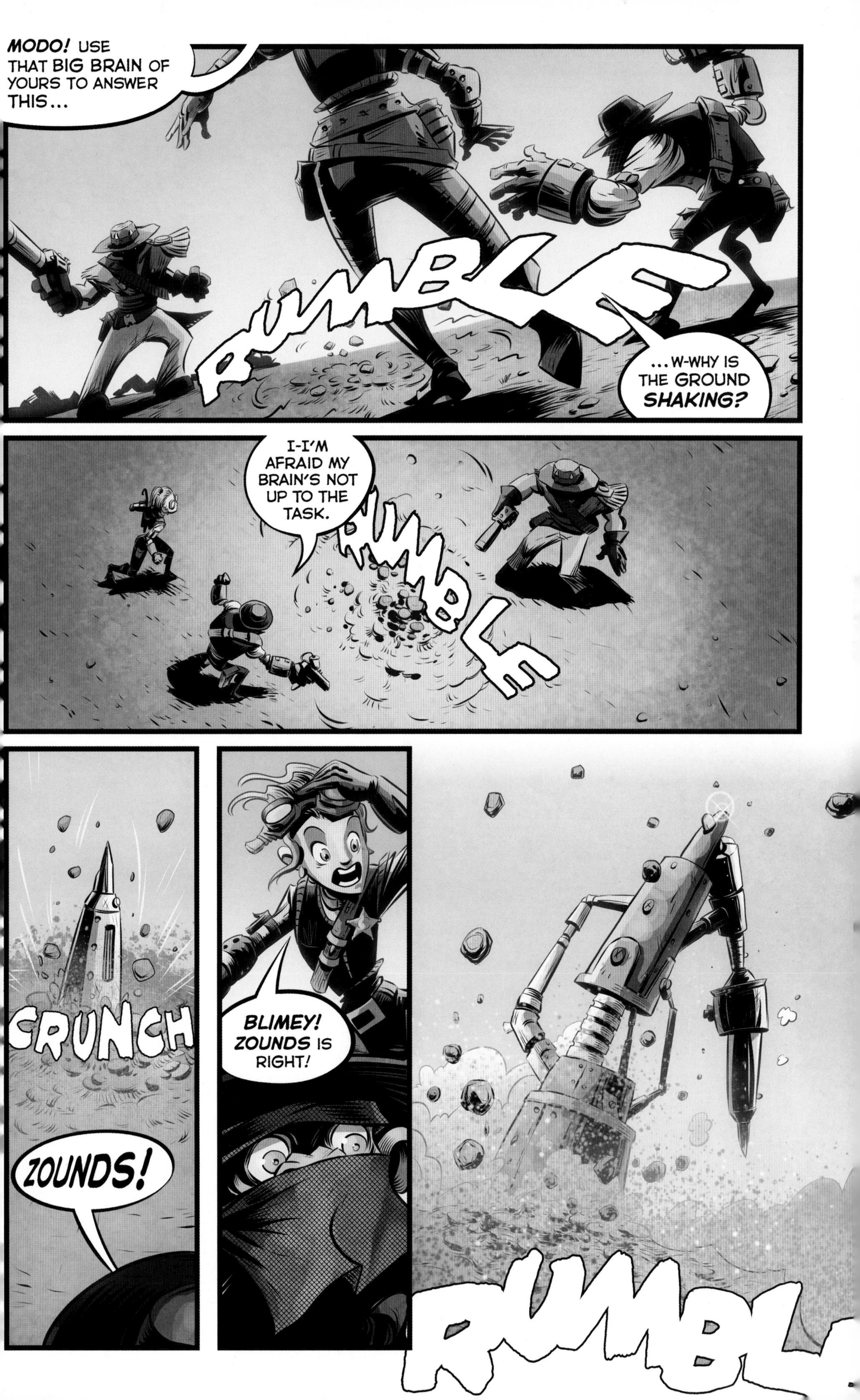
MODO! USE THAT BIG BRAIN OF YOURS TO ANSWER THIS...
RUMBLE
...W-WHY IS THE GROUND SHAKING?
I-I'M AFRAID MY BRAIN'S NOT UP TO THE TASK.
RUMBLE
CRUNCH
ZOUNDS!
BLIMEY! ZOUNDS IS RIGHT!
RUMBL

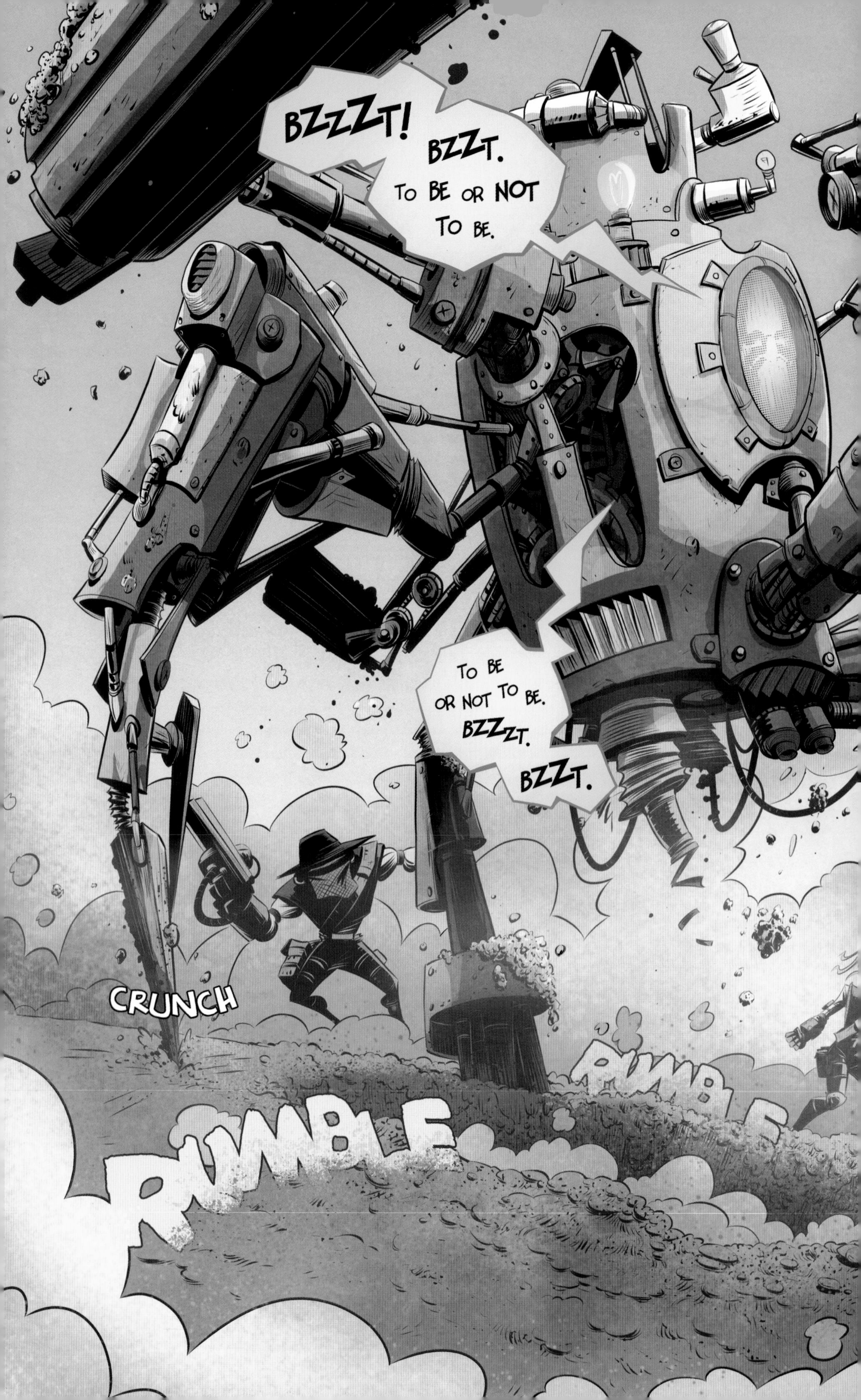
BZZZT! BZZT. TO BE OR NOT TO BE.
TO BE OR NOT TO BE. BZZZT. BZZT.
CRUNCH
RUMBLE
RUMBLE

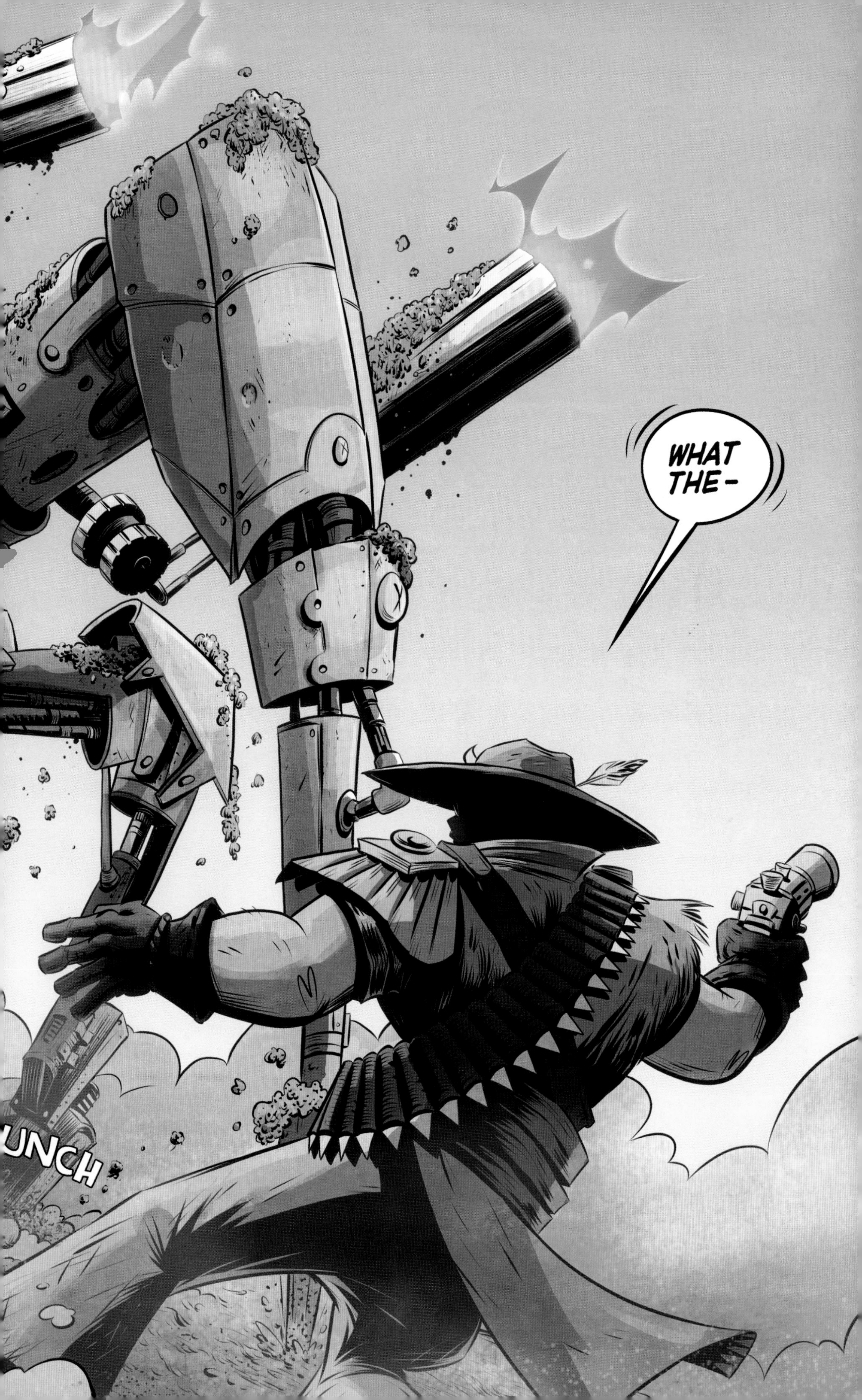
WHAT THE-
UNCH

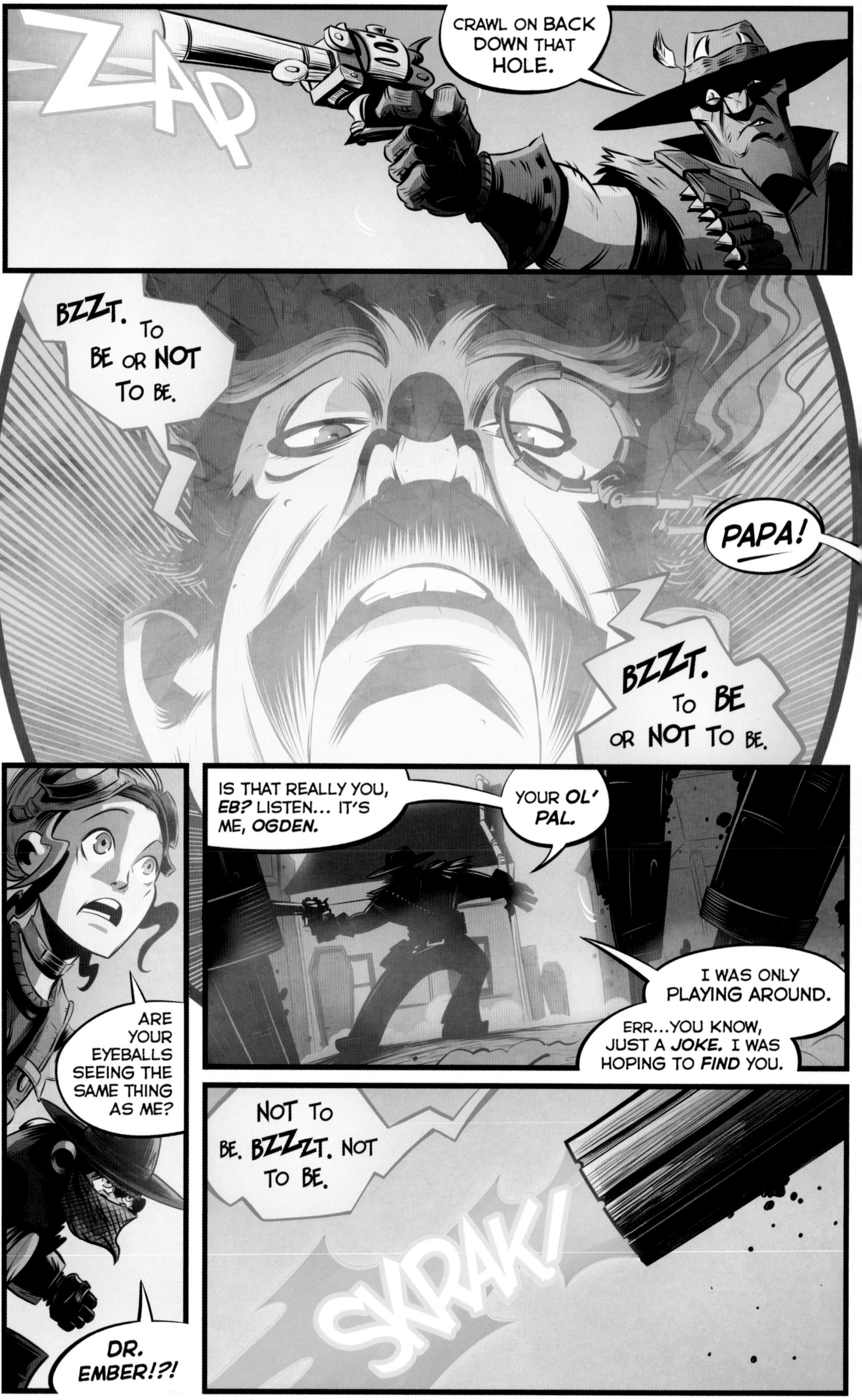
ZAP
CRAWL ON BACK DOWN THAT HOLE.
BZZT. TO BE OR NOT TO BE.
PAPA!
BZZT. TO BE OR NOT TO BE.
ARE YOUR EYEBALLS SEEING THE SAME THING AS ME?
DR. EMBER!?!
IS THAT REALLY YOU, EB? LISTEN... IT'S ME, OGDEN.
YOUR OL' PAL.
I WAS ONLY PLAYING AROUND.
ERR...YOU KNOW, JUST A JOKE. I WAS HOPING TO FIND YOU.
NOT TO BE. BZZZT. NOT TO BE.
SKRAK!

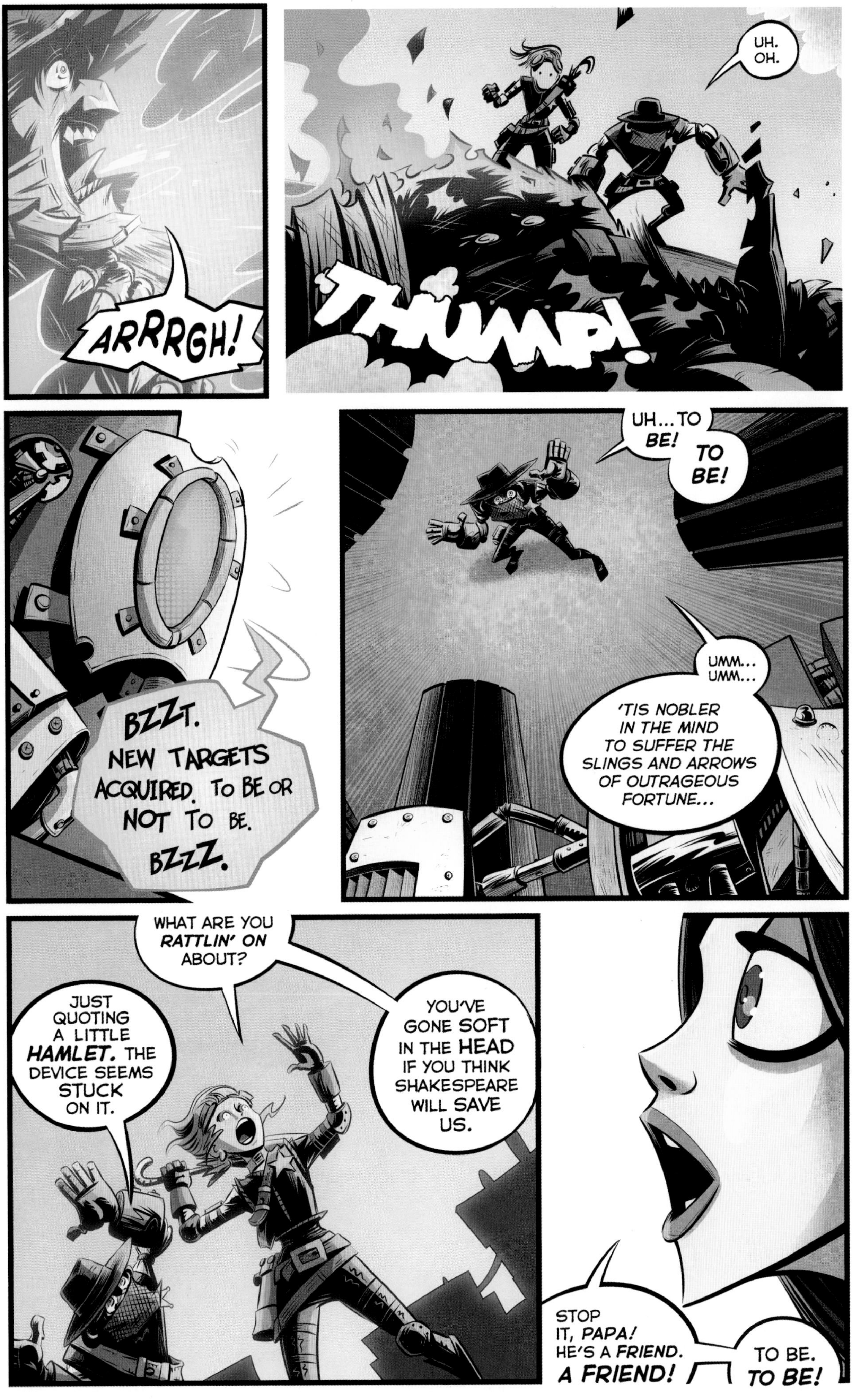
ARRRGH!
UH. OH.
THUMP!
BZZT. NEW TARGETS ACQUIRED. TO BE OR NOT TO BE. BZZZ.
UH...TO BE!
TO BE!
UMM... UMM...
'TIS NOBLER IN THE MIND TO SUFFER THE SLINGS AND ARROWS OF OUTRAGEOUS FORTUNE...
WHAT ARE YOU RATTLIN' ON ABOUT?
JUST QUOTING A LITTLE HAMLET. THE DEVICE SEEMS STUCK ON IT.
YOU'VE GONE SOFT IN THE HEAD IF YOU THINK SHAKESPEARE WILL SAVE US.
STOP IT, PAPA! HE'S A FRIEND. A FRIEND!
TO BE. TO BE!

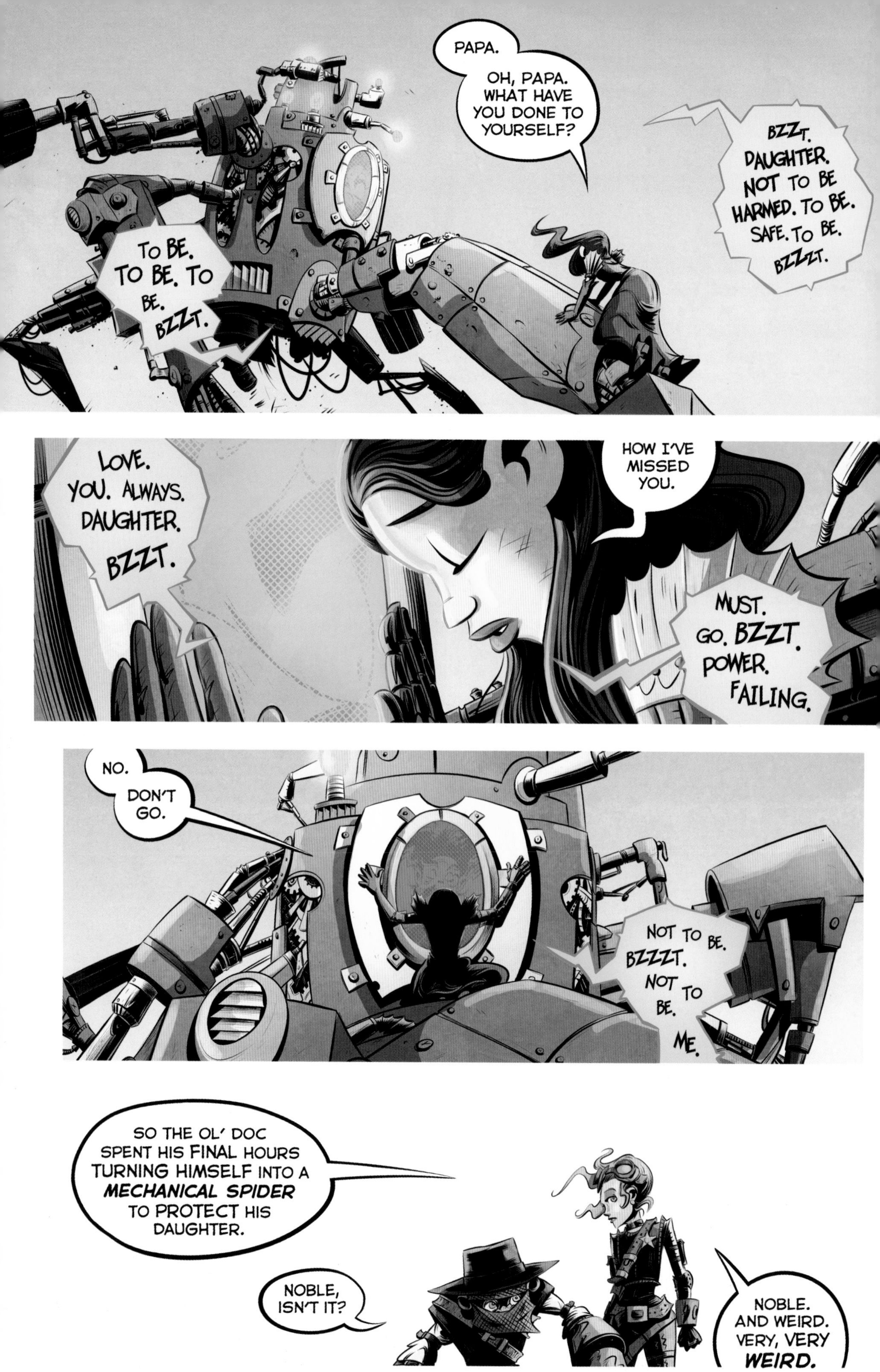
PAPA.
OH, PAPA. WHAT HAVE YOU DONE TO YOURSELF?
BZZT. DAUGHTER. NOT TO BE HARMED. TO BE. SAFE. TO BE. BZZZT.
TO BE. TO BE. TO BE. BZZT.
LOVE. YOU. ALWAYS. DAUGHTER. BZZT.
HOW I'VE MISSED YOU.
MUST. GO. BZZT. POWER. FAILING.
NO.
DON'T GO.
NOT TO BE. BZZZT. NOT TO BE. ME.
SO THE OL' DOC SPENT HIS FINAL HOURS TURNING HIMSELF INTO A *MECHANICAL SPIDER* TO PROTECT HIS DAUGHTER.
NOBLE, ISN'T IT?
NOBLE. AND WEIRD. VERY, VERY *WEIRD.*

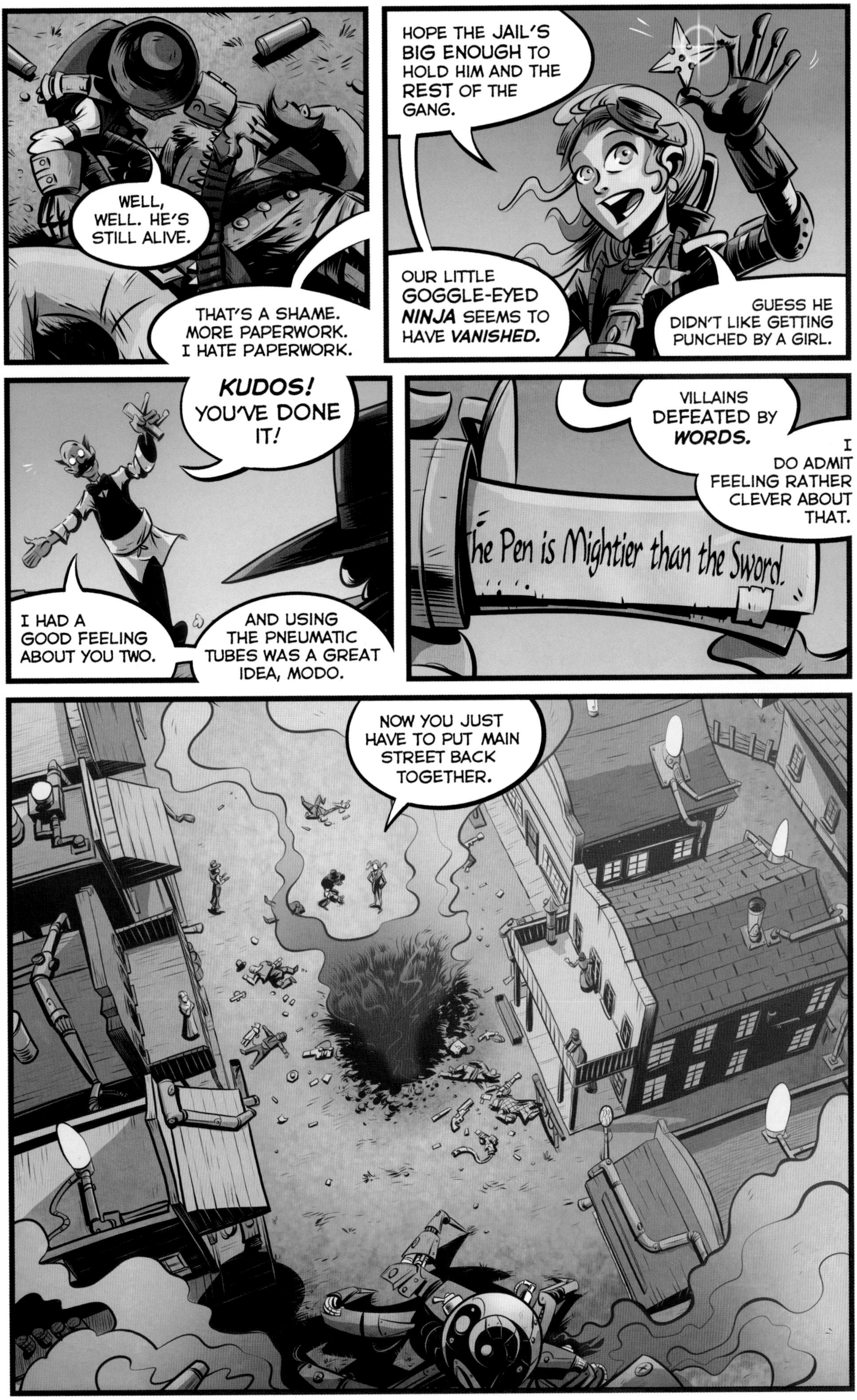
WELL, WELL. HE'S STILL ALIVE.
THAT'S A SHAME. MORE PAPERWORK. I HATE PAPERWORK.
HOPE THE JAIL'S BIG ENOUGH TO HOLD HIM AND THE REST OF THE GANG.
OUR LITTLE GOGGLE-EYED NINJA SEEMS TO HAVE VANISHED.
GUESS HE DIDN'T LIKE GETTING PUNCHED BY A GIRL.
KUDOS! YOU'VE DONE IT!
I HAD A GOOD FEELING ABOUT YOU TWO.
AND USING THE PNEUMATIC TUBES WAS A GREAT IDEA, MODO.
VILLAINS DEFEATED BY WORDS.
I DO ADMIT FEELING RATHER CLEVER ABOUT THAT.
he Pen is Mightier than the Sword.
NOW YOU JUST HAVE TO PUT MAIN STREET BACK TOGETHER.

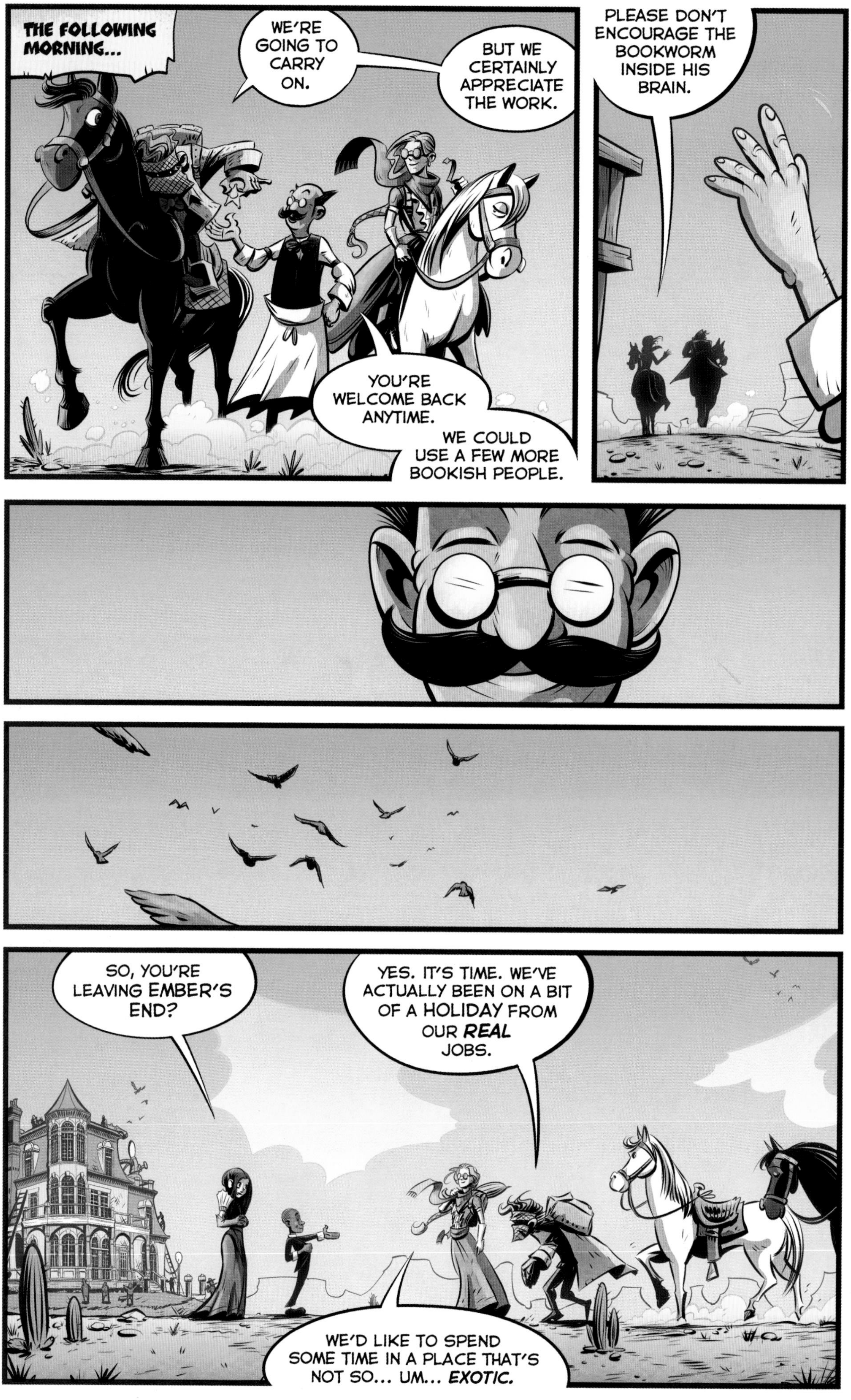
THE FOLLOWING MORNING...
WE'RE GOING TO CARRY ON.
BUT WE CERTAINLY APPRECIATE THE WORK.
YOU'RE WELCOME BACK ANYTIME.
WE COULD USE A FEW MORE BOOKISH PEOPLE.
PLEASE DON'T ENCOURAGE THE BOOKWORM INSIDE HIS BRAIN.
SO, YOU'RE LEAVING EMBER'S END?
YES. IT'S TIME. WE'VE ACTUALLY BEEN ON A BIT OF A HOLIDAY FROM OUR REAL JOBS.
WE'D LIKE TO SPEND SOME TIME IN A PLACE THAT'S NOT SO... UM... EXOTIC.

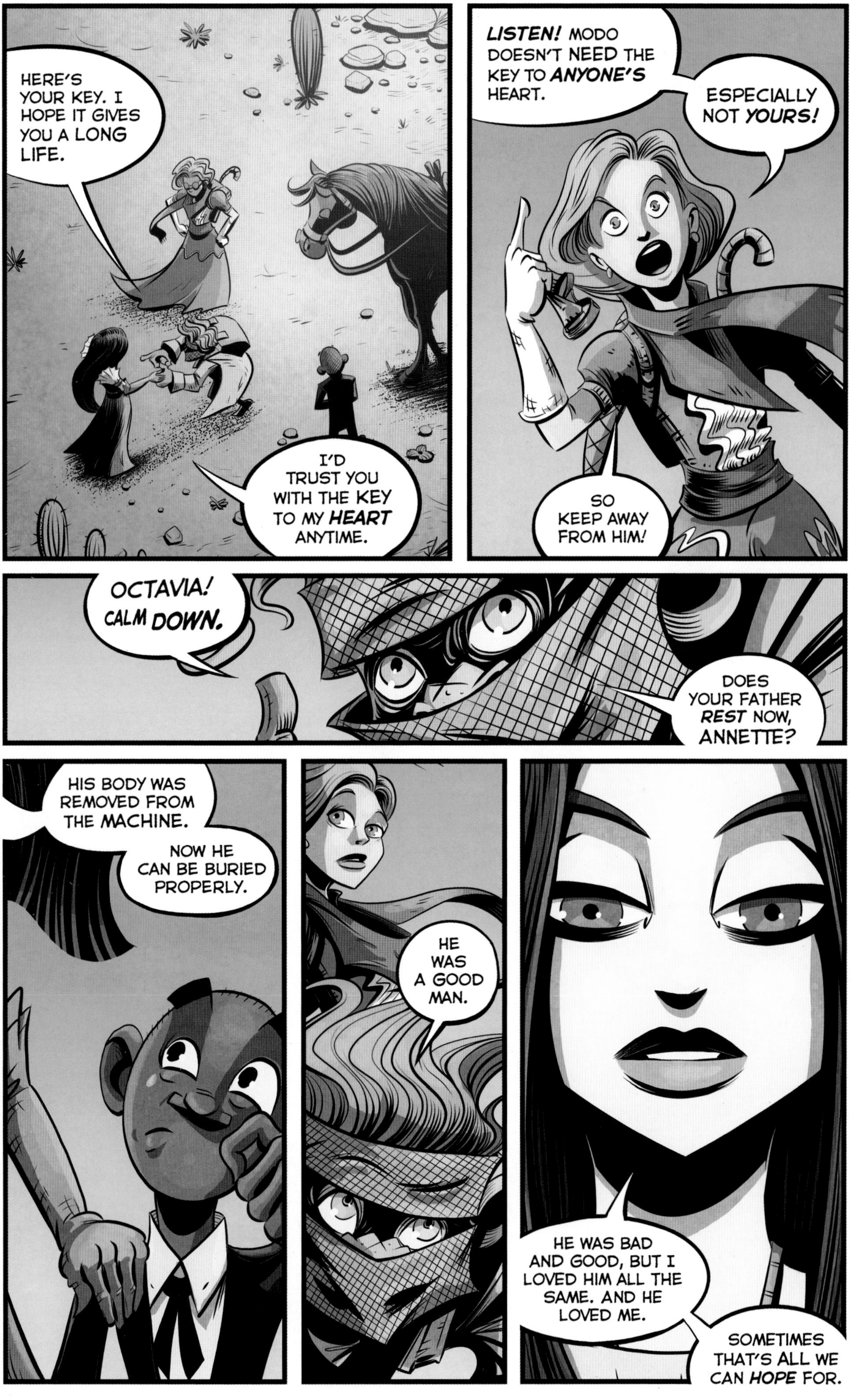
HERE'S YOUR KEY. I HOPE IT GIVES YOU A LONG LIFE.
I'D TRUST YOU WITH THE KEY TO MY HEART ANYTIME.
LISTEN! MODO DOESN'T NEED THE KEY TO ANYONE'S HEART.
ESPECIALLY NOT YOURS!
SO KEEP AWAY FROM HIM!
OCTAVIA! CALM DOWN.
DOES YOUR FATHER REST NOW, ANNETTE?
HIS BODY WAS REMOVED FROM THE MACHINE.
NOW HE CAN BE BURIED PROPERLY.
HE WAS A GOOD MAN.
HE WAS BAD AND GOOD, BUT I LOVED HIM ALL THE SAME. AND HE LOVED ME.
SOMETIMES THAT'S ALL WE CAN HOPE FOR.

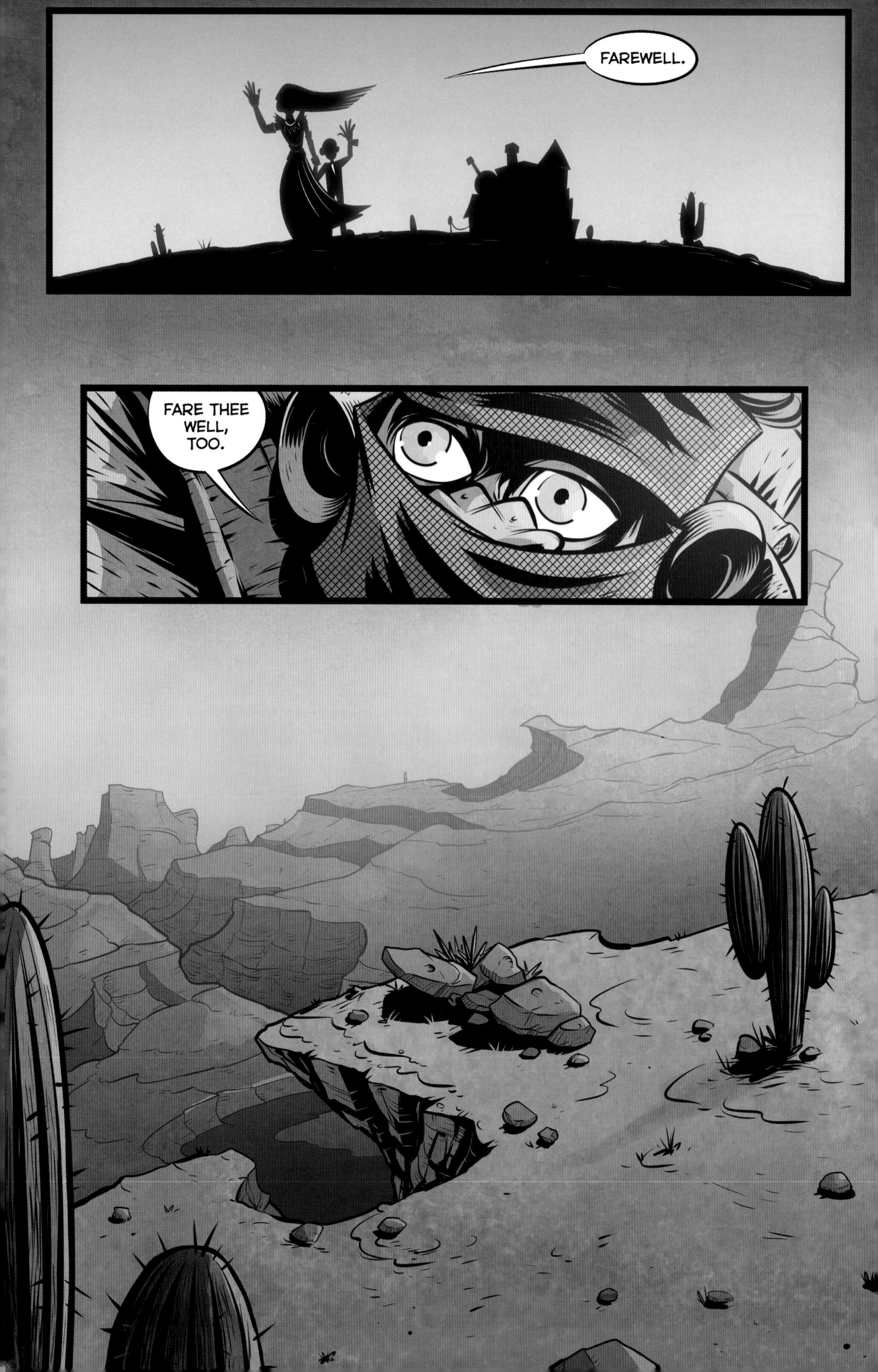
FAREWELL.
FARE THEE WELL, TOO.

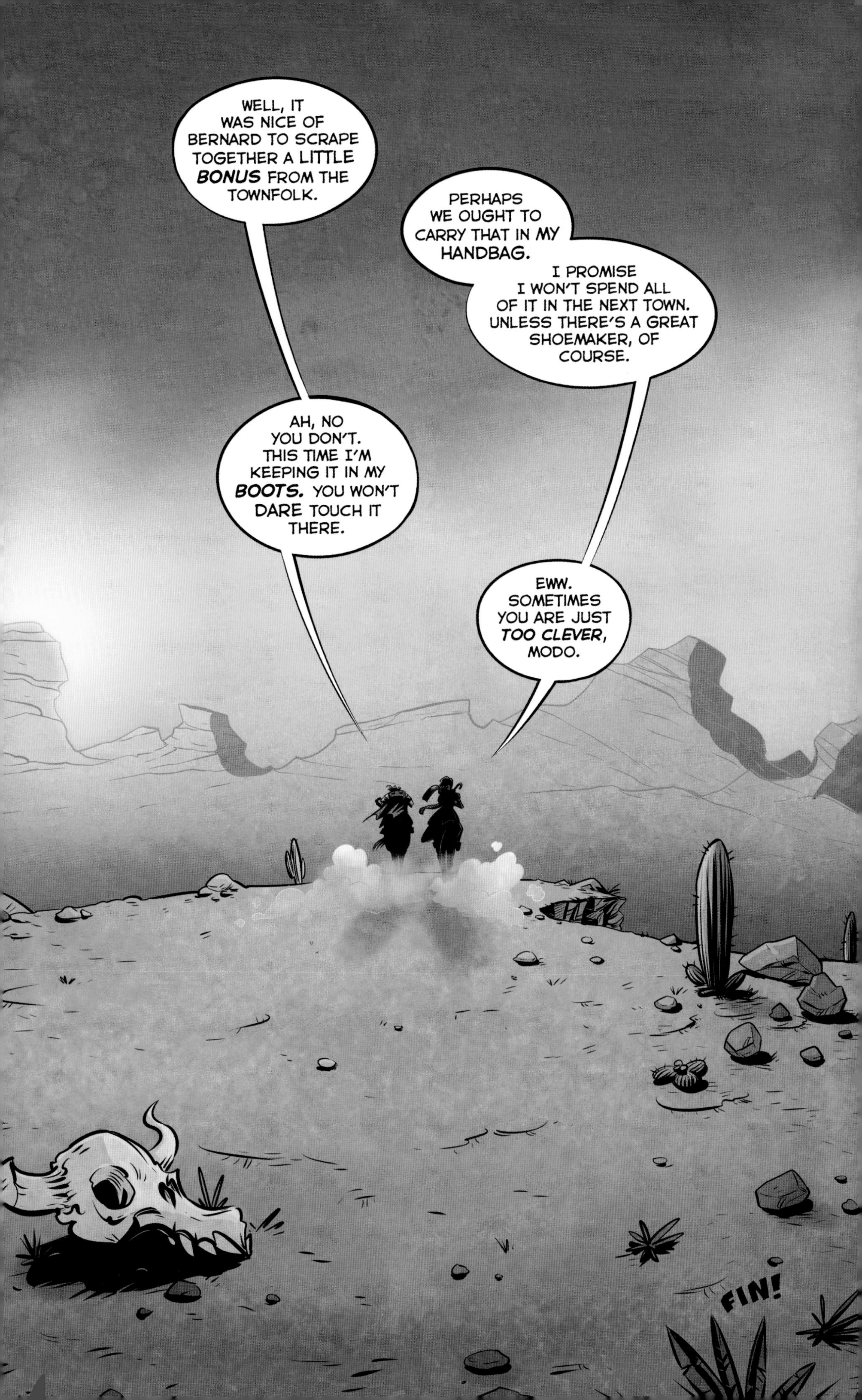
WELL, IT WAS NICE OF BERNARD TO SCRAPE TOGETHER A LITTLE BONUS FROM THE TOWNFOLK.
PERHAPS WE OUGHT TO CARRY THAT IN MY HANDBAG.
I PROMISE I WON'T SPEND ALL OF IT IN THE NEXT TOWN. UNLESS THERE'S A GREAT SHOEMAKER, OF COURSE.
AH, NO YOU DON'T. THIS TIME I'M KEEPING IT IN MY BOOTS. YOU WON'T DARE TOUCH IT THERE.
EWW. SOMETIMES YOU ARE JUST TOO CLEVER, MODO.
FIN!

MODO: EMBER'S END SKETCHBOOK

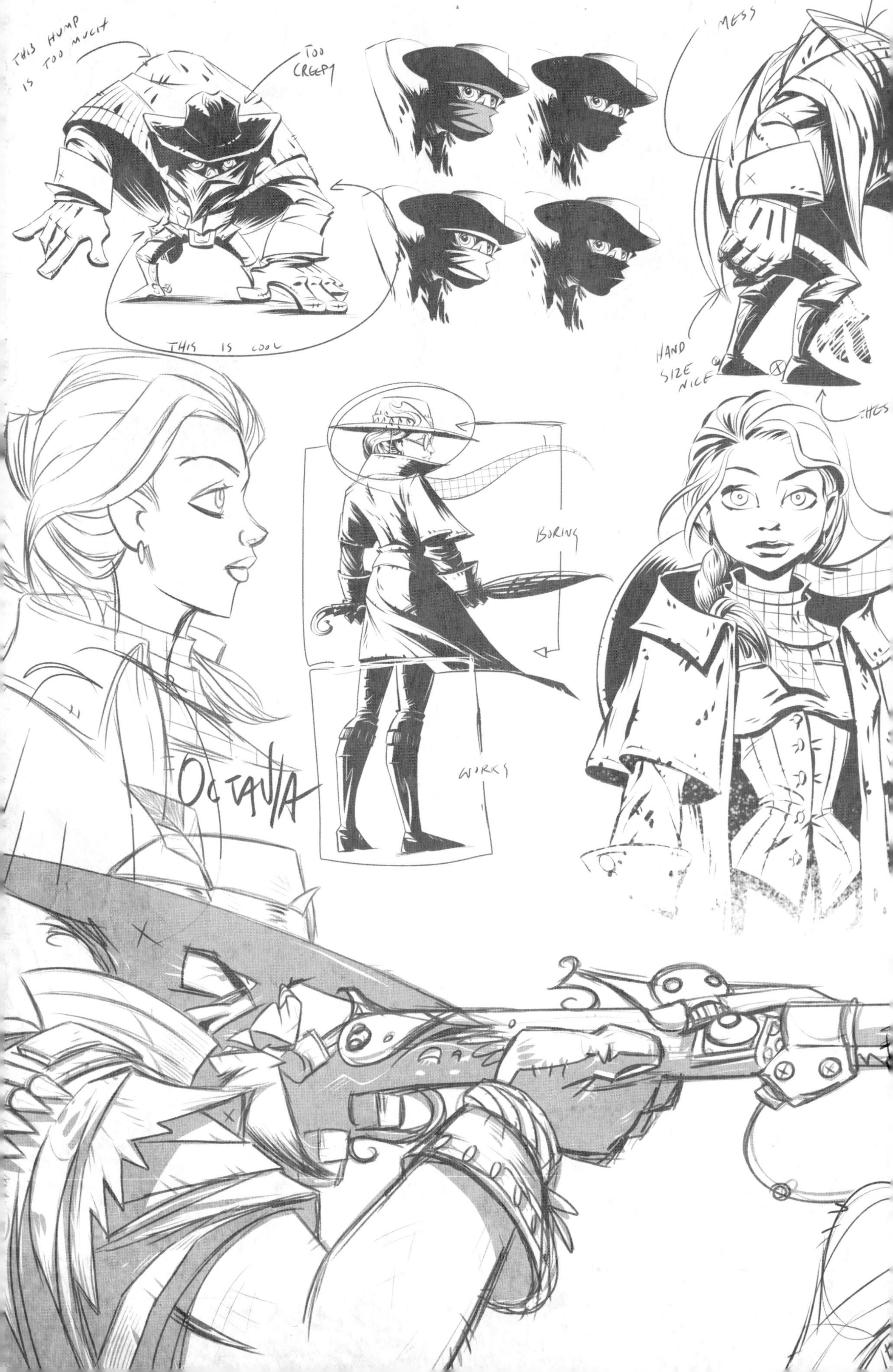
THIS HUMP IS TOO MUCH
TOO CREEPY
THIS IS COOL
MESS
HAND SIZE NICE
BORING
WORKS
OCTAVIA

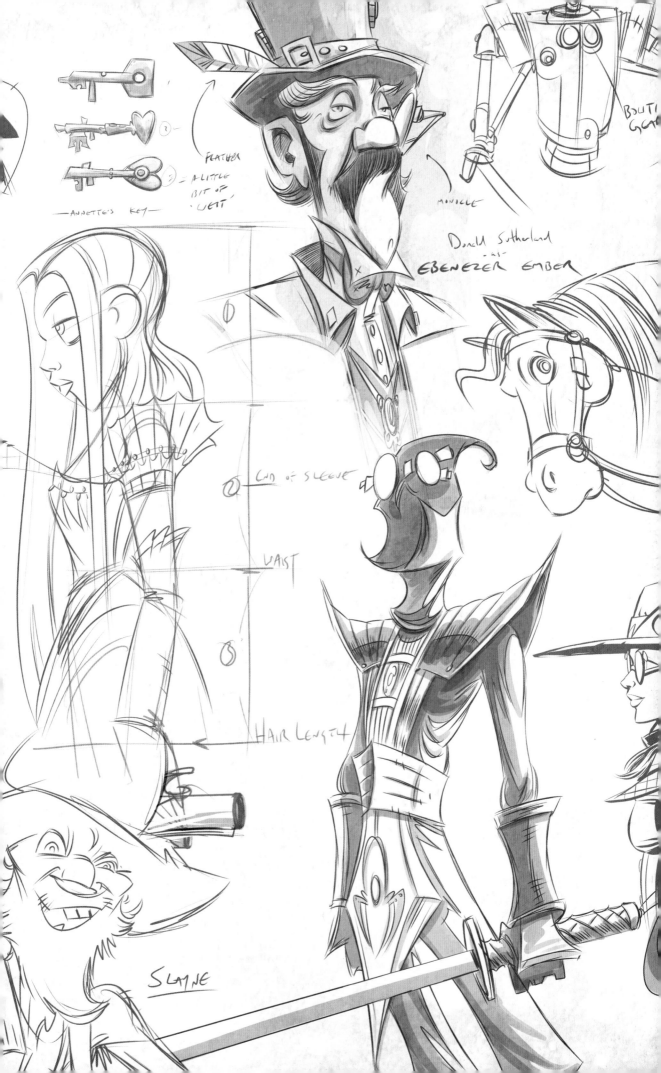

ANNETTE'S KEY

FEATHER

A LITTLE BIT OF 'WETT'

MONICLE

Donald Sutherland AS EBENEZER EMBER

END OF SLEEVE

WAIST

HAIR LENGTH

SLAYNE

ARTHUR SLADE was raised on a ranch in the Cypress Hills of Saskatchewan. He is the author of nineteen novels for young readers, including *The Hunchback Assignments*, which won the prestigious TD Canadian Children's Literature Award, and *Dust*, winner of the Governor General's Award for Children's Literature. He lives in Saskatoon, Saskatchewan. For more information, visit www.arthurslade.com.

CHRISTOPHER STEININGER has done storyboards for numerous
shows and video games, including Marvel's *Avengers Assemble* and
Spec Ops: The Line. He's also created concept art for a variety of projects,
such as Warhammer 40K and *Iron Maiden: Legacy of the Beast.* Currently,
he's illustrating *In Search of Hannibal*, a historically accurate retelling of
Hannibal's epic battle against Rome, and working on the next book in his
Dead Heaven fantasy series. He lives in Inglewood, Ontario. For more
information, visit www.christophersteininger.com.

Cataloguing in Publication information availble from Library and Archives Canada

ISBN 978-1-4598-1721-0 (softcover).—ISBN 978-1-4598-1722-7 (pdf).—
ISBN 978-1-4598-1723-4 (epub)

This edition was first published in the United States in 2018
Library of Congress Control Number: 2017949688

Summary: In this graphic novel for middle readers, a young spy with a special ability must prevent a villain from getting his hands on an all-powerful weapon.

MIX
Paper from responsible sources
FSC® C013314

Orca Book Publishers is dedicated to preserving the environment and has printed this book on Forest Stewardship Council® certified paper.

Orca Book Publishers gratefully acknowledges the support for its publishing programs provided by the following agencies: the Government of Canada through the Canada Book Fund and the Canada Council for the Arts, and the Province of British Columbia through the BC Arts Council and the Book Publishing Tax Credit.

Cover and interior artwork by Christopher Steininger
Coloring by Donna Gregory
Color flats by Alexa Rosa

ORCA BOOK PUBLISHERS
www.orcabook.com

Printed and bound in China

21 20 19 18 • 4 3 2 1